"How long do y[ou] take you to pac[k...] want to bring?"

Nick's eyebrows snapped together. "Bring with me where?"

"Back to Chicago, of course." Claire struggled to keep the impatience out of her voice. "Where I live. Where you're going to live with me."

The mulish look in Nick's eyes only strengthened his resemblance to her sister. "I'm not moving to Chicago. My mum wanted me to live in Monroe. I'm staying here."

"I can't leave you here."

"Why not? I'm nothing to you," he said.

"You're my nephew. My sister's only child. I care about you."

Nick gave a derisive snort. "Yeah, right. If you care so much about me, how come you never came around when Mum was alive?"

Available in August 2006
from Silhouette Superromance

Hometown Girl
by Margaret Watson
(Suddenly a Parent)

The Chosen Child
by Brenda Mott
(Count on a Cop)

A Little Secret Between Friends
by CJ Carmichael

Coming Home
by Jean Brashear
(Mother & Child Reunion)

Hometown Girl

MARGARET WATSON

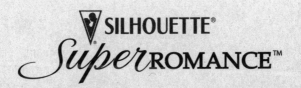

SILHOUETTE®
Super ROMANCE™

First published in Great Britain 2006
Silhouette Books, Eton House, 18-24 Paradise Road,
Richmond, Surrey TW9 1SR

© Margaret Watson 2005

Standard ISBN 0 373 71258 8
Promotional ISBN 0 373 60489 0

38-0806

Printed and bound in Spain
by Litografia Rosés S.A., Barcelona

Dear Reader,

There's something compelling about returning to our roots—how can you resist watching a woman return to the places and people of her past? Especially if that past includes a hometown she's vowed to leave behind forever. In *Hometown Girl* I've given Claire Kendall many reasons to stay as far away from Monroe, Illinois, as possible—and one reason to return that she can't resist. After her sister is killed in a car accident, leaving Claire's nephew Nick an orphan, she has no choice but to hurry back to Monroe to be with him.

The challenges of becoming an instant parent to a teenager overshadow Claire's dread of being back in Monroe. And when Claire meets Tucker Hall, the handsome, charismatic man who is Nick's teacher and football coach, her life is thrown into even more turmoil.

None of us has a perfect past. We all have people and places we'd rather forget, issues that we'd rather not face. But life doesn't work that way. We all struggle to grow and change. Sometimes, if we're very lucky, we can get past our fears and pain to find that our heart's desire is right there in front of us, waiting for us to recognise it.

I hope you enjoy Claire, Tucker and Nick's journey of discovery. These three people hold a very special place in my heart, and I'm delighted to share their story with you.

I love to hear from readers! You can e-mail me at mwatson1004@hotmail.com or visit my website, www.margaretwatson.com.

Sincerely,

Margaret Watson

For Mum, my biggest fan.
Thanks for all your support and
encouragement.

PROLOGUE

THE TWO LITTLE GIRLS FLED from the house, angry voices following them into the trees at the back of the property.

"Hurry, Claire," the older one panted, grabbing her sister's hand. "Faster."

Frightened tears poured down nine-year-old Claire's face as she raced for the refuge of the trees and the crude shelter she and Janice had built. It was their fort, their secret hideaway, the place they hid when their parents started yelling and fists began flying.

When they reached the tangle of dead branches and pine boughs that concealed their hideaway, Janice pulled her inside and wrapped her arm around Claire's shoulder. "They won't find us here," Janice whispered with the certainty of her twelve years. "Don't worry."

Trembling, Claire clung to Janice and listened for the angry voices to come closer. When they didn't, she wiped her runny nose on the sleeve of her sweater and pressed more closely into her sister.

"Maybe she found our fort," she whispered, her voice breaking. "Maybe she's coming to get us."

If her mother's angry face appeared in the door of

their fort, Claire knew she'd pee in her pants again. That would make her mother scream even louder.

"She doesn't come into the woods," Janice said. "Neither does he."

"They'll find us, Janny. They will," she sobbed.

She squeezed her eyes shut against the memory of their father taking off his belt. His breath would have that funny smell when he called their names and she'd see that scary look in his eyes as he reached for Janice.

"I won't let them find us," Janice said, her voice fierce.

"I'm scared," she whispered.

Anger flashed in her sister's eyes and her mouth tightened. "I know, Sissy. But you don't need to be scared. I'll take care of you. I promise. I'll make sure she doesn't yell at you. And I won't let him hurt you."

Moisture from the damp ground seeped through Claire's jeans, making her wonder if she'd peed in her pants after all. She shivered in the cool autumn air and burrowed into Janice's arms.

The voices from the house gradually faded away, the green light from the trees dimmed, and her eyelids grew heavy. Huddled close to her sister's warmth, Claire's fear subsided. As dusk deepened to twilight, she tightened her grip on Janice's sweater and fell asleep.

CHAPTER ONE

CLAIRE KENDALL STARED BLINDLY down into the open grave. She didn't see the casket that held the body of her sister, she didn't see the face of Nick, Janice's son, standing next to her, she didn't see the mourners clustered around the yawning hole.

In her mind, two little girls fled from a dark house into the green safety of the woods.

She could smell the freshness of the trees and the heavy scent of decaying leaves and dirt as her older sister whispered that she was safe, that no one would hurt her.

Janice had kept her word. Her parents had never touched Claire. Their preferred target was Janice, whose eyes flashed insolence and defiance, whose words dripped scorn and contempt. It was Janice who stood up to them, Janice who took the fists and the belt, Janice who shouted back. Sick with guilt and fear, Claire had crept around the house hoping they wouldn't notice her.

Janice had saved her. But she couldn't save herself.

Her sister's self-destructive behavior had culminated in a pregnancy at seventeen. Refusing to name the father of her child, she'd run away from home and Claire had heard from her only sporadically for the next sixteen years.

Until the late-night phone call four days ago.

A sympathetic voice identifying himself as a Monroe police officer had informed Claire that her sister had died in an automobile accident. As Janice Kendall's only known relative, Claire was now responsible for Janice's fifteen-year-old son. If Claire didn't come to Monroe immediately, Nick would have to be placed in a foster home.

The droning voice of the minister stopped, and Claire snapped back to the present. The minister waited, and Claire frantically tried to figure out what he'd just said.

"You're supposed to take a flower," Nick muttered, shooting her a black look. "Or don't you care?"

His jaw muscles jumped as he grabbed a rose from the arrangement next to him. He gripped it tightly in his hand, then hurled it into the open grave. A bright red spot of blood blossomed on his hand before he curled his fingers into a fist.

She chose a small rose just beginning to unfurl and dropped it gently into the hole in the ground. Then she turned away, reaching for Nick's hand. The boy jerked his arm back and walked out of reach.

Their movement away from the grave broke the silence of the mourners clustered behind them. She hadn't expected many of the eight thousand people who lived in Monroe to attend the services, but she'd been surprised. As the crowd began to leave, they offered quiet condolences.

"Thank you for coming," she replied mechanically, over and over. Several people took her hand and Claire gave them a tight smile.

When the last straggler slammed his car door and left, she turned to Nick, fumbling for the right thing to say. "Are you hungry?" she finally asked. "Do you want to get something to eat?"

It was a safe question. In the past four days she'd learned one thing about Nick—he was always hungry.

Nick shrugged. "I don't care."

She took that as a yes. "Anywhere you'd like to go?"

"I don't care."

Claire tried to swallow the mounting panic. Nick was now her responsibility. Since she had no idea who his father was, she was all he had. If he wouldn't talk to her about where he wanted to eat, how would they talk about the important stuff?

"I saw a restaurant on my way into town," she said, praying for patience. "How about that?"

"Fine." He shoved his hands into his pockets and hunched his shoulders.

Neither of them spoke on the way to the Golden Coin Restaurant. The shops and stores of downtown Monroe flashed past the windows of the car, bringing back the past with a painful clarity. It was only a couple more days, she told herself. She could handle two days. Maybe even three. But as soon as they could pack Nick's belongings, she and her nephew would drive away from Monroe forever.

The interior of the restaurant was cool and dimly lit. The décor had been fashionable in the 1970s, but now looked tired and slightly shabby.

The young waitress at the restaurant took their order, gazing at them with bright curiosity in her eyes. Clearly she'd heard all the stories about the Kendalls.

Claire's family was notorious in Monroe. The death of her father, and his victim, in a drunken accident twelve years earlier had only capped a lifetime of gossip and averted eyes. Janice's car accident would have started the tongues flapping all over again.

The gossip could no longer hurt her, Claire reminded herself. And neither could the averted eyes. She'd escaped Monroe and erased it from her life years ago.

After they'd ordered their meals, Claire leaned toward Nick. "How long do you think it will take you to pack all the stuff you want to bring with you?"

His eyebrows snapped together. "Bring with me where?"

"Back to Chicago, of course." Claire struggled to keep the impatience out of her voice. "Where I live. Where you're going to live with me."

Nick stared at her, the mulish look in his eyes only strengthening his resemblance to her sister. "I'm not moving to Chicago. My mom wanted me to live in Monroe. I'm staying here."

"You can't stay here, Nick. I live in Chicago."

"Then go back to Chicago. No one's stopping you."

"I can't leave you here."

"Why not? I'm nothing to you," he said. He crushed a dinner roll into the table with his fingers, grinding it into the wood.

"You're my nephew. My sister's only child. I care about you."

Nick gave a derisive snort. "Yeah, right. If you care so much about me, how come you never came around when Mom was alive?"

Why was she surprised at Nick's bluntness? Janice had been exactly the same.

"Your mom and I had a…complicated relationship. She didn't want to spend time with me."

Scorn filled Nick's eyes. "You never asked."

"I invited you both to visit many times. Your mother always found a reason she couldn't make it."

"Mom didn't want charity. She wouldn't go crawling to her rich sister."

Claire flinched as though the boy had hit her. Is that how Janice thought of her? As the rich sister who would dispense largesse to her down-and-out sibling?

"I loved your mother. She was my only sister," Claire said, staring fiercely at Nick, willing her tears not to fall. His features blurred together and softened, making him look eerily like Janice. "She took care of me when I was little. But every time I asked her to visit, she was busy."

"Of course she said she was busy," he said scornfully, holding her gaze and leaning toward her. She resisted the urge to back away from him. Nick burned with the same intensity she remembered in Janice. "What was she supposed to say? 'We'd love to come visit, but the car died last week and we don't have the money for a bus ticket'?"

Even pitching his voice in a falsetto couldn't hide Nick's anger. He shoved the table, and it slid painfully into her stomach.

Claire pushed the table away gingerly, sadness and regret twisting through her. "Then all I can do is tell you how sorry I am," she said. "I can't apologize to Janice, but I can to you. I'm sorry, Nick. I should have made more of an effort to see you and your mother."

"Whatever," he said. "We didn't miss you."

"I'm sorry for that, too," she said softly. "I missed you. You were ten years old the last time I saw you."

"I'm not ten anymore, and I can take care of myself. Go on back to your fancy house and your fancy job in Chicago. I'm staying in Monroe."

Losing her temper wouldn't accomplish a thing, she reminded herself. It would only give Nick more ammunition. She spotted the waitress and closed her eyes with relief. "Here's our food. We'll finish talking about this later."

"How soon before you head back to Chicago?" Nick sprawled in one of the chairs in the living room and watched her, challenge on his face.

"I'm not going anywhere without you, Nick," she answered, struggling to remain calm. He was fifteen, on the cusp of manhood, but he was still a child who had lost his mother. Of course he was defensive and scared.

"Then I guess you're not going anywhere," he drawled. "Because I'm sure as hell not."

"Don't swear at me." Anger swelled inside her, masking the growing desperation. She would not stay in Monroe. Images of the people who'd whispered about the Kendalls but did nothing to stop the abuse, nothing to help the two children, rose up inside her. Her ex-husband's sneering face joined them, and she closed her eyes against the images.

"I wasn't swearing at you," he retorted. "Swearing at you would be saying 'go to hell.' I didn't say 'go to hell.' I said hell to emphasize my determination."

A reluctant smile leached away her anger. "You must have kept Janice on her toes. How often did she complain about living with a smart kid?"

He scowled. "My mom never complained about living with me." She saw his mouth tremble. "She never said anything about living with a smart kid."

"I'm sorry, Nick," she said. "I know Janice adored you. She wouldn't have complained." She sighed. "I was trying to make a joke. You know? Lighten the mood?"

"Yeah, well, it wasn't very funny." He got out of the chair and towered over her. He was tall and gangly already, with an awkward body that would fill out as he got older. "I'll be in my room when you want to say goodbye."

His limp was more noticeable tonight. Her heart ached as she watched him try to disguise his unbalanced gait. The congenital dislocation of his hip had been repaired when he was an infant, but the joint would never be normal. Nick disappeared up the stairs, and she heard the defiant bang of his door slamming shut. Moments later his stereo blasted out Eminem.

He would be horrified if he knew she liked Eminem.

Shoving her hands into the pockets of her tailored slacks, she wandered around the first floor of the house, trying to banish the memories. Apparently Janice had been able to get past those memories and the pain they evoked. When their mother had died earlier that year, her sister had said she wanted the house. Nick needed stability, she'd said. They were going home.

Claire leaned against the kitchen counter and looked out the window. The trees stood guard at the back of the house, a wall of darkness and refuge. If she walked into the woods, could she find any remnants of the fort she and Janice had made?

Of course not. After so many years, the branches they'd used would have rotted into sawdust. The fort was gone as surely as Janice.

Very little else about the house had changed. The butcher-block pattern of the Formica counters had faded to white in patches, the dark wood kitchen cabinets were covered with nicks and scratches, and the appliances were at least as old as she was. Janice had tried to put some brightening touches in the room, like the vase of cheerful flowers, now wilted, on the scarred wooden table and the bright dish towels hanging from the rack, but it was the same kitchen Claire remembered.

The living room, too, had changed little. The furniture was more shabby, more faded and worn, as was the carpet, but that was all.

"Why did you come back to Monroe, Janny?" she whispered. "How could you bear to live in this house?"

The ghosts of her parents haunted every room. The echoes of angry voices reverberated in the walls and the sounds of fists meeting flesh shivered up from the floor.

There was no way she could live in this house.

No way in hell. As Nick would say.

Ten years ago, she'd left and vowed never to return. Although she and her mother had made an uneasy peace after her father died, their infrequent visits had all been in Chicago. And now here she was, living in the place of her childhood nightmares, a place drenched in misery and unhappiness.

And she couldn't get Nick to leave.

He and his mother had only been living in Monroe for three months when Janice was killed in the car crash. Now Nick would be uprooted once again, transplanted to the foreign territory of Chicago.

Her condominium in Lincoln Park was big enough for both of them. There were rooms she never even used. Nick would adjust to the change. Kids were very adaptable. He'd be fine.

Would he? The small voice nagged at her from deep within her conscience.

Of course Nick would be fine! He would attend the most exclusive private school in the city, only blocks from her house. He'd get the best education money could buy, much better than Monroe High School. He'd make friends and get involved in all sorts of clubs and activities. What teen wouldn't love growing up in a city like Chicago?

Maybe Nick wouldn't, the mocking voice inside her suggested. She had no idea, because she didn't know her nephew. Not in any of the ways that mattered.

"Damn it!" She picked up a tattered pillow from the couch and heaved it against the wall. It struck a picture, which clattered to the floor. The frame cracked and fell into pieces on the wood floor.

"Good! I always hated that picture," she said under her breath.

"What's going on?" Nick called from the stairs.

"Nothing." She pushed heavy strands of hair away from her face. "Nothing at all."

He peered over the banister, frowning at the picture

and its shattered frame. "What did you do? Why are you wrecking my house?"

She wanted to remind him that it wasn't his house, that they owned equal shares. But she clamped her mouth shut. One immature child in the house was enough.

"I'm not wrecking the house, Nick. The picture came off the wall. It was falling apart anyway."

"That was my favorite picture." He scowled at her.

She glanced at the canvas leaning against the wall. Dull, dusty fruit, most of it unidentifiable, was painted onto a bilious green background. "Yeah, I can see why," she said.

He gave her a sharp look but didn't respond. After staring at the picture for a moment, he turned and headed back up the stairs. "Make sure you clean it up," he said over his shoulder.

She bit off her instinctive, angry retort. Now wasn't the time to get into a fight. She was tired, upset and on edge. A bad combination. It was the worst possible time for a confrontation with her nephew.

She lowered herself onto the worn couch, sinking deep into the cushion. She couldn't stay in Monroe. Ugly memories of fear and anger swept through her in a roiling wave. No one could expect her to stay in Monroe.

She'd paid her penance in this town for the first twenty years of her life. An ugly childhood followed by an uglier marriage had destroyed any wisps of fondness, any nostalgia she might have felt for Monroe.

But would Chicago really be the best place for Nick? that small voice asked again. He must have friends here. Maybe he had a job. A girlfriend.

She'd never asked him, she realized with a surge of shame. She'd assumed he'd gladly pack up and leave.

"Nick," she called up the stairs. "Could you come down here for a moment?"

His door opened. "What?" he yelled.

"I need to talk to you."

"About what?"

"Just come here, will you?"

After a moment she heard him on the stairs. As soon as he could see her, he stopped. "What?"

"Come and sit down," she said, the effort to be patient grinding against her temper.

He stared at her for a long moment, then shuffled down the stairs and threw himself onto the chair farthest from the couch.

"Tell me why you want to stay in Monroe," she said.

He studied her, his face wary, clearly wondering what she was up to. Finally he scowled and looked away. "This is the place my mom wanted to live," he said. "Okay? She said a new start would be good for both of us." His voice thickened and he stood up, ramming his hands into the pockets of his baggy jeans. The pressure of his fists pulled them even lower on his narrow hips.

"What else did your mom say?" she asked quietly.

"She had a job, you know." He whirled to face her, anger filling his face. His eyes were shiny with unshed tears. "She said we'd be just like everyone else in town. I'd go to high school, she'd go to work. We wouldn't have to move around all the time. We'd be a normal family, just like the other kids. That's all I ever wanted to be."

His voice caught on the last words and he turned

away from her again, furtively wiping his hand across his eyes.

"You could have the same things in Chicago," she said softly. "There's a wonderful school a few blocks away from my condo. I have a job, too, but I'd be home every evening. I'll never take your mother's place, but we could make a home together."

"I don't need a home in Chicago. I have one here." His voice was thick and he cleared his throat.

"And I have a job in Chicago."

Her job as the owner of a small accounting firm gave her a lot of flexibility, she admitted reluctantly. With a few adjustments, it was a job she could do from Monroe.

She could stay in Monroe for a few weeks. She could give Nick a chance to get to know her before she took him back to the city.

Her stomach spasmed, and dread rushed through her at the thought.

Monroe.

The town she feared. The town where she had never been in control of any aspect of her life. The town that starred in all her nightmares.

The town where her ex-husband still lived.

It was a matter of what she wanted versus what Nick needed. Her stomach twisted even tighter. He was a child. His needs had to come first.

It was the least she could do for Janice. She'd failed her sister when they were children, allowing her older sister to absorb all the punishment from their parents.

And she'd failed Janice as an adult. She should have made sure her sister and her nephew were provided for.

She drew a deep, trembling breath. Forcing the words out of her mouth, she said, "How about we compromise? We'll stay in Monroe for a few weeks while we get to know each other. When you're comfortable with me, and vice versa, we'll go back to Chicago."

Nick turned around slowly, distrust in his eyes. "I thought you had a job in Chicago."

The faint flicker of hope behind the anger and suspicion in his eyes filled her with another rush of shame. She'd been in such a hurry to leave Monroe she hadn't considered Nick's feelings at all. "I do. But I can work from Monroe, at least for a little while."

She saw his hands bunch into fists inside the pockets of his jeans. "What is this important job you do?"

"I didn't say it was important," she answered, her voice mild. "It's only important to me." She hesitated. Would her job make him even more resentful of her? "I own a small accounting company."

He scowled. "You're going to just let your business go to hell?"

"I can do my job from Monroe," she said, resisting the urge to tell him not to swear. He would no doubt like nothing better than to redirect their discussion.

"You're going to make all the rich people come to Monroe?" he asked with a sneer.

"Not at all. I can do a lot of my work over the phone, with a fax machine and a computer. I can get by without face-to-face meetings for a while."

Hope struggled to surface in his eyes. She watched as he crushed it. "Don't bother to get everything set up. I'm not going to change my mind."

"Let's not worry about that right now." She looked around the room as dread filled her again. "School opens in two weeks. Let's see how we're doing by then."

CHAPTER TWO

"YOU DID WHAT?"

Incredulous, Claire turned her chair from her computer to face Nick. He stared back at her insolently, the always-present anger swirling like storm clouds in his eyes. Nothing had changed in the three weeks since Janice's funeral.

"I joined the football team."

"You can't play football!"

"Says who?" he sneered.

"Says me. And your doctors. And the school! They know about your hip and your asthma. I can't believe they let you sign up to play football."

"Coach Hall said I could be on the team." Nick stuck his chin out. "He said it would be good for me."

"And how would Coach Hall know what's good for you?"

"Tucker Hall knows everything about football," Nick responded hotly. "He said he could make me a kicker."

"I don't care what he said he could do. And I don't care how much he knows about football. He doesn't know what's best for you."

Was Tucker Hall the same man who'd been the football coach when she'd attended Monroe High School? She had no idea, but the name sounded vaguely familiar.

"He's a good coach," Nick said. "All the guys say so. Of course, you wouldn't know that. You don't know a thing about football." His voice dripped with scorn.

"Guilty as charged," she said, her voice dry. "But I do know a few things about you."

Beneath her nephew's defiance she could see his hunger to be accepted, to be merely one of the guys instead of the newcomer with a limp. She'd learned that much about him in the past three weeks. Remembering her childhood as the one who never fit in, the child the other kids whispered about, the one who was *different*, her heart ached for him.

But it didn't mean she could let him play football. It was a dangerous, ridiculous idea. "I guess I'll have to straighten out this Coach Hall."

"Let's go back to school right now," Nick said. "You can talk to him after practice."

She wanted to refuse, to tell Nick there was no way he was playing football and that was the end of the discussion. But she hesitated. This was the most animated she'd seen him since his mother had died. And even if there *was* no way she could let him play football, she could at least explain the reasons to the coach.

"All right, Nick. I'll go over to the high school and talk to him. I'm sure once he understands your medical problems he'll agree with me."

"I don't have any medical problems." Nick's eyes

took on the mulish expression that was becoming too familiar to her. "I keep telling you that."

"You have asthma. And your hip is fragile."

"There's nothing wrong with my hip," he shot back. "I had surgery on it when I was a baby. It's fine."

"Yes, your hip was repaired, but it's not as strong as it should be. You can't play a contact sport, even if you didn't have asthma."

"Kids with asthma play sports all the time," he said scornfully, as if this was something she should have known. "They use inhalers and sh—stuff."

"Do you even have an inhaler? I haven't seen you use it once in the past few weeks." She noticed the near slip into swearing, and the way he caught himself. He was listening to at least some of the things she'd said. It might be a tiny step, but it was progress.

He hunched his shoulders and turned away, a response she'd learned was typical when she was right and he knew it. "I haven't had any reason to use it," he muttered.

"All right. I'll call the school tomorrow and make an appointment to talk to the coach."

"No! We have to go right now!"

He faced her, and for the first time wasn't trying to hide how he felt. The pleading look in his eyes made her heart constrict. "I need to start tomorrow. I can't do that unless you talk to Coach today. I've already missed two weeks of practice!"

She glanced at the spreadsheet she'd been working on. It wasn't nearly as important as her nephew. Clicking it closed, she stood up.

"All right. We'll go over to the high school now."

TUCKER HALL STOOD on the practice field, watching carefully as the sixty-four players on his team ran laps around the track, still wearing their pads and helmets. The crushing heat of a central Illinois summer had relented just a little today. He didn't have to worry as much about heat-related illnesses, but he still assessed each boy as he trotted past.

A car door slammed in the distance, and a voice called, "Coach Hall! Coach Hall!"

He turned to see Nick Kendall hurrying toward him, trying hard not to limp. The kid's face was lit with excitement, and Tucker felt something squeeze his heart.

Trailing behind him was a slight woman. Even from a distance he could see the resolve in her squared shoulders and determined stride. So this was the aunt. The woman Nick described as a combination jailer, tyrant and Cruella DeVil.

"All right, guys, take a water break," he yelled to his team. "And keep walking while you're drinking."

He strolled over to the edge of the field and nodded to Nick. "Hey, Kendall. Brought your aunt, huh?" Tucker crossed his arms and waited for the woman to catch up.

"She says I can't play football. Tell her she's wrong."

The raw eagerness in Nick's eyes made him look like a typical fifteen-year-old. It was the most unguarded Tucker had seen him since school had started.

Tucker watched as the woman approached. She was shorter than Nick—the gangly teen towered over her. And slender in a pair of shorts and a T-shirt. But she had curves in all the right places. He felt a quickening of interest as she got closer.

Her short, sleek, dark-red hair brushed her cheek as she walked. Her legs were firm and smooth, and her eyes were deep pools of mysterious green.

And faint, disapproving determination.

She stopped in front of him and had to look up to meet his eyes. "Mr. Hall? I'm Claire Kendall. Nick's aunt."

She held out her hand. Her grip was firm and businesslike. But her skin was smooth and creamy.

Startled by the thought, he dropped her hand and took a step backward. The air was suddenly too dense and heavy.

"I'm Tucker Hall," he said, and waited for the inevitable recognition to seep into her eyes.

She frowned, and he braced himself. But all she said was, "Your name sounds familiar. But you're not the football coach I remember."

"Tom Peters retired last year," he said, letting out the breath he'd been holding. "I took his place."

"I see."

She continued frowning, as if trying to place him, then shook her head. "That doesn't matter. Nick says you told him he could play football. I'm afraid that's impossible." Her voice was brisk and firm. "He has a congenital weakness in his hip, and he can't play any contact sports."

"Nick told me all about his hip. And his asthma," Tucker answered.

He saw the flicker of surprise in her eyes. "He did?" Then she recovered. "So you must see that football wouldn't be a wise choice for him."

"Not at all. I think football would be an excellent choice for him."

Her eyes narrowed. "Perhaps you didn't understand, Mr. Hall. Nick—"

He interrupted, holding one hand up to stop her. "Hold on a minute. Nick," he turned to the boy, "why don't you go on over and start walking with the team. You've got some catching up to do to get in shape."

Nick grinned and his whole face lit up. "Yes, sir!"

"Johnson!" Tucker shouted. "Walk with Kendall."

Nick ran toward the other boys and fell in beside a couple of other sophomores.

Tucker turned to Claire. "Booger Johnson is a sophomore, too. He's in a couple of Nick's classes."

"Booger?"

Tucker grinned. "It's a teenage boy thing. You probably don't want to know the details."

He glanced over at the boys again, then back at Claire Kendall. "You were saying?"

Her jaw tightened and her eyes flashed. "You had no right to tell him to go practice with the team. He can't play football!"

"He's not practicing. He's just walking. That's not going to hurt him, is it? Or is walking prohibited, too? With his hip problem and all?"

He was baiting her and it was a mistake. But he wanted to see those sparks flash in her eyes again.

He wasn't disappointed. "Do you understand plain English? Or are you going to prove that dreary stereotype of the athlete as a Neanderthal? Nick can't play *football!* It's cruel to get his hopes up like that."

"I don't agree. Nick can and should play football. Come on over into the shade so we can talk."

He touched her arm and she jerked away from his hand. "Didn't you listen to a thing I said? He was born with a dislocated hip. It's been surgically repaired, but it's still fragile. And on top of that, he has asthma."

He took her elbow and steered her toward a tree, tightening his grip when she tried to free herself. He wanted to keep touching that velvety skin of hers.

Don't do it, a voice warned. *She's definitely not your type. Everything about her says sleek, sophisticated city woman.*

He released her when they reached the tree and she backed up a step, rubbing the spot where he'd held her. He hadn't held her that tightly, he thought, watching the sweep of her fingers over her skin. His muscles tightened. Apparently sleek city women *were* his type.

Was it possible she'd felt the same tiny frisson of electricity when he touched her?

It didn't matter if she did. She was here to talk about Nick. And that was all.

"Ms. Kendall, are you aware that Nick is having trouble in school?"

Her eyebrows shot up to her hairline. "What kind of trouble?" She took a step toward him, then caught herself.

"Not the kind you're thinking of." He wanted to touch her arm again, to reassure her, but he kept his hands to himself. "He's in my U.S. history class, and he's a good student. Bright, hardworking, conscientious. But he isolates himself from the rest of the students. He doesn't talk to anyone, doesn't sit with anyone at lunch. And it's not as if no one tries. I've seen several kids make overtures to him, but he pushes them away."

Worry filled Claire Kendall's eyes. "I wondered if he was making any friends at school," she said. "He never calls anyone, and no one calls the house for him."

"School is as much about learning social skills as it is about learning math and reading," he said. "That's why I'm concerned."

"I appreciate that," she said, and swallowed once. Pain filled her eyes and was quickly hidden. "His mother died very recently. Nick has a lot to deal with."

"I know about his mother. I'm sorry for your loss and his, and I think it would help him to get involved in an activity. He wants to play football."

"There are a lot of other activities that would be more suitable."

"Probably. But football is what he wants to do." He leaned forward, trying to make her understand. "Do you know he's been at practice every afternoon since school started? He stands against that fence over there and watches from beginning to end. Every day."

"I didn't know he wanted to play football that much. I wish it was possible," she said in a low voice. Her gaze wandered and he could see she was watching her nephew. "I want him to find something he loves, something to be passionate about. But his hip can't take the kind of beating he'd get playing football."

"I think you're wrong," he said, his eyes on the boy. Nick was talking to Booger. He was more animated than Tucker had ever seen him. "Do you know anything about football, Ms. Kendall?"

"Not a thing," she said, tearing her gaze away from Nick. "Do you?"

He wanted to tell her exactly how much he knew about football. He caught himself in time. The fact that she didn't recognize his name meant she knew nothing about the game. And he was asking her to entrust her nephew to his care, a boy with physical drawbacks.

"Yes, I know a lot about football. I've been playing it for twenty years."

Her gaze flickered over him, then she nodded. "All right. Tell me how Nick could play football."

Her small concession had him moving a step closer. "Every team needs someone to kick the ball. For field goals." He pointed to the uprights at each end of the field. "We get three points if we kick the ball through those poles."

"I do know that much about football," she said, her voice wry. "I live in Chicago. I'd have to be living in a cave not to learn something about football."

She hadn't learned much, or she would have recognized his name. And thank God she hadn't.

"All right. We need a field goal kicker. We also need a punter. He kicks the ball when we have to give it to the other team."

"And you think Nick could be a kicker?"

"Yes, he could. The kicker rarely gets tackled. The other team is concentrating on the ball more than the kicker, and the kicker usually ends up just standing on the field after the play is over."

"It's the 'rarely' and 'usually' parts of what you just said that bother me, Mr. Hall."

"I'll teach him how to avoid tackles. This is the one time in his life that his hip problem will actually be an asset, rather than a liability."

She frowned. "How can that be?"

"His right leg is weaker than normal because of his problem. That means his left leg is a lot stronger. If he can kick with his left leg, he'll have a big advantage."

"And you think you can teach him all this?" Her eyes held skepticism.

The competitor in him leaped to attention. He'd never been able to resist a challenge. And Claire Kendall was clearly challenging him.

"Yes, I can teach him that. That's my job. And I'm damn good at it."

She tore her gaze away from her nephew. "I'm glad to see that you have a healthy ego, Coach. Although I've never found that trait attractive in a man, it doesn't matter if you can help Nick."

"You don't pull your punches, do you?" he said.

"No, I don't," she answered coolly. "What would be the point?"

Oh, yeah. This one was a ball-breaker. "Any other concerns you'd like to share with an egotistical Neanderthal? Before I get back to the kids?" he asked.

Pink washed over her creamy skin. But she lifted her chin. "Nick has asthma, you know. That's another reason he can't play football."

"There are several other boys on the team with asthma. They all handle it just fine with their inhalers and medication." He raised his eyebrows. "Maybe you should see his doctor."

"Nick already has an inhaler. He won't use it."

"He will if he wants to be on the team. That's rule number one. If you need medication, you use it. If not, you're off the team."

She watched him for a moment, then nodded. "All right, Mr. Hall. I'll give you a chance. Nick can play."

He searched her gaze, startled. He'd been certain she wouldn't give in, even though he'd answered all her questions. "Thank you," he finally said. "And no one calls me Mr. Hall. The kids call me Coach Hall. You can call me Tucker."

She gave him a cool look. "I can't imagine I'll have much reason to talk to you, Mr. Hall."

He let his gaze sweep over her once. "You might be surprised."

A faint blush of color bloomed in her face once more. "I'll be monitoring Nick closely," she said, ignoring his faint come-on. "If I think this isn't working, I'll take him off the team."

"I hope you'll talk to me about it first," he said.

"Of course. And one other thing. Nick may not even be here for all the games. As soon as he's more comfortable with me, we're moving back to Chicago."

"Is that so?" Of course they were moving back to Chicago, he told himself harshly. The confident look in her eyes, the challenging tilt of her head, the smooth sophistication of her clothes and hair were definitely out of place in Monroe. Claire Kendall had *city girl* stamped all over her.

"Yes. I don't know when we'll be leaving, but don't count on Nick for the whole season."

"Does Nick know about this?"

Her gaze slipped over his shoulder, and he guessed she was watching her nephew again. Uncertainty and pain filled her eyes. "We've talked about it in general terms."

"Well, in general terms, I think Nick expects to be here for the season. It ends in November."

"I'll keep that in mind when we're making plans," she said, cool and collected again. "How soon before practice is over?"

"About five minutes. I like to talk to them as a group before we call it a day."

"What equipment is Nick going to need?" she asked.

"The sports store in town has a list. You can get everything there."

"Thank you." She held out her hand, and he wrapped his larger one around it. She felt fragile and unsubstantial. But Claire Kendall was anything but weak. She might be small, but she packed a wallop.

"I'll see you at the first game," he said.

She nodded. "I'll be there."

CLAIRE STOOD under the tree and watched as Tucker Hall talked to his team. His voice was low-pitched and quiet, and she couldn't hear what he said. But every boy listened to him intently, their attention completely focused on him.

She wasn't surprised. Tucker Hall was the kind of man who commanded attention. It wasn't just his size, although he towered over her and all the boys. He wasn't bulky, but his broad shoulders and lean build would make him stand out anywhere.

It was more his quiet assumption of authority, the way he carried himself, as if no one would think to question his leadership.

Apparently it worked with teenage boys. It had certainly worked with Nick. He never paid that much attention to her.

A few minutes later the meeting ended and the boys began to straggle toward the school. Tucker stopped Nick with a hand on his shoulder. Moments later, her nephew's face lit up. He nodded vigorously, then turned and ran toward her.

"Thank you," he said breathlessly, but she noticed he still wouldn't call her by name. Not once had he called her Aunt Claire, or even Claire. "Coach Hall told me you said I could play. I'll use my inhaler every day," he promised. "Can we go get my gear now?"

"Sure," she said, glad to see Nick so excited. "What are you going to need?"

As they walked to the car, Nick babbled about cleats and practice jerseys. Claire was almost glad she'd allowed him to play.

Almost.

Besides her worries about his health, football was another tie binding him to Monroe. As excited as he was about being on the team, there was no way he'd agree to leave before the season was over. She'd have to endure at least two more months of Monroe.

She could do it, she told herself. She'd been here three weeks and survived.

Of course, she hadn't gone anywhere. She'd holed up in the house, working. She'd ventured out only to get groceries and school supplies for Nick, and she'd driven to the next town for that. But she couldn't avoid everyone in Monroe for two more months.

This trip to town would be her first. It was long overdue. She'd never thought of herself as a coward, but she'd been cringing in her house like a whipped puppy.

Not anymore, she vowed.

She tuned out Nick's chatter as she parked the car, then she took a deep breath and slid out onto the hot asphalt. Downtown Monroe didn't look any different than it had when she'd left.

A few stores had different names, some facades had been updated, but most of the buildings looked the same. The library still occupied the old Rogard mansion, an elaborate, graceful Victorian set back from the street and surrounded by stately oak trees. City hall was still across the street, solid and sturdy in an old brick house. She couldn't help looking at her ex-husband's law office. It hadn't changed, either. She reminded herself that she was a different woman from the girl who had fled Monroe, but the old shame and anxiety bloomed inside her anyway.

"Where's the sports store?" Nick asked, craning his head as they scanned the stores on Main Street.

"It's around the corner. This way."

Nick hurried to keep up with her, and she forced herself to slow down. She was an adult, she reminded herself sharply. A successful adult who'd built a good life for herself. She didn't have to scurry around Monroe, ashamed and scared. If she did, she knew what would happen. It was just like dealing with a vicious animal—

if she showed any sign of weakness, the people of Monroe would be merciless.

They'd almost made it safely to the Monroe Sports Shop when the door of the barbershop opened and a man stepped into her path. She stopped in time to avoid a collision, but not before he'd recognized her.

"Well, well, well. Look who's in town," Roger Vernon drawled, flashing an ugly smile. "I'd heard you'd moved back to Monroe. What are you doing here, Claire? Slumming?"

Claire stood on the sidewalk, frozen in the summer heat, and stared at her ex-husband.

CHAPTER THREE

CLAIRE RECOVERED quickly, but not quickly enough. Roger had seen her moment of weakness and he pounced.

"Who would guess you'd be back in Monroe?" he continued, sneering. "I didn't think we were good enough for you."

"You certainly weren't," she retorted, her voice crisp.

He flushed with anger, and she had to stop herself from cringing away from him. She was no longer twenty years old and married to him, she reminded herself sharply.

"This must be Janice's son," Roger said, measuring Nick with his eyes.

"Nick Kendall, Roger Vernon," she said, her voice cold. "Sorry we can't stay and chat, but we're busy."

Stepping past Roger, she grabbed Nick's arm and dragged him around the corner.

Nick stared at her, astonishment in his eyes. "Wow," he said. "Who was that dude? You shut him down big-time."

"Roger Vernon isn't worth the time it takes to talk about him," she said. "Here's the store. Let's get your gear."

They emerged from the store forty-five minutes later,

Nick clutching the bag of equipment close to his chest. Back in the store, picking out shoes and practice clothes, he'd been the happy, sweet kid she remembered from her last brief visit with Janice. Five years ago, she reminded herself, guilt washing over her in a hot wave.

A lot can change in five years.

As they went by, Nick glanced into the window of the town's small restaurant. The Dixie Diner had been a fixture in Monroe for as long as she could remember.

"Did you eat here when you lived in Monroe?" he asked.

She gave him a sharp glance. He never initiated conversations. But she saw no sarcasm in his eyes, just the painful longing of a child gazing at a denied treat.

"Not very often," she said in a neutral voice. "My parents couldn't afford to take us to a restaurant."

That wasn't the complete truth. Even if they'd had the money, neither her mother nor her father would have thought of spending it on a family outing. The idea would have been completely foreign to them.

"Did you and Janice eat here before…" She couldn't force the words *before the accident* out of her mouth.

Nick didn't seem to notice her hesitation. "Nah. Mom always said it wasn't our kind of place."

But Nick desperately wanted to go to the diner. She could see it in his eyes. And suddenly she understood.

When she was in high school, all the kids had hung out at the diner, and that probably hadn't changed. When she'd been Nick's age, she'd secretly hungered to go there, too. But there'd been no money for Cokes and French fries after school. So she'd walked past it every day, pretending she had no interest in the gathering at the diner.

"Let's have dinner here," she said impulsively. "We both need a break from cooking."

"Really? Are you sure?" He glanced at the modest menu posted in the window. "The prices seem kind of high."

Another wave of shame washed over her. She could have made Nick's life, and Janice's, so much easier. Janice hadn't wanted charity, but she could have found some way to help them. The trust fund she'd set up for Nick's college education now seemed pitifully inadequate.

"Let's splurge," she said, forcing herself to smile. "Including hot fudge sundaes for dessert."

Nick was already pushing open the door to the restaurant. A tinny bell rang and the hostess looked up. "Table for two?" she asked brightly.

"Please." Claire looked around, remembering her desperate longing to be included in the gatherings here after school. She was pretty sure that the landscapes and lake scenes decorating the walls were the same ones from years ago. The chairs and tables looked old, as well, but the restaurant held an air of vitality. Apparently it was still the nerve center of Monroe.

The hostess led them to a place in the middle of the diner, and Claire followed Nick into the booth. The air smelled of fried food and the turquoise vinyl seats were cold and stiff against her legs. Nick pored over the menu, his bag of football equipment tucked under his arm.

Maybe, for one evening, they could pretend to be a normal family.

They were halfway through dinner when Nick looked up. Wariness flickered in his eyes, then he glanced at her.

Claire turned around to see what had disturbed him. She was dismayed to see Roger Vernon and a young woman standing by the door. Roger had his hand on the young woman's back, a proprietary stance Claire remembered all too well.

Coldness spread deep inside her. Had Roger married again? Or was he thinking about it?

Roger spotted her staring at him and gave her a smug smile. He held her gaze as he followed the hostess through the restaurant, maintaining his contact with the woman's back. The triumph and satisfaction in his eyes sparked a flare of anger inside her.

He slowed as they passed her booth, and impulsively Claire jumped to her feet. She held out her hand to the startled young woman and said, "Hi. I'm Claire Kendall. I don't think we've met."

The woman looked puzzled, but she held out her hand obediently. "I'm Andrea Vernon. Nice to meet you." She studied Claire's face. "Do you live in Monroe?"

"I just moved back here." She glanced at Roger, who seemed furious, then back at Andrea. "I'll see you around town."

"Sure." Andrea gave her another bewildered look, then Roger steered her away. Claire slowly slid back into the booth.

Nick watched her with curiosity in his eyes. "You haven't talked to anyone since you got to Monroe," he said. "Why did you introduce yourself to her?"

She stared at him, startled and surprised. Apparently

he'd been watching her more closely than she realized. She struggled to frame her answer carefully. "Impulse." She shrugged. "I thought maybe she could use a friend."

With the unselfconscious curiosity of the young, Nick turned around and looked at Roger and Andrea. "Why?"

Roger caught his glance and glared at him. She saw Nick's shoulders hunch, then he turned back to face her.

Before she could answer his question, Roger was standing next to their booth. He put his hands on the table and leaned toward her. "You stay away from Andrea and keep your nose out of my business," he warned her, his voice full of venom. "Do you understand?"

Claire stared right back at him. "No, I'm not sure I do." Her voice was steady, but she was shaking inside. Stupid, cowardly reaction, she told herself. But the instinctive response was too powerful, too ingrained to be ignored.

Roger leaned closer. "I think you know what I mean," he said. If she didn't back away, he'd be touching her. Revulsion crawled over her skin, and he smiled with satisfaction.

Before she could react, another voice spoke over her shoulder. "I didn't expect to see you here. Hello, Nick, Ms. Kendall. Vernon." The soft southern drawl was completely neutral in tone.

It was Tucker Hall. Roger straightened and gave him an angry stare, then returned to his table. Claire watched his young wife, who gave her husband a frightened look. Claire vowed to call Andrea Vernon at the first opportunity.

The football coach took Roger's place next to the table. "Looks like you got some gear there," he said.

Nick glanced over his shoulder at the Vernons, then looked back at Tucker. His eyes brightened. "Yeah. We got everything on the list. I'll be ready to go tomorrow."

"Great. You've got some catching up to do. But you're a smart kid. You'll pick it up right away." Tucker's smile swept over both of them, and Claire felt as if she'd been punched in the gut.

Tucker glanced at Claire. "You two come here for dinner often? I don't remember seeing you."

"It's our first time," she said. "How about you?"

"I eat dinner here most nights," he said with an easy smile. "Best way I know to keep tabs on what my kids are up to." He nodded at Roger's table. "Looks like you've met our esteemed lawyer already."

Was that a hint of contempt she heard in Tucker's voice? "I knew him years ago," she said, expressionless.

She gave him a polite smile and prepared to dismiss him. She didn't like the way her stomach reacted when he smiled at her. But before she could say anything, Nick leaned across the table. "You want to have dinner with us?" he asked eagerly. "We've got plenty of room."

Tucker didn't hesitate. "Sure. Thanks for the invitation." He gave Claire another smile, and her stomach dipped again. "If that's okay with you, Ms. Kendall?"

"Of course," she managed to say. She tried to signal Nick to move over so Tucker could slide in next to him, but the coach was already easing onto the bench next to her.

One side of his mouth curled up in a grin as he nodded at the bag of football gear clutched under Nick's arm. "You going to sleep with that equipment tonight, Kendall?"

Claire tensed, waiting for the explosion from Nick. She'd learned quickly that any hint of teasing only resulted in sarcasm, sneering or anger.

To her surprise, he grinned at his coach. "Maybe I will. Do you think it would help me learn faster?"

"You never know."

Tucker glanced over at her. She recognized the spark of interest in his eyes, the appreciative flash of male approval. An involuntary response shivered through her.

Apparently he'd taken a shower after practice, because his short, sun-bleached blond hair now gleamed dark gold with water. The crisp scent of his soap seemed to surround her, and the heat of his body burned into her. His leg was inches from hers, and the conservative khaki slacks he wore did nothing to hide his powerfully muscled thighs. She felt ridiculously small sitting next to him.

In spite of the signals her body was giving her, she was not interested in Tucker Hall, she told herself firmly. He was too big, too male, too cocky, too overwhelming.

And he lived in Monroe.

That fact alone was the death knell of any possible relationship. She wouldn't stay in Monroe a second longer than absolutely necessary. No matter how attractive she found the man sitting next to her.

"…one of the conditions of being on the team," Tucker was saying to Nick. "You avoid contact with the other team, as much as possible."

Nick frowned. The mulish glint of resistance she'd come to know so well over the past three weeks flared in his eyes. "You're supposed to get hit in football. You're supposed to hit the other team."

"Not the kicker," Tucker answered. He leaned back in the booth and draped his arm over the top of the seat. His forearm brushed against the nape of her neck in a fleeting caress, then was gone. Sensation crashed through her, and she snapped her head around to look at him. Engrossed in his conversation with Nick, he appeared not to notice.

Apparently the contact had been accidental.

She wasn't sure if she was disappointed or relieved. Heart pounding, she pretended she hadn't noticed, either.

"The kicker is off-limits to the other team," he was explaining to Nick. "When his leg is in the air, he's completely defenseless."

"Where's the fun in that?" Nick grumbled.

"The fun is in contributing to the team," Tucker answered, holding Nick's gaze. "Knowing that you're playing as a team. That's what football is all about."

He sat back and gave Nick another easy smile, and her stomach did a flip. "Besides, a good kicker is vital in football, and you're going to be an important part of Monroe's success this year. I don't want you to take any chances that will hurt the team."

Nick glowed, and Claire felt a rush of gratitude. She suspected it had been a long time since Nick had heard praise like that. He was too prickly, too defensive. Tucker was saying exactly what Nick needed to hear.

Tucker's dinner arrived and he ate quickly, as if he only swallowed the food because he needed fuel. Nick talked about football while he ate, and Claire marveled at the difference in her nephew.

"You've been here for a few months now. How do you like Monroe?" Tucker asked as he pushed his empty plate toward the center of the table.

Nick shrugged. "Monroe is okay, I guess."

His eyebrows rose. "Just okay?"

Nick looked away. "There's not much to do here."

"There's plenty to do, if you're interested in finding it," he said, his voice mild. "The parks commission organizes all kinds of stuff for kids during the summer. Did you check that out?"

Nick hunched his shoulder and scowled. "Nah. It all sounded pretty lame to me."

"Suit yourself." Tucker leaned back against the seat, and Nick glanced at him, surprised. Claire knew he'd expected the coach to give him the stock speech about making his own opportunities.

"How about you?" Tucker turned to Claire.

"How do I like Monroe?" she asked. "I can't wait to get back to Chicago."

"Why's that?"

"It's where I live. Where I work. And Monroe—" She clamped her mouth shut, shocked that she'd almost blurted out her reasons for hating the town to this stranger.

"Monroe..." he prompted.

"I don't fit in Monroe," she said coolly. "I'm much more comfortable in the city."

"I see." The cheerful, uncomplicated smile in his eyes was gone, replaced by a bland gaze that hid everything he was thinking. "What is it that you do in Chicago?"

"I own an accounting business."

"Sounds interesting." His tone said he thought otherwise.

"It is," she said with a tiny emphasis. "I'm very happy in Chicago."

"I told her she didn't have to stay here," Nick said from across the table. He glared at her, frowning.

"Nick, you know I wanted to stay," she replied. "I can work from Monroe almost as easily as from Chicago."

"You can't wait to get out of here."

"That's right. My home is in Chicago," she said, struggling to keep her voice level. "Naturally I want to go back there. But I already told you we'll stay here until you're ready to leave."

"I'm not ready to leave," he said defiantly.

"I know that. And we have a lot of work to do on the house," she said briskly. "That's going to take a while."

"Why bother to work on the house if we're going to leave?" Nick challenged.

She felt Tucker's gaze on her but didn't look over at him. "We'll need to sell the house," she said gently. "It looks like your mom started to fix it up. We'll finish what she started."

Nick flicked a stray French fry off the table. "She would have done more," he said defiantly. "She was just busy with her job."

"She worked over at city hall, didn't she?" Tucker rested his elbows on the table and gazed at Nick.

"Yeah. She had some big job over there."

"What did she do?" Claire asked, curious.

"I don't know." Nick shrugged. "She worked in an office." After a moment, he muttered, "She liked it, the work and the responsibility. She said it was the first decent job she'd ever had."

"It sounds like your mom was glad she'd come back to Monroe," Tucker said gently.

"She was." Nick's eyes glittered with unshed tears. "She said it was a new start for both of us."

"I'm so sorry about her accident," Tucker said.

Nick stared at them, the challenging, angry look back on his face. "It wasn't an accident," he said, his voice thick. He wiped his arm across his eyes to catch any tears that threatened to fall. "My mom was killed."

CHAPTER FOUR

"What?" Claire's gasp fell into the sudden silence.

"You heard me. She was killed." Nick's gaze met hers defiantly and he sniffled again. "Someone called her that night. She told me she had to go meet someone."

"Just because she went to meet someone doesn't mean she was killed," Claire said softly.

"She was worried about something." Nick's expression dared her to disagree. "She was worried before that night."

Claire's heart ached for the boy. Nick had said goodbye to his mother, knowing she was upset, and had never seen her again. Of course he wanted to believe it wasn't an accident that had killed Janice. Claire took his hand. "I'm sorry, Nick."

He yanked his hand from her grasp. "I'm not some stupid kid who doesn't know what he's talking about," he retorted.

"I don't think you're stupid, Nick." Claire wanted to hug him. He'd been completely alone after Janice died. He must have been so frightened, wondering what would happen to him. "I'm being clumsy. It's just that no one mentioned this as a possibility."

"You think I'm making this up, don't you?" Nick's mouth hardened with determination.

"Of course not," she said. "I'm surprised."

"You think it doesn't matter now that she's dead." He crossed his arms in front of his chest and gave her a stubborn stare, so much like Janice that her heart ached.

"Kendall." Tucker's voice was like a whip in the shocked silence. "Apologize to your aunt."

"Don't tell me what to do. You're not my father," Nick shot back.

"Right now you're damn lucky that I'm not," Tucker said grimly. He stared at Nick, his face hard. "But I *am* your coach and you *will* respect me. As well as your aunt." He leaned across the table, his face close to Nick's. "Do you understand?"

Shocked at Tucker's transformation from easygoing dinner companion to dangerous male, Claire watched the silent battle of wills.

Nick looked away first. "Yeah," he muttered.

"Yeah what?" Tucker said.

"Yeah, I understand."

"That's good." Tucker settled against the back of the booth again, but he didn't take his eyes off Nick. When Nick didn't say anything, Tucker leaned toward him again. "Don't you have something to say to your aunt?"

Nick's eyes darted in her direction. "Sorry."

Tucker didn't look away. He kept his gaze locked on Nick's until the boy muttered, "Sorry, Aunt Claire."

The tension surrounding Tucker eased as he nodded at Nick. "Thank you. Now do you think you can discuss this with your aunt like an adult?"

"Yeah." Nick's voice was surly, but his eyes flickered when Tucker used the word *adult.*

"The police told me her car slid off the road into the lake," Claire said carefully. "They didn't say anything about it not being an accident."

Nick snorted in derision. "Of course not. Why would they listen to a kid?"

"You've talked to the police?" Claire asked.

Nick gave her a guarded look. "Yeah. I told the police officer who came to…who told me what happened."

"That was smart thinking. What did he say?"

"He said he'd look into it. But he didn't," Nick burst out. "He didn't do anything."

"Are you sure? Maybe he looked into it and found out that it really was an accident," Claire said gently.

"He didn't." Anger sparked in Nick's eyes. "I asked him later if he found anything and he hadn't even tried."

"How do you know?" Claire asked.

"He gave me all that sympathy crap and told me he knew it was hard, blah blah blah, but sometimes accidents happen." Nick's voice rose. "I could tell he never checked a thing."

"I'll talk to the police," Claire promised. "I'll make sure it was an accident."

"Yeah? You will?"

Claire could see both hope and doubt in Nick's eyes. "Of course. Janice was my sister. I need to know. And you have a right to know what happened to your mother."

"He'll blow you off, too," Nick muttered.

"I don't see Seth Broderick blowing off your aunt," Tucker said, his voice dry.

"Why not?" Nick asked, his eyes guarded as they moved from Tucker to Claire.

"She's a tough city woman, used to getting what she wants. I suspect she doesn't take kindly to 'no,'" Tucker said. "She'll get to the bottom of it."

Somehow it didn't sound like a compliment when Tucker called her a tough city woman. Not bothering to suppress the glimmer of resentment that she'd been judged already and found wanting, Claire ignored him and focused on Nick.

"Mr. Hall is right," she said firmly. "I won't take no for an answer."

Nick looked doubtful, but he nodded. "Okay."

An uneasy silence settled over the table. Claire adjusted her used silverware on her plate and wished Tucker wasn't sitting so close. She felt the tension flowing from him, felt his efforts to calm down.

She didn't want to be this aware of him. Finally, after several edgy moments, she put her hands on the table and plastered a smile on her face.

"Well. We don't want to keep you, Mr. Hall. I'm sure you have things to do tonight. And Nick has homework," she said with a glance at her nephew.

Tucker didn't move. He just shifted in his seat and glanced down at her, his blue eyes sharp with understanding. "Yeah, I should get going. I have a few chores to do." He smiled. "The cave I live in requires a lot of maintenance, you know."

Claire flushed, remembering her remark about Neanderthals earlier in the day. "Then we won't keep you. I'm glad you joined us for dinner." And if he bought that, she was a better liar than she'd thought.

Real amusement lit his eyes. "I enjoyed myself, too. We'll have to do it again."

"Absolutely," she lied. She followed him out of the booth, careful to stand far enough away from him to avoid the force field that crackled around him.

"I'll see you tomorrow in class, Nick," Tucker said. "And I'm looking forward to having you on the team."

"Thanks, Coach." The bruised look in Nick's eyes faded just a little.

Tucker turned to her. She felt tiny next to the tall, broad-shouldered coach, and she took another step away from him. A flicker of his eyes told her that he'd noticed. "Thank you for letting Nick join the team," he said quietly. "You won't be sorry."

As she watched him walk out the door of the diner, she murmured to herself, "That remains to be seen."

Nick stared after him as she paid their bill. "Jeez, where does he get off yelling at me about personal stuff? I thought he was a lot cooler than that," he muttered.

"I still think he's cool," she answered lightly. Unfortunately, she thought as she watched Tucker stroll down the street, *cool* was the last word she'd choose to describe her reaction to Nick's new football coach.

Nick gave her a disgusted look, then twisted his hand around the bag of football equipment and walked out of the restaurant without waiting for her.

She swallowed hard. His enthusiasm for football and

his excitement about his new equipment had apparently vanished. Feeling helpless, she followed him to the car.

He stood impatiently at the car, waiting for her. Desperate for a way to spend more time with her nephew, she scanned the stores along Main Street. An ice cream shop caught her eye, and she turned to Nick.

"Did you forget those hot fudge sundaes?" she asked brightly. She nodded at the store. "How about dessert?"

He looked at the store and his expression lightened for a moment. Then he shrugged. "I don't care," he said, his voice carefully disinterested.

"I'd like some ice cream. Wouldn't you?" she pressed.

He shrugged again. "I guess."

"Let's put your stuff in the car," she said as she unlocked it. Once the gear was safely stowed, she headed across the street. This time Nick walked next to her.

She'd take tiny steps of progress wherever she found them.

As they reached the shop, she saw that it was jammed with people. Her hand on the door was suddenly sweaty, and she wiped it on her shorts. Then, lifting her head, she strode into the shop.

Nick stopped abruptly, staring at the petite blond girl behind the counter, scooping out the ice cream. She must have felt his gaze, because she looked up and saw him.

"Hi, Nick," she called with a smile.

Dark red color flooded Nick's face. "Hi," he tried to say. But it came out as nothing more than a strangled croak. He cleared his throat. "Uh, hello," he finally managed.

The crowd milling around in front of the freezer

cases glanced over at them. Several people's gazes sharpened when they saw her. She nodded to them, her stomach twisting into a knot, but didn't say anything. Grabbing a ticket, she pressed it and some money into Nick's hand.

"Order me a small hot fudge sundae," she said, edging toward the door. "Get whatever you want. I'll wait by the door."

Nick looked at her, a hint of panic in his eyes. "You sure you don't want to order? Maybe you should check out the flavors."

Understanding swept over her. Glancing at the young woman behind the counter, she steered Nick to a corner. "Is the girl behind the counter a friend of yours?"

"She's in a couple of my classes." He turned bright red again.

This was dangerous, sensitive territory. Remembering her own teenage crushes, she prayed she'd handle it right.

"That's nice, but don't try to start a conversation with her. She's too busy to talk," she said briskly, knowing that a conversation with the girl was Nick's deepest fear. "Just ask her how she's doing, then give her your order."

"Okay." The panic eased in his eyes. He started toward the counter, then stopped and looked back at her. "You sure you don't want to order?"

"Positive. I'll let you fight the crowd."

He glanced toward the counter, fear and anticipation swirling in his eyes. She gave him a reassuring smile, then watched as he squared his shoulders and walked toward the counter as if heading for a firing squad.

As she threaded her way through the crowded shop, most of the people she passed smiled and said hello. She didn't see anything more than warm welcome in anyone's eyes. By the time she reached the door, she'd relaxed enough to smile back and murmur her own hellos.

"Here's your ice cream."

Slashes of red streaked his cheekbones when Nick handed her a sundae, but his eyes were animated. The knot of worry that had lodged in Claire's stomach as he'd headed for the counter eased just a little.

She watched, bemused, as he attacked his own sundae, remembering the enormous hamburger and the huge pile of fries he'd just eaten. Apparently even hormones and adolescent self-consciousness couldn't interfere with a teenage boy's appetite.

"I guess you must have been starving, huh?"

"Yeah," he said, concentrating on his treat.

"Are you ready to head home?" she asked.

"I guess." Nick glanced over his shoulder at the girl behind the counter.

"What's your friend's name?" Claire asked, holding her breath.

Instead of the explosion she'd feared, Nick shuffled his feet. "Caitlyn," he muttered. "Caitlyn Burns."

"She seems very nice," Claire said, glancing at Nick out of the corner of her eye. "I had a friend in high school named Molly Burns. I'd say they might be related, but Molly moved away before we graduated."

Nick shoved a huge spoonful of ice cream into his mouth, a signal Claire took to mean the conversation was over. She turned to go, but found the doorway blocked by a handsome older man with wavy white hair and a florid face.

"If it isn't Claire Kendall," he boomed. "Welcome back to Monroe."

Claire froze. "Hello, Chief Denton," she said, keeping her voice expressionless.

"I'm not the chief of police anymore. We needed someone with more energy for that," he said with a wink. "I'm the mayor now."

"Congratulations," Claire said, her voice flat.

"It's always nice when our young people return to Monroe," he said, his voice carrying over the murmurs of the crowd. "Brings new life to the town."

"It does bring back memories," she said, her voice wooden.

"Sorry about your sister," he said. "A fine woman."

"Thank you, Mayor."

She nudged Nick toward the door, but the mayor had taken his hand, clasping it between both of his.

"Dreadful accident," he said to Nick, "dreadful. My deepest sympathies."

Claire saw the mutinous look gather on Nick's face and stepped between the two. Until she'd had a chance to investigate, the last thing she wanted was to hear Nick tell Denton that his mother had been murdered.

"We should go, Nick," she murmured, putting her hand on Nick's arm.

For once he didn't shake her off. "Yeah."

He edged around the mayor and followed her out the door.

"Asshole," he muttered, glancing back over his shoulder at the mayor.

"Nick!" she exclaimed. "Don't use that word."

"Why not? That's what my mom called him." Nick stuck his chin out. "She didn't like him. She talked about him sometimes, said he was a nothing but a blowhard politician."

"He wasn't the mayor when I lived in Monroe," she said. "He was the chief of police then."

"I'll bet he was an asshole police chief, too."

She should tell him again not to use that word. Instead, sighing, she said, "Yes, he was."

Nick shot her a startled look. Clearly, he'd expected her to correct him.

"Did your mom work for him?" Claire asked.

"No. But she worked in city hall. She saw him around all the time." Nick's mouth tightened. "I think he was trying to hit on her."

"What did your mom think of that?"

"She said he was married and that made him a slimeball. And that even if he wasn't married, she wouldn't go out with him if he was the last man on earth."

"Your mom was a smart woman," Claire said. "She knew how to handle men like that."

Nick gave her a careful, measuring glance. "I thought maybe Denton was the one who called her that night."

Claire froze, a spoonful of ice cream halfway to her mouth. "Really? Why did you think that?"

"Because she wasn't too happy about going out."

Claire glanced down and saw fat white splashes of ice cream hitting the asphalt. Shoving the spoon back into the melting mess, she tossed it in the nearest trash can. "Let's not talk about this here," she said quietly.

Nick looked around again and nodded. Claire opened the car and slid in. Not even the heat rolling out the door could warm the chill that settled in her heart. Nick thought his mother had been killed.

And he thought Fred Denton was involved.

She stared at city hall as they drove away. She didn't know what Janice had done there. But she'd find out.

As far-fetched as Nick's theory sounded, she owed it to him to find out exactly what had happened to his mother.

And she owed it to Janice to make sure she hadn't been killed. Janice had been denied justice for all the years of abuse she'd suffered.

If her death had been anything but a tragic accident, Claire vowed, she'd find justice for that now.

CHAPTER FIVE

CLAIRE PAUSED to toss another bunch of bananas into her cart, eyeing the growing mound of groceries with bemusement. Her normal trips to the grocery store were infrequent and hurried. A few frozen dinners, some fruits and vegetables, and she was on her way.

Now her cart was filled with meat, vegetables, snack food, pasta, milk and more fruit than she'd eat in two months. And she'd be back in a few days to load up again.

Nick's appetite was both astounding and unnerving, and it didn't seem to matter what she set in front of him. He ate an enormous breakfast and took a huge sack lunch to school. When he walked in the door after football practice, he'd devour anything edible he could find.

The night before, she'd watched as he'd eaten a container of yogurt, an apple, more cookies than she could count and two glasses of milk. Then he'd announced he was starving and asked when they were having dinner.

She glanced at her watch and pushed the cart a little faster. Nick would be home in a few minutes, and she didn't want him returning to an empty house.

Her cell phone chirped in her purse and she reached for it, frowning. It was too late for anyone from the office to call her. Nick had her cell phone number, but he'd never used it.

"Ms. Kendall?"

She recognized Tucker Hall's voice immediately. Her hand tightened on the phone. "Yes?"

"I need you to come and get Nick."

His voice sounded grim and fear grabbed her by the throat. "Is something wrong?" she asked, her hand trembling on the phone. "Is Nick all right?"

"He's fine. But you need to pick him up."

"Why? What happened?"

"Nick is fine," he repeated. His drawl was oddly reassuring. "We'll talk when you get here. Come to the trainer's room." He hung up without waiting for an answer.

Her heart pounding, her stomach tight with fear, she abandoned the cart of groceries and flew out of the store. By the time she ran into the trainer's room, she was sick with dread.

Two treatment tables stood against one wall. A desk stood in the corner and cabinets lined the other walls. Nick was pushing a wide broom across the floor.

"Don't kick that towel into a corner, Kendall," Tucker said sharply. "Put it where it belongs."

Nick flung the towel into a tall bin, but it caught on the side and fluttered there for a moment. With a quick glance over his shoulder, he nudged it into the container.

"When you finish that, you can clean out the icing buckets," Tucker told him.

"What's wrong?" she asked, hurrying over to Nick. "Are you all right?" She grabbed his shoulders and turned him to face her, scanning him from head to toe.

To her surprise, he didn't jerk away from her. He looked down at the floor and muttered, "I'm fine."

Without letting him go, she turned to Tucker, who stood watching them as he methodically folded elastic bandages into tight rolls. Claire glanced at his hands as they moved quickly and competently, then looked away.

"What's going on? What's wrong with Nick?" she demanded.

Tucker placed another rolled bandage into a drawer. "He's fine now," he said. "He wasn't so fine fifteen minutes ago."

Her hands tightened on her nephew, and she studied him frantically. He wouldn't meet her eyes.

"Nick didn't use his inhaler before practice today," the coach said. "He had an asthma attack fifteen minutes before practice ended."

"Nick!" Her hands tightened on his shoulders. "Are you all right now? Can you breathe?"

"I'm fine."

There was a catch to his voice, as if he was going to cry. He turned away from her and resumed pushing the broom across the floor.

"Kendall." Tucker's voice was sharp. "Tell your aunt what happened."

Nick kept his head turned away from her. "I couldn't breathe. Coach had to stop practice early."

"That's right." Tucker leaned back against the trainer's table, his face hard. "Not only did he endanger himself, but he ended practice for the rest of the team."

She gently turned Nick around to face her. "Why didn't you use the inhaler?"

He slid his eyes away. "I don't like it," he muttered.

"What don't you like?" she asked.

"I don't like the way it tastes. And I don't like the way it makes me feel."

"How does it make you feel?"

"It makes my heart race. I feel all jittery."

"Then we should go back to the doctor, see if there's some other kind of medicine you should be using."

He shrugged. "I guess." He stepped away from her and continued sweeping.

Claire watched him, feeling overwhelmed. She had no idea how to handle him, what to say or do.

"I've handled the team part of the problem." Tucker said. "How you deal with Nick is up to you."

"What do you mean, you've 'handled the team part of the problem'?" she asked.

"Instead of practicing tomorrow, Nick will help Mr. Tracy clean the training room. And he's benched for the first half of the game on Friday." He glanced over at the boy. "I sure hope we won't need any punts or field goals."

Dull red swept up the back of Nick's neck. "I'm sorry, Coach," he mumbled without turning around.

"So is the rest of the team, Nick. They're sorry you won't be able to help them on Friday. They're sorry they didn't get to practice that last play today. Now go collect your gear."

Nick put the broom into a small closet and slipped out the training room door. Claire gazed after him helplessly.

"It's not the end of the world," Tucker said as the door closed behind Nick. "He's not the first kid who didn't want to use his inhaler."

She looked up at Tucker, who was standing close enough to touch. "But it's the first time I've had to deal with it," she said.

He studied her, his face softening. "It must be tough becoming an instant parent," he said. "You seem to be doing okay so far."

"That depends on your definition of okay," she said wearily. "Nick and I butt heads constantly."

A smile hovered around Tucker's mouth. "That just means he's a teenage boy. Some of your friends in town must have teenagers. They'll tell you the same thing."

"I don't have a lot of friends in town," she said stiffly. "I lost contact with them when I moved away."

"Really?" He tilted his head as he watched her. "That surprises me. I took you for the social type."

"Why is that?" she asked, her voice cool. But she was surprised at his perception. She *was* social when she was home in Chicago.

He held her gaze silently, his eyes heating as he watched her. An answering response trembled inside her and she finally looked away.

"I'll take Nick home," she said, feeling awkward as a teenager herself. "I'm sorry he disrupted your practice."

"Don't worry about it," he said, holding her gaze. "I don't think it'll happen again."

"Thank you," she said with a sigh. "I'll talk to him tonight."

"Good." He straightened from the training table, and suddenly he was in front of her. She'd never seen a man as big as Tucker move so fluidly. Or so fast.

Her heart tripped in her chest, then began to pound.

"Is Nick going to the team pasta party on Thursday?" he asked.

"I don't know." Her mouth was suddenly dry. "He hasn't said anything about a party."

"The guys have a pasta party the night before every game." He smiled, and her heart fluttered. "A different parent hosts it every week. It's great for team bonding. See if you can get him to go."

"How is he doing?" she asked impulsively. "Is he making friends on the team?"

Tucker turned his head toward the door, and she heard footsteps approaching. Nick had collected his gear.

"Let's have dinner together on Thursday and we can talk about it," he said. "I'll pick you up at 6:30."

Before she could answer, Nick pulled the door open. The mesh bag that held his equipment was slung over his shoulder. "Let's go," he said.

She looked at Tucker. She should refuse, she told herself, but didn't know how without sounding churlish. She'd asked him about Nick, after all. The twinkle in Tucker's eyes told her that he recognized her dilemma.

"See you later, Kendall," he said, his voice easy. "You too, Ms. Kendall."

His mouth curled into a grin as he turned away, and Claire stared at him for a moment. They were going to discuss Nick, she told herself firmly. It was a parent-teacher conference.

It was *not* a date.

NICK THREW HIS BAG of gear into the back seat and slid into the car without looking at his aunt. He jammed the seat belt together and stared out the windshield, determined not to blubber like a baby in front of her.

"I'm sorry this happened," she said softly. "Can we talk about why you did it?"

Oh, man, he hated when she used that quiet voice on him. He pressed his lips together as his eyes tingled. Why couldn't she yell at him like his mother had?

"I don't know."

"You don't know why you didn't use your inhaler?"

She looked at him out of the corner of her eye, and he squirmed in the seat. "I don't know."

"You don't know much, do you?" she said with a sigh.

He braced himself for the yelling. But she pressed her lips together and waited.

"No." He was ashamed of the short, surly answer, but he banished the feeling. She didn't want to be stuck in this Podunk town, he reminded himself. The sooner she figured out that he didn't need her, the better.

She didn't say anything for the rest of the short trip home. When he got into the house, he headed for the stairs and the safety of his room.

"Nick," she said. "Come back down to the kitchen."

He stopped on the stairs but didn't look back at her. His hand tightened on his bag of gear.

"I want to talk to you, Nick."

"I don't feel like talking right now."

"I don't care."

She was standing at the bottom of the stairs now, and he slowly turned around. He knew that voice. That was the same voice his mom used when he was in trouble.

"Fine," he said, dropping the gear deliberately on the stairs. She looked at it but didn't say anything.

She had a glass of milk and a carton of cookies on the table, and his stomach reminded him how long it had been since he'd eaten. He threw himself into a chair and looked away from the cookies.

She sat down across from him and took a cookie, then pushed the box toward him. "How about a cookie, Nick?"

"Fine," he muttered. He ate one cookie and was reaching for the next before he caught himself. But she wasn't looking at the damn cookies. She was looking at him, with disappointment on her face.

He shoved another cookie into his mouth and slouched lower on the seat.

"I remember hearing Coach Hall tell you the rule about using your inhaler," she said. "So why didn't you?"

"I told you. It makes me jittery. And it tastes like sh— it tastes bad." He flicked a tiny piece of chocolate chip onto the floor.

She frowned. "I thought football was important to you. I thought you wanted to be on the team."

"It is. I do," he muttered. She was making him feel stupid. She was doing it on purpose, he told himself as he fanned the embers of his temper.

"I don't understand," she said. "I'm just trying to understand why you did it. Can't you tell me that?"

He shoved the chair back and heard it crash to the floor. "Because I did, okay? I didn't want to use the f— the inhaler, okay?" Tears burned in his eyes. "Just forget it." He moved away from the table, caught his leg on the chair and stumbled.

He kicked the chair out of his way. He hated his stupid hip, hated that he limped. Hated that he couldn't do anything about it. But he was in charge of his inhaler.

She looked at him steadily. "Are you going to do it again?"

"I guess not," he muttered.

"All right."

She watched him for a moment, and he squirmed. "Can I go now?"

She nodded. "I think you've been punished enough," she said softly.

He wanted to storm out of the room, slam his bedroom door behind him. But something in her eyes stopped him. She looked sad, he realized. Sad for him?

He pushed the thought away. Of course not. How could you feel sad for someone you were stuck with? And she was stuck with him. He didn't care how much she said she wanted to stay with him. How much she said she wasn't going anywhere without him.

Sooner or later, she'd leave.

That's what everyone did.

CHAPTER SIX

TUCKER PUSHED Claire's doorbell, both anticipation and uneasiness humming through him. He jiggled the coins in his pocket as he waited. What if she was upset at the change in plans?

"Hi," Claire said as the door opened. "Come on in."

His hand stilled as he looked at her. A slim green dress flowed down her body, hugging all the curves he'd already noticed. The color of the dress mirrored her eyes. Her hair was a smooth, shiny wave that rippled around her shoulders when she moved.

Oh yeah. Claire Kendall definitely made his hormones stand up and pay attention. He was almost grateful to Nick for screwing up with his inhaler. It had given him the perfect excuse to ask Claire to dinner.

Her hand tightened on the door when she noticed what he was wearing. "It looks like I'm way overdressed," she said, looking at his cutoff shorts, T-shirt and sandals.

"Don't apologize for that dress," he said, dragging his gaze to her face again. "You look great." He wondered if the material was as silky as it looked. "But there's been a slight change of plans," he said.

"What happened?"

"The team pasta party has been moved to my house." He shot her an easy grin. "The parents who were supposed to host it had a plumbing emergency. Their toddler wanted to see if his stuffed puppy could swim."

Her mouth curled in an answering smile, then she shrugged. "Don't worry about it. We can get together some other time to talk about Nick."

"I'm counting on that. As far as tonight goes, I'm throwing myself on your mercy. You're not going to make me face that houseful of boys alone, are you?"

"I'm having trouble dealing with one teenage boy, let alone a whole team of them. Are you sure you want me to help you with the pasta party?" She looked at him as if he was out of his mind.

"Absolutely." He smiled, enjoying her awkwardness. He guessed Claire Kendall didn't get flustered too often.

"All right," she said, doubt in her voice. "I'll give you a hand."

"Great." He looked at the green dress again. "But you should probably wear something different," he said, real regret in his voice.

She looked down and smoothed her hands down the material. "Right. It'll just take me a minute to change."

She ran up the stairs, and he closed the door and looked around. The house was clean, but everything inside it looked tired. The furniture was lumpy, the upholstery faded. Dull paint covered the walls, and the woodwork was chipped and yellowing. The carpeting on the stairs to the second floor was worn on every tread.

"Depressing, isn't it?" Claire reappeared at the top

of the stairs and headed down, dressed in shorts and a T-shirt. She followed his gaze into the living room. "I don't think my mother did anything to this house in the last twenty years."

"It looks like it needs a lot of work."

"It does." She looked around the room. "I'm hoping Nick and I can bond over paint chips and floor sanders," she said. Her voice was light, but he heard the pain beneath her words.

"If you need any help, give me a call. I can find my way around a lot of remodeling projects."

"Thanks," she said, pushing a strand of hair away from her face. "But I'm not even sure where to begin."

"Make sure there are power tools," he said, shoving his hands into his pockets to keep them from tucking that shiny curl of hair behind her ear. "Males can't resist power tools."

"I'll keep that in mind." She flashed him a quick smile.

He held the door open and waited for her to precede him into the sunlight. Her light, flowery scent brushed past him as she walked by, and he took a deep breath before he could stop himself. Her hair gleamed like fire in the sun and she lifted her face to the sky.

"It's a beautiful evening," she said.

"Yeah, it is," he murmured. Sunlight warmed her skin and made it look almost translucent. What would it feel like beneath his palm?

She glanced over at him and caught him watching her. A hint of color washed her cheeks, then she looked away.

"How do these parties work?" she asked as they drove toward his house, and he smiled to himself at the breathy tone in her voice. She didn't sound quite as cool and collected anymore.

"The kids bring the ingredients and the parents throw everything together. Enormous quantities of pasta, garlic bread and salad are consumed, and the team spends time together outside of practices and games. It's a little corny, but the kids love it and it's a sacred tradition."

"You're saying you need help boiling water and chopping lettuce?" She raised her eyebrows.

"I need help keeping my sanity," he answered easily. "Without a female presence, the testosterone level would be dangerously high."

"Maybe I should have brought a whip and chair," she said.

"Not necessary. That quelling stare of yours will settle them right down."

"I do not have a quelling stare," she said, indignant.

He snorted. "You could cut glass with that look, honey. I was shaking in my shoes when you came marching to practice to confront me."

She settled back against the seat with a rueful chuckle. "You have never shaken in your shoes in your life."

"You're wrong. You pretty much knocked me out of my socks that day," he said softly.

She straightened with a startled look, but before she could answer he swung into his driveway and stopped. "Here we are. Madhouse central."

She glanced at the house and stilled on the seat. Finally she turned to him. "This is your house?" she asked.

He shrugged and draped his arm across the back of her seat as he followed her gaze. "Yeah."

Teenage boys raced across the wraparound porch and down the stairs, whooping and hollering. The sinking sun highlighted the gingerbread trim, painted in shades of blue, green and violet, against the mellow glow of the pale-yellow Victorian house.

"I remember this house," she said, wonder in her voice. "The windows were mostly broken and the porch was full of holes. We all thought it was haunted when I was a kid." She shifted in the seat to look at him. "It's beautiful. The transformation is amazing."

"Yeah, well, teachers don't have a lot to do during the summer," he said. He rolled his shoulders. "I had a lot of time on my hands when I moved here two years ago." Remodeling the house had saved him when he'd first come to Monroe. Exhausting physical labor was the only thing that kept the demons of guilt and loss at bay during the endless nights.

"You did this yourself?"

"I had some help," he said.

She slid out of the car and walked up the steps. He opened the front door for her, but she stopped abruptly.

"I'm impressed, Tucker," she said softly.

"It's just a house," he said, but he couldn't keep the pride out of his voice. "The kitchen is back here."

The sound of female voices drifted down the hall, and he felt her hesitate beside him. Then she squared her shoulders, lifted her chin and walked into the kitchen. He noticed the wary, guarded expression on her face and filed it away for future reference.

When Claire walked into the kitchen, she saw three women moving around the enormous room, already at work. They looked up, smiling, when Claire and Tucker walked in.

"It seems the cavalry has ridden to the rescue," Tucker said with a smile. "How did you know I needed you?"

A woman with short dark hair grinned at him. "Sue Berger called and told me about the switch. You didn't think we'd make you deal with this by yourself, did you?"

"The thought of it had me cowering in fear. So I went out and found a rookie who didn't know what she was agreeing to," Tucker said.

The woman with the dark hair turned her attention to Claire. She gave her an appraising glance, then smiled. "Hi," she said. "You must be Nick's aunt."

"I'm Claire Kendall," she said, putting a little distance between herself and Tucker. The woman's eyes were a little too shrewd.

"I'm Judy Johnson," the woman answered, and introduced the other two women. "What job would you like?"

"Whatever you need me to do."

The woman gave an approving nod. "How about making the salad?"

"Sounds good."

She pulled open the commercial refrigerator and set the salad ingredients on the granite counter. Judy caught her eye as she surveyed the kitchen.

"Quite the place, isn't it?"

"It's amazing."

Judy grinned. "It's a sin for a single man to have a kitchen like this. We're all green with envy."

"I can see why. It's gorgeous," Claire said.

"If the teaching and coaching don't work out, he definitely has a future in construction," one of the other women said with a smile.

"And word is he looks great in a tool belt," the other woman said.

All of the women laughed, and Tucker rolled his eyes.

"You keep talking like that, I'm going to have to leave," he said. "Once this kind of talk starts, a smart man knows it's time to disappear."

"You think this is rough talk? If you abandon us to those boys we'll really get down and dirty," Judy teased.

"You're a hard woman, Judy Johnson," Tucker said. He looked over at Claire. "See what I have to put up with?"

"Yeah, I can see you have a rough life," she said.

"You're ganging up on me, too?" he asked Claire, his face a picture of disappointment. But his eyes twinkled at her. "And here I thought you'd be on my side."

Something fluttered in her chest at that twinkle. Anticipation shivered through her.

"Women stick together," Judy said, pointing a knife at Tucker. "You'd be smart to remember that."

"I can't seduce you to the dark side?" he asked Claire. His mouth curled up in a half smile, but something hot flashed in his eyes, something meant only for her.

An answering ribbon of lust uncurled inside her. She struggled to keep her voice light. "I'm going with the majority here, mister. Judy has a knife."

He threw his hands into the air. "All right, ladies. I know enough to make a strategic retreat when I'm outnumbered. I'm going to sit at the table, roll the cutlery into the napkins and mind my own business."

"I like a man who knows his place," Judy said with a grin. "Doing the menial labor. At least you're good for something."

Tucker raised one eyebrow. "Oh, we're good for one or two other things." He let his gaze drift to Claire, held hers for a long moment. She fumbled with the vegetables on the counter, heat creeping up the back of her neck.

Judy slid a cutting board toward her, and Claire grabbed it. Tucker leaned back in his chair, folding plastic knives and forks into napkins. He was completely at ease with the teasing. In fact, he was having fun.

Tucker was a man who truly enjoyed women, she realized. Another spurt of lust shot through her.

Time to change the subject. "What you've done with this house is amazing."

"You like it?" Tucker asked.

"We used to call this the haunted house when I was a kid," Claire said, letting her gaze wander around the bright, welcoming kitchen. Keeping her gaze away from Tucker. "It's hard to believe it's the same place."

"You grew up in Monroe?" Judy asked, her eyes sharpening with interest. Tucker stopped folding and looked over at her.

"Yes. I moved away when I was twenty." Claire braced herself for the shock of recognition in Judy's eyes.

Judy gave her a sympathetic look. "I remember hearing that when your sister was killed. It's nice to be able to come home. My husband and I moved here five years ago," Judy said, slathering butter on garlic bread. "It's a great town."

"Nick seems to like it." Claire concentrated on cutting the lettuce. Was it possible that Judy hadn't heard the rumors about the Kendalls?

"You moved here to be with Nick?" one of the other women asked, polite curiosity in her voice.

"Temporarily." Claire forced a smile. "I planned to take him back to Chicago, but we decided it would be better to stay here for a while."

"You picked up and left your job, moved all the way here from Chicago?" the third woman said, awe in her voice.

"He's my nephew and he needed me," Claire said with a shrug.

Out of the corner of her eye, Claire saw Tucker stop folding napkins and turn to study her. Her neck tingled and her stomach jittered. Did the other women notice?

"What did you do in Chicago?" Judy asked with a friendly smile.

She could do this. This was nothing more than a typical get-acquainted conversation. Judy and the other two women didn't care about her history in Monroe. They were just parents with kids on the same team, getting together to make a dinner for their sons.

And she was enjoying it, she realized with a shock. She was enjoying the camaraderie of the women, the fun of ganging up on Tucker, the easy conversation.

"I'm an accountant," she said, relaxing. "It was easy enough to work from Monroe for a while."

They continued to talk, discussing the school, their kids and the football season. Finally, when the food was ready and waiting in large bowls on the counter, Tucker walked to the back door and called the kids for dinner.

He turned around and grinned at Claire. "You might want to brace yourself."

The boys swarmed through the kitchen, piling their paper plates with enormous mounds of spaghetti, bread and salad. Shreds of lettuce littered the counter, and blobs of bright red sauce splattered on the tile floor. The boys sprawled on every chair and available inch of the floor, wolfing down the food.

They ate until the food was gone, including the various desserts that replaced the spaghetti on the counters, then they charged out of the house again. In moments, they were playing a noisy game of touch football in Tucker's huge backyard.

"Now you see why I didn't want to face this alone," Tucker said to her with a grin. "It's a scary sight."

"It's a little overwhelming," Claire admitted. "You do this before every game?"

"That's what I've been told."

"That's right, you told me this was your first year as coach."

"Yep. I'm learning right along with the kids," he said, his voice easy.

Judy rolled her eyes. "As if there's anything you don't know about football," she said.

"There are plenty of things I need to learn," Tucker protested. "I never coached before."

One of the women noticed Claire's questioning look.

"Tucker was in the NFL. He used to play football for Chicago."

Judy snorted. "Play for them? Heck, he was the team." She shot Claire a grin. "There are plenty of fans in Monroe. And they were pretty excited when they heard that Choo Choo was coming to teach at Monroe High. For the past two years they've been salivating at the thought of him coaching the team."

"Choo Choo?"

Judy laughed again. "His nickname. Because he ran people over like an express train. Mr. Easygoing here hit so hard that the other player didn't want to get up off the ground. They said he was the meanest SOB in the NFL."

"The meanest man in the NFL?" Claire stared at him, shocked. "And now you're coaching our boys?"

Tucker waved his hand. "That stuff is all marketing and hype," he said, but there was a shadow in his eyes. "A way to sell the team and the products that sponsor it."

"Oh," she said faintly. Tucker Hall was clearly more than the easygoing man she'd met so far.

"A lot of the parents want you to teach their boys how to hit like you did," one of the women said to Tucker.

There was a flash of irritation in his eyes. "I don't care what a lot of the parents want," he said, leaning against the table and crossing his arms over his chest. "My priorities are teaching them how to play a clean game and be good sports."

Judy smiled at Claire. "Everyone in town is excited about the game tomorrow. We all want to see what Tucker's done with the kids. Are you coming to the game?"

"Of course. I wouldn't miss it."

They talked easily as they washed and dried the dishes. Tucker's past wasn't mentioned again, and Claire slowly relaxed. The Tucker she'd seen so far didn't seem like a violent man. And surely the school wouldn't have hired him if he weren't a good teacher.

When they finished, Judy and the other two women smiled and said their goodbyes. "We'll see you at the game tomorrow," they called as they closed the front door.

"Come sit on the porch with me," Tucker said, holding the screen door for her.

She eased into a chair next to him and searched for Nick. To her surprise, he was laughing and running with a group of boys, tossing a football back and forth. His limp didn't seem as noticeable as usual.

Tucker must have followed her gaze. "Being on the team has been good for him so far," he said quietly.

"It has been. We got some new asthma medication, and he doesn't mind the taste," she said. "And he looks so happy," she said, unable to tear her gaze away from her nephew. He looked like the carefree child she remembered from her last visit with Janice.

"He seems to be. He's always one of the first ones out to practice and one of the last to leave."

"If he likes it so much, why didn't he use his inhaler?" She looked at him in the gathering darkness.

His eyes softened. "I think it's a control issue. His life is in turmoil right now and there's not a lot he can do about it. His mother is dead, he thinks it wasn't an accident, he's living with an aunt who's a virtual stranger. You want to take him back to Chicago, which is another thing he can't control. When and where to use his inhaler is something he *can* control. I'm not surprised he refused to use it."

"You like working with these kids, don't you?" she asked, her voice soft.

He gazed out at the kids in the yard and his eyes darkened. She couldn't read his expression, but it made her want to reach out and touch his hand. Before she could move, he shrugged and the smile was back in his eyes.

"They're a lot of fun. I was a teenage boy once and I remember what it was like."

"You went out of your way for Nick," she said.

"He was desperate to play football." He gazed out into the yard, where the boys were indistinct shadows. "He reminds me of myself at that age."

"Cranky, contrary and argumentative?" she said in a light voice.

"Oh, yeah," he said. "I was a major pain in the butt."

"That's hard to believe," she said. Instead of the teasing she'd intended, her voice came out softer, more tender. More intimate.

He turned to her, studying her through the darkness for a moment. Then he shrugged. The smile curving his mouth didn't quite reach his eyes. "I was a typical teenage troublemaker. Football gave me the discipline I needed."

The night air was fragrant and still around them, and the darkness wrapped them in intimacy. It felt like the most natural thing in the world to reach out and touch his hand. "Thank you for noticing Nick. Thank you for reaching out to him."

Before she could draw her hand away, he slid his

palm against hers and twined their fingers. "It was my pleasure," he said. "Meeting Nick's aunt was an unexpected bonus."

Her heart hammered against her ribs, and she told herself to take back her hand. But awareness swirled around them in the dark and she didn't move. The sweet, heavy scent of a night-blooming flower drifted on the breeze, and the air between them thickened with anticipation.

"Hey, Coach! Come and play!"

The excited voice ripped through the spell binding them together, and Tucker slipped his hand away from hers.

"Nah," he called. "You guys are too fast for me. I don't want to be publicly humiliated."

As the boys hooted and jeered, Claire stood up. "I should go," she said, nervously tugging at the hem of her shorts. "Should Nick come home with me?"

"Nope." Tucker stood up. "That's part of the tradition. The older guys on the team drive the younger ones home after the party."

"All right." She stared into the darkness. It was impossible to identify any of the dark shapes running through Tucker's deep back yard.

"Don't worry. The team captains will break it up in a few minutes. All the kids have homework to do."

Tucker followed her into the kitchen. He waited while she picked up her purse, then settled one hand on her lower back to guide her to the front door.

The warmth of his palm burned through her T-shirt and she could feel the separate imprint of each of his fingers. When he pushed the door open, his arm brushed her chest and she sucked in a breath.

He looked down at her, his eyes heating. Then he stepped aside to let her pass in front of him.

By the time she settled herself in his car she'd managed to control her breathing. When he slid in the driver's side, he watched her for a moment, then started the car.

"Thanks for helping out tonight," he said. "Consider this your baptism by fire."

"It was fun. I liked watching the kids goof around. Watching Nick act like a kid," she admitted.

"They were a little more wild tonight than usual," he said. "They needed to blow off steam. They're all excited about the first game."

"You're very good with them," she said.

"I learned from the best. My high school football coach was one in a million."

"I'll bet he's proud of what you've done," she said.

He stilled and she could see his hands tighten on the steering wheel. "I hope so."

"How could he not be proud of you?" she asked. Tension rippled through him and she wanted to reach out for his hand again. But she didn't move.

He rolled his shoulders as he drove down the deserted street. "I'll never measure up to Coach Bo," he said.

His quiet words were tinged with pain. She wanted to know why, to dig beneath Tucker's charming surface for the man he kept hidden. But before she could ask him anything, he pulled into her driveway.

He slid out of the car and came around to open her door. When he settled his hand at her waist again as they walked to her front door, she wanted to lean into him.

Get control of yourself. What on earth was she thinking? This was Nick's teacher, a man who was part of the fabric of Monroe. He wasn't leaving this town, and she wasn't staying.

She moved away as she unlocked the door. Before she could step inside the house, he took her wrist.

"I'm sorry I made you work for your dinner." He drew her hand up to his mouth and kissed her palm, and her heart fluttered in her chest. "I'll make up for it next time."

"Next time?" She raised her eyebrows. "You're so sure there's going to be a next time?"

He smiled, heat and temptation in his eyes. "Oh, yeah. There most definitely is going to be a next time."

He cupped her face in his hands and pressed his mouth to hers. The kiss was quick and light, but it left her shaking.

He smoothed his thumbs along her jaw, then stepped back. "You'll want to go in and turn on the lights before Nick gets home. I'll see you at the game tomorrow."

CHAPTER SEVEN

CLAIRE WAS too fidgety the next morning to work. It was the perfect time to keep her promise to Nick and talk to the police about Janice's death.

At least she wouldn't have to deal with Fred Denton, she told herself grimly as she got into her car. The glad-handing old windbag had looked the other way at anything that would inconvenience the powerful in Monroe. Apparently, his willingness to do so had gotten him elected mayor.

Maybe they'd hired a police chief from outside the department. It would be easier to talk to someone she'd never met before, someone with no history in Monroe.

It didn't matter who was chief, she reminded herself as she slid out of the car at the tiny police station on the edge of the downtown area. She'd promised Nick she'd talk to him. And she was determined to keep her promises to Nick.

She suspected that he'd had too many broken ones in his young life.

A middle-aged woman looked up from a desk as Claire walked in the door, a start of recognition in her eyes. "Claire Kendall, isn't it?" the woman said, her eyes warming. "I heard you were back in Monroe."

"Yes." Claire pasted a smile on her face and looked at the woman's name tag. Josie Williams. She vaguely remembered her family. "Hello, Josie. How are you?"

"I'm just fine. How about you?" Josie settled back in her seat, preparing for a long chat.

"I'm good. Is the chief of police available?" Claire asked, her voice polite.

"Yes, he's here." Disappointment flickered in Josie's eyes. "I'll see if he has time to talk to you."

"Thank you," Claire murmured.

Josie pushed away from her desk and disappeared into an office. A few moments later, she reappeared, followed by a tall, broad-shouldered man Claire didn't recognize.

"Ms. Kendall?" the man said. "I'm Seth Broderick, the chief of police. You wanted to talk to me?"

"Yes." She walked over to the man and shook his hand. Broderick had a face that looked lived-in, with lines around his eyes and a cleft in his chin. But his brown eyes were shrewd. She'd guess he, unlike Fred Denton, didn't miss much. "Can we go into your office?"

"Sure." He led the way, then closed the door after her. "Have a seat," he offered.

"I'm here about my sister, Janice Kendall."

Broderick nodded. "I'm very sorry for your loss."

"Thank you." Claire knotted her fingers together. "Can you tell me the details of the investigation?"

Broderick's eyebrows rose. "There aren't a lot of details to tell. It was a rainy night, the roads were slick and she skidded off the road into the lake. There's a fifty-foot drop-off where she went in, and it looked as if her car bounced a couple of times on the way down." He paused. "If it's any comfort to you, or her boy, she was probably dead before she hit the lake. Her neck was broken."

"Thank you," Claire said in a low voice. It was painful to hear the details of her sister's death recited so dispassionately. "But I wondered if you investigated the possibility that her death wasn't an accident."

The chief's eyebrows went up again. "Do you think it was a suicide?"

"Not at all," she said. Her hands were cold, and she pressed her palms together. "My nephew said she got a phone call just before she went out that night. He said she didn't want to go, but apparently she was supposed to meet someone." She swallowed, suddenly fighting back tears. "I want to make sure she didn't have help going into that lake."

"There was no evidence that it was more than a tragic accident," the chief said.

"Did anyone search for evidence?"

He studied her for a moment, then wheeled his chair around. "I'll get the report."

He opened a file cabinet and pulled out a manila folder. She could see, even from the other side of the desk, that it was painfully thin. After reading it, he looked up. His eyes were cool. "There's no mention here of evidence that would indicate foul play. But there's also no mention of anyone looking for evidence."

"I'm not trying to embarrass you or the department," Claire said. "My nephew and I just need answers."

The chief's eyes softened a bit. "It's hard for a child to lose his mother."

"Yes, it is. Especially when his concerns are brushed over by the authorities," she said, her voice even.

The softness disappeared from his eyes. "No one brushed aside his concerns," he said.

"Nick told the officer who came to the house that he was afraid his mother had been lured away that night. As far as he could tell, the officer never followed up."

The chief glanced back down at his notes. After a moment, he looked back at her, his jaw clenched. "There's no mention of your nephew saying anything to my officer."

"My nephew didn't lie." Her voice was firm. "If he says he talked to the officer, he did. I suggest you ask the officer."

"You can be sure that I will." There was no sympathy in his eyes now. He looked like a typical police officer, his eyes cold and flat, giving nothing away.

"What happened to Janice's car?" she asked.

"It was totaled." He glanced down at the report. "The responding officers had it towed to C&J Wrecking. That's in Bakersville," he said, naming the large city closest to Monroe.

"Thank you, Chief," Claire said, reaching to shake his hand. "Will you get back to me after you talk to the officer who spoke to my nephew?"

He gave her a curt nod. "Count on it."

"I appreciate it."

She walked out of his office and continued out of the building. She was shaking with reaction.

Fred Denton was no longer the police chief, but it

seemed as if nothing had changed in the Monroe Police Department. They still saw only what they wanted to see.

Maybe that wasn't fair, she conceded. She assumed the new police chief was just like Fred Denton, but maybe she'd been mistaken about Seth Broderick. The new chief of police hadn't ignored her concerns. And he hadn't patronized her.

Had Janice been murdered? Had her "accident" actually been carefully arranged?

Nerves jumped beneath her skin and dark whispers of foreboding stirred as she drove back through town. Apprehensive, full of edgy energy, her eyes narrowed when she saw a familiar figure walking into the Dixie Diner. Andrea Vernon, Roger's current wife.

And she was alone.

Before Claire could stop and think, she pulled into a parking spot. Hurrying down the street, her attention focused on Andrea and the diner, she jumped when someone reached out and touched her arm.

"Hey there, Claire," Tucker said, his eyes warming. "You look like you're in a hurry."

Yanked out of her thoughts, she stared at Tucker, disoriented. Finally she managed a smile. "I was thinking about something."

"I could see that. I've been thinking about a lot of things lately, too," he answered, shoving his hands into his pockets and smiling down at her. "And then you appeared in front of me. Like magic."

Her heart thumped against her ribs at the barely hidden heat in his eyes. "That's pretty smooth. And so early in the morning. I'm impressed," she said. Her voice sounded breathy and weak.

"I'm a morning person," he answered, a gleam in his eye. "Always have been. Mornings are the best time for so many things."

She raised her eyebrows, trying to ignore the sharp stab of hunger. "They're also the time for school. Are you playing hooky?"

"I wasn't, but it sounds like a good idea. Want to sneak off with me?"

She was shocked by her urge to say yes. And relieved to see the teasing light in his eye. He wasn't serious.

She hoped.

"Afraid not," she said, clearing her throat. "In fact, I'd better steer clear of you. You're a bad influence, trying to tempt me away from work."

The corner of his eyes crinkled as he gave a wicked grin. "A bad influence? Honey, you have no idea how bad I can be."

She was afraid she had a very good idea—and appalled to realize she wanted to find out. "Why aren't you in school?" she asked, trying to change the subject.

The twinkle in his eyes told her that he recognized her ploy, that he'd let her get away with it. For now.

"This is one of my free periods," he said. "I needed to pick something up at the sports store."

"I'll let you go, then."

When she tried to move past him, he laid a hand on her arm. "What are you doing after the game tonight?"

"I don't know," she said. Her skin warmed beneath his touch. When she found herself leaning toward him, she moved away. "I hadn't thought about it."

"A lot of the kids go to Sparky's for pizza," he said. "So do some of the parents."

"I'll ask Nick if he's interested." She smiled up at him. "Thanks for letting me know. Is that another one of the football team's traditions?"

"You got it." He smiled easily at her. "We've got a million of them."

"Good luck tonight," she said.

"Thanks."

Neither of them moved for a moment, then they both moved at the same time. He reached out to steady her, then stepped back.

"Take care, Claire," he said, his voice soft. "Maybe I'll see you tonight."

His voice was husky with promise, a promise she acknowledged she wanted to explore. She swallowed, nodded and slipped past him. She could feel his eyes on her back as she stepped into the Dixie Diner.

She stood by the door for a moment, letting her eyes adjust to the dim light, letting her thundering heart slow down. Putting Tucker firmly out of her mind and taking a deep breath, she stepped up to the hostesses' station and scanned the restaurant.

Andrea was sitting at a booth in the corner with a cup of coffee. Claire smiled at the hostess and nodded toward Andrea. "I'll just join Mrs. Vernon," she said.

"Okay." The hostess gave her a puzzled smile, as if no one ever met Andrea Vernon at the restaurant. As she walked toward Andrea, Claire resolved to make sure the young woman knew she wasn't alone.

She was involving herself in Monroe by talking to Andrea. That was a good thing, she realized with a spurt of understanding. She'd been a child when she left. Now she was an adult, and it was time to act like it.

"Hi, Andrea," Claire said in a low voice.

Andrea looked up and eyed Claire warily. "Hello."

"Do you mind if I join you for a moment?"

Andrea's eyes flickered anxiously to the front of the diner. "Um, I'm not sure. I'm, um, meeting someone."

Claire knew that expression far too well. It meant that Andrea didn't want to be caught talking to her. Her resolve hardened. "Are you expecting Roger?" she asked.

"No," she said. "He's in court today."

"Great. Then you won't mind if I sit down until your friend joins you, will you?"

"Ah, no." Andrea bit her lip and looked out the front window of the diner again. "I guess not."

She was checking for Roger, Claire realized with a burst of anger. Andrea was afraid Roger would see his wife talking to Claire.

As soon as she was seated, the waitress came over, bright curiosity in her eyes. "Can I get you something?"

"A cup of coffee, please," Claire said.

Andrea's eyes followed the waitress away from the table, and Claire recognized the expression in them. Andrea was sick with fear that the waitress would tell Roger that she'd talked to Claire.

"Did you grow up in Monroe, Andrea?" Claire asked.

"No." Her gaze returned to Claire. "I grew up in Clinton." It was the county seat, twenty miles away.

"Is that where you met Roger?" Claire pasted what she hoped was a pleasant, nonthreatening smile on her face.

"Yes." The younger woman relaxed a little. "I was working in the county clerk's office. He came in to get some records, and we started talking." Her gaze slid to her cup, and she lifted it to her mouth with a shaking hand. "One thing led to another, we got married and here I am."

There was a small bruise on the inside of Andrea's wrist. A bruise the size of a man's finger.

"It sounds like he swept you off your feet," Claire said. She smiled through clenched teeth.

Andrea nodded. "We got married after three months."

"It sounds very romantic," Claire said.

A shadow passed over Andrea's face, then disappeared. "It was," she said, lifting her chin defiantly.

Good, Claire thought. At least she has a little spirit left. "Were your parents happy you got married?" she asked.

Andrea's mouth trembled. "My mom and dad died in a car accident a few months before I met Roger."

"I'm sorry," Claire said gently. "That must have been hard for you."

Andrea stared out the window of the diner and didn't answer.

Claire slid her coffee cup to the side. "Did Roger tell you who I am?" she asked.

Andrea glanced at her, pink tinting her skin. "He said you were a former client," she mumbled. "He said you'd had a disagreement, that you'd tried to get him in trouble with the police and the bar association."

Claire gave a rueful laugh. "I guess that's one way of putting it." She leaned forward and touched the other woman's hand. "I'm sorry you have to hear this way, but I was a lot more than a disgruntled client. I was married to Roger for two years."

"What?" Andrea's face paled. "That's impossible."

"Why do you think so?"

"Roger never told me he'd been married before."

"I'm not surprised. Roger doesn't take losing well. And believe me, he didn't give me a divorce voluntarily."

"I don't believe you." Andrea stared at her, shaking her head. "I don't know why you're making this up, but you're lying. You were never married to Roger."

"I'm not lying, Andrea." Claire ached for the young woman who looked so confused. And so frightened. "If you used to work in the County Clerk's office, you know you can look up our marriage license. And our divorce decree."

"Why would he lie to me?"

Claire held her gaze, then reached across the table and touched the bruise on Andrea's wrist. "You know why."

Andrea followed her gaze to the bruise, then slid her hand into her lap again and lifted her head. "I think you should leave now."

"I will. I don't want Roger to find out about this meeting any more than you do. Because I know what will happen if he does."

Andrea shot her a frightened look but didn't answer.

"What he's doing is wrong, Andrea. He has no right to hit you." She reached across the table to touch Andrea's arm, and the other woman flinched. Anger swelled inside Claire. "I can help you," she said quietly.

Claire scribbled her home and cell phone numbers on the napkin, then pressed it into Andrea's hand. "I got away from him," she said. "I can help you get away, too."

"But I love him," Andrea whispered. "And Roger loves me."

Claire knew better than to argue. "That doesn't give him the right to hurt you. I want to help you, Andrea. Call me anytime."

She laid some money on the table for her coffee, then slid out of the booth and tried to smile at Andrea. She knew too well how the young woman felt—she'd been cowed and terrified herself during her marriage to Roger.

But Claire wasn't a child anymore. She was an adult, and she wouldn't allow Roger to intimidate her. Shaking with anger, she vowed to help Andrea.

As she slid back into her car, she saw Roger turning into the parking spot in front of his office. Her anger flared again. How many times had he told her he'd be gone all day, only to show up unexpectedly, hoping to catch her doing something he'd forbidden?

Thank goodness she'd left the Dixie Diner when she had, Claire thought as she watched the lawyer hurry over to the restaurant. She didn't want Andrea to suffer because of their conversation. And if Roger knew Claire and his wife had been talking, Andrea would definitely suffer.

Call me, Andrea, Claire prayed as she drove away. *Call me soon.*

CHAPTER EIGHT

"THANKS," Nick yelled as he slammed the door and loped toward school. Guilt kept him from turning around to watch his aunt's car pull away. He knew she wanted him to call her Aunt Claire. He saw it in her face every time he didn't.

He couldn't make the words come out of his mouth.

He clutched his uniform more tightly to his chest as he ran. He didn't need her. He didn't need anyone.

It didn't matter if he called her Aunt Claire. She'd still leave.

He opened the locker room door and slipped inside, quickly surrounded by the familiar smells of overripe gym socks and mildew. Those smells soothed him, reminded him that there was at least one place where he belonged.

He was part of this team and no one could take that away from him.

"Hey, Kendall," an excited voice called from the other side of the room. "Are we going to kick some Acadia butt tonight, or what?"

Nick wove his way past his teammates to give Booger Johnson a high five. "You got that right, man," he said.

Booger grinned at him. "Wait until you see the cheer-leaders tonight. They'll be hot, man. Carly Horton will be out there. She's the hottest of all."

"Cool." Nick didn't much care if Carly Horton would be on the field, but he wondered about Caitlyn Burns. She was in the band. Would she be playing at the game? He'd wanted to ask her, but his mouth wouldn't form the words.

Nick stripped off his clothes and began to dress for the game. The shoulder pads felt bulky and awkward and he adjusted them nervously, trying to make them feel more natural. As he pulled on the stretchy pants, he examined his legs. Did the tight material make his bad leg look funny? Would the other guys laugh at how skinny it was?

"Hey, Kendall, get a move on. It's almost time to go," Booger said.

Nick bent to tie his shoelaces hiding the furious red of his face. Booger must think he was a total dork.

"You guys about ready to warm up?" Coach Hall spoke from the door, and the chatter in the locker room stopped immediately. Nick grabbed his helmet and stood up.

"You've been working hard for the last few weeks, and this is it. Are you guys ready to play?" The room erupted into cheers, and he grinned. "I've been looking forward to this game as much as you have. Now let's go out there and play some football."

Coach gave the guy closest to him a high five. "Captains, lead the way."

Nick followed the rest of the team out the door, his

heart pounding with excitement as he ran toward the stadium. The lights were already on, even though it wasn't dark yet. The stands were filled with people, and they stood up and cheered as the team ran onto the field. He stopped dead, staring at the crowd.

"How are you doing, Kendall?"

Coach Hall appeared beside him, and Nick nodded, unable to speak. His throat was too thick.

"Your leg feel good tonight?"

"Yeah," he managed to say.

"Good. You go out on the field and do your warm-ups, then I'll show you where to practice your kicks." He gave Nick a shrewd glance. "Nervous?"

Nick swallowed. "A little."

"That's good," Coach said, slapping him on the back. "I'd be worried if you weren't. Now get out there and loosen up your leg."

Coach turned to another player and Nick trotted onto the field. The grass was thick and cushiony beneath his feet, and the sweet scent of it drifted up to him. It made him think of one of the last days he'd spent with his mom. They'd made sandwiches and taken them into the backyard. Sprawled in the grass, his mom had told him how well her job was going. She'd asked him if he liked Monroe, told him it was a good place for them to be. She'd said they'd be staying in Monroe for a long time.

He blinked fiercely to clear his vision. He wished his mom were here tonight, watching him play football.

As he straightened from his stretch, he saw Aunt Claire walking up the bleachers. He rolled his eyes when he saw she was wearing fancy clothes, clothes he'd labeled her city clothes. She didn't look anything like the other parents. Jeez, was she trying to embarrass him?

All the other parents wore Monroe Bulldogs sweatshirts or T-shirts, and jeans or shorts. His mom would have worn a Bulldog T-shirt.

He kept one eye on her while he followed the captain's directions for warming up. She sat down with someone who looked like Booger's mom. Why was she talking to Mrs. Johnson? He stared at them for a moment, trying to figure out what they were saying. Were they talking about him?

Coach blew his whistle and they all headed to the bench. Booger ran at him and jumped into the air, banging his helmet against Nick's. Nick staggered backward, his head ringing, then grinned. He and Booger jumped up at the same time and banged helmets again. Then all the guys on the team were banging heads and doing high fives. Nick's heart swelled until it almost burst out of his chest.

They got into a circle, put their hands together and yelled, "Go, Bulldogs!" The starters trotted onto the field and the rest of the team settled on the bench.

Nick sat down at the end of the bench, afraid to watch the guy who was going to kick off. If Tompson screwed up, it would be Nick's fault. Coach hadn't relented about benching him for the first half of the game, and Tompson hadn't been too happy about having to kick.

The crowd groaned, and Nick knew Tompson had screwed up. He lifted his head and saw that the ball had only gone a few yards. His heart sinking, his gut churning, he watched the other team exchange high fives. His stomach burned with shame.

The rest of the half was a nightmare. Every time they tried to kick the ball, it squirted out of someone's hands or dribbled weakly to the ground. When the other team laughed, Nick shrank further into himself.

He could hardly bear to look at the crowd, but a flash of bright green caught his eye. His aunt Claire was on her feet, cheering when the Bulldogs gained a few yards. He watched her out of the corner of his eye. She was paying attention to the game, he admitted grudgingly. And she was cheering in all the right places.

He narrowed his eyes. It looked as if she was even asking Mr. Johnson about the game. She was just putting on a good front for the Johnsons, he assured himself. But a tiny voice told him he was being unfair to his aunt.

He didn't want to hear it. He didn't want to care what his aunt did.

Finally the whistle blew for the end of the half and he shot up from the bench. He practically sprinted into the locker room, ahead of almost everyone else. He just wanted to go and hide somewhere.

TUCKER STOOD on the sideline, watching the boys as they warmed up for the second half of the game. He'd have to go talk to Nick, he thought. The kid looked completely miserable.

As he started to walk over to him, he found the green shirt in the bleachers that told him where Claire was.

She had come down to the front of the stands and leaned over the railing, clearly searching for Nick. Tucker couldn't tear his eyes away from her. Then she turned to look at someone who'd apparently called her name.

Derek Joiner sidled up next to her, and Tucker scowled.

Why was that smooth-talking metrosexual sucking up to Claire? His slick blond hair gleamed in the lights and his smile flashed. His teeth were probably whitened.

A hot bolt of jealousy stabbed through Tucker when Joiner laid his hand on Claire's arm. Tucker would bet big bucks that Joiner's manicured fingers would gleam in the lights, too. He watched them, brooding, his hands itching to tear the little weasel away from Claire.

"Coach?"

One of the captains interrupted his thoughts, and he turned to the boy with a start. "Yeah, Coolvin?"

"Same starting lineup?" the boy asked.

Tucker cursed himself for allowing Claire to distract him. These boys deserved his full attention. "Yeah, same starters," he said.

He avoided looking at the stands, wouldn't allow himself to look at Claire as he watched the first plays unfold. They weren't going to score on this drive. Hell, they'd be lucky if they scored at all tonight.

He looked to the end of the bench, where Nick sat with his hands between his knees, his head bent. "Kendall," he barked. "Come here."

Nick jerked his head up and stood up. The hope in his eyes was heartbreaking. He hurried over to Tucker.

"It looks like you're going to have to punt," Tucker said. "You ready?"

"Yeah," Nick said. "I'm ready, Coach."

"Okay. When you get out there, you take a few deep breaths and relax. You've done a good job in practice this week. Just pretend you're still practicing. Keep your leg straight and you'll be fine."

"Right, Coach. I'll remember." Nick nodded vigorously as he shifted from foot to foot.

A few moments later, Tucker patted him on the back. "You're up, Kendall."

Nick bounded onto the field, got into position and kicked the ball. It rose into the air, then slowly fell back to the ground.

As soon as the boy who caught the ball had been tackled, Nick trudged off the field, his head down. Tucker intercepted him before he reached the end of the bench.

"You'll do better next time, Kendall," he said.

Nick nodded and kept walking.

"Let's walk through a kick again." Tucker slung an arm around Nick's shoulders, feeling the tension that hummed through him. "Even the pros walk through before they take a kick."

Nick listened as Tucker broke down a punt, step by step. By the time he'd finished, the tightness had disappeared from Nick's face. Then he went and stood on the sideline instead of retreating to the bench.

WHEN THE GAME ENDED, Tucker shook hands with the opposing coach, then watched as his team filed down the field, exchanging hand-slaps and muttered "good games" with their opponents. He couldn't bear to look at the scoreboard, the evidence of their failure. *It's just a high school game,* he told himself as he walked away.

He'd damn well better pull himself together before the post-game locker room speech.

He swallowed the bitter-tasting anger and disappointment and managed to smile as the kids trooped off the field. "Sophomores, you grab the water coolers," he said. "Juniors and seniors, pick up any equipment on the field. Freshmen, make sure there's nothing lying around beneath the bench. Then I'll see you in the locker room."

He headed into the building, then locked himself in the washroom and paced from one side to the other. He hated to lose, loathed it with a fierceness that still burned. When he'd been the one wearing a uniform, a loss like this would have had him punching a hole in the locker room wall.

A metal garbage can stood in his way and he kicked it with a vicious swing of his foot. It flew through the air and smashed into the wall. The noise of it crashing to the floor rang in his ears like the echo of a hundred cymbals.

The sound jerked him abruptly back to reality. This wasn't an NFL game. This was Monroe High School, and the players were boys who would be studying him to see how he reacted to the loss.

It was his responsibility to teach them the important things about sports.

He closed his eyes, took a deep breath and reached for his composure.

Ten minutes later, the team sat uneasily on the locker room benches or leaned against a wall, holding their helmets. None of them would look him in the eye.

"All right, guys, what do you think about our first game?" Tucker asked.

No one said a thing.

"Captains? Porter? Coolvin?" Tucker asked with a raised eyebrow.

Finally one boy muttered, "We sucked."

Tucker waited, looking around at the others, but no one else said a thing. "Is that what you all think?" he asked. "That we sucked?"

Grunts and curt nods were his only answers.

"Want to know what I think?" He waited for a moment, but no one said a thing. "Sucked is the last word I'd use to describe how we did." He met each boy's gaze, one by one.

"I'm proud of you. Every single young man on this team played hard. Every one of you gave it all you have. And every one of you played a clean game."

He paused. "Those are the things that are important. The final score isn't the final measure of a game. In all the ways that count, you guys were winners tonight. You should be proud of yourselves."

The boys shuffled their feet, but their faces began to relax. Had they been afraid he was going to chew them out?

"Now get out of here," Tucker said with a smile. "It's Friday night. Don't you guys have anything better to do than hang around a locker room?"

Suddenly, the tension broke and the boys were laughing and joking with each other. Tucker watched them for a moment, then went into his tiny office.

As he wrote some notes about the game and what they needed to work on, he sensed someone in the door. When he looked up, Nick Kendall stood there, looking miserable.

"Kendall," he said. "Come on in. What do you need?"

"I think I should quit," he muttered, standing stiff and tense.

"Quit?" Tucker raised his eyebrows. "Quit what? Quit flirting with pretty girls? Quit eating ten pounds of junk food every day? What do you want to quit?"

His face flamed. "I think I should quit the team."

Tucker leaned back in his chair and studied the boy. "Why is that, Nick?" he asked in a quiet voice.

"Because I really did suck tonight," Nick said. He looked close to tears. "I didn't help the team at all."

"Seems to me you kicked two punts and tried a field goal. Did I miss something?"

"No, I'm the one who missed," he burst out. "I missed the field goal and only got a few yards on the punts. The team needs a better kicker than me."

"You're the best kicker we have, Nick. Do you really want to quit and let the team down?"

"They'll be better off without me," he muttered.

Tucker leaned farther back in his chair and laced his hands behind his head. "Is this a private pity party or can anyone join?"

Nick shot him a startled glance. "I'm just trying to do what's best for the team."

"Then you'll come to practice on Monday and work on your kicks," Tucker said. He beckoned to Nick. "Sit down, Kendall."

When Nick was sitting rigid in a chair, Tucker said, "Yeah, you missed your field goal. You didn't get as much distance on your punts as you wanted. But you tried, Kendall." He tilted his head, watched Nick for a moment. "No one wanted to be our kicker until you joined the team, Nick. Want to know why?"

He waited until Nick nodded. "Because it's a job with a lot of responsibility. When you're kicking the ball, everyone is watching you. If you screw up, everyone knows it." He leaned forward. "Not everyone can handle that kind of pressure, Kendall. I think you can."

The flash of pleasure in Nick's eyes was blinding, but quickly hidden. "All right," he said, rubbing at a grass stain on his pants. "I'll stay." He looked up at Tucker. "I'll see you on Monday, I guess."

"Damn straight you will." Tucker stood up. "Come on, let's get out of here. We spend enough time in this locker room during the week."

He clapped Nick on the back and the boy staggered. Upset that he'd forgotten about Nick's weak leg, he started to apologize, but Nick turned and gave him a brilliant smile. "Okay, Coach."

Somehow, he'd managed to say and do just the right thing. His earlier frustration and disappointment at their loss drained completely away. As he grabbed his briefcase and flicked out the lights in the now-empty locker room, Tucker realized that the boys weren't the only ones who'd learn something this year.

CHAPTER NINE

"WHAT COLOR DO YOU LIKE, Nick?" Claire asked the next morning as they stood in the paint aisle of the Home Helper store. She held three paint strips, trying to decide how they'd look in the living room of the house.

"I don't care," he said impatiently. He glanced at the paint chips and stabbed a finger at one. "That one."

"I can tell you gave that a lot of thought," she said with a wry smile.

"I said I'd help you paint," Nick retorted, hiking up his baggy pants. "I didn't say anything about picking out a stupid color."

Two weeks ago, Nick's answer would have had her bristling. She must be mellowing, because now she just laughed. "Spoken like a true male," she said. "I think we'll try this one." She tapped her fingernail against a creamy light yellow. "If we don't like it on the walls, we can try something else."

"Whatever," Nick said, pointing to a complicated collection of tubes. "Are we going to get one of these?"

"A power paint roller?" She read the box and rolled her eyes. "I don't think so." She had a mental picture of her and Nick struggling with the device, unable to control it as paint sprayed in every direction. "I think we'll stick to the old-fashioned way."

"Good idea," a voice said behind her. "The old-fashioned way usually works for me."

She spun around to see Tucker standing behind her. He wore ragged shorts and a paint-spattered T-shirt that hugged his upper body. She dragged her gaze away from the impressive muscles in his chest and shoulders.

"Hi," she said, rattled. "You're up bright and early." She shuddered inside at her inane words.

Tucker didn't seem to notice. "I told you I was a morning person," he said in his sexy drawl. "Looks like you two are getting ready to do some serious work."

"Hi, Coach Hall." Nick turned away from his contemplation of the paint sprayer. He hunched his shoulders self-consciously. "We're going to paint the living room this weekend."

"Yeah? I was planning on some painting, too," he said, giving Nick a "males stuck in the same boat" look.

Nick straightened, and Claire watched as his chest seemed to swell. "I was trying to tell her that we need one of these things." He gestured to the power painter, clearly hoping to get another male on his side.

"Nah," Tucker said. "You don't want one of those things. Takes all the fun out of painting."

"But it looks so cool," Nick protested.

"Looks can be deceiving, kid." He held Claire's gaze for a beat too long, then leaned against the shelves as if he had all day and glanced into their cart. His lips twitched. When he looked up at her, his eyes were laughing. "How much painting have you done, city girl?"

"Not very much," she admitted. "But Nick and I should be able to figure it out. How complicated can it be?"

Tucker pushed away from the shelves. "Painting is a tricky business. It would take days to cover all the subtleties," he assured her, his eyes twinkling. "I'll allow you to take advantage of my vast experience and give you a hand."

"That's not necessary," she said firmly, although her stomach jumped when she pictured him holding her hand, guiding a brush down the wall. "We're perfectly capable of doing it ourselves. Right, Nick?"

Nick's face fell, but he shrugged. "Yeah, whatever."

"Besides, you must have work to do this weekend," she added quickly. "Or you wouldn't be here."

"Believe me, my painting can wait. The entertainment value alone will be worth it." He grinned as he plucked two brushes out of her cart. "What were you going to use these for?" he asked.

"To paint, of course." She scowled. "What else would we use them for?"

"I wondered, seeing as how they're for staining wood siding."

"What? Let me see."

She snatched them out of his hand and read the fine print. Sure enough, it said their ideal use was on rough wood siding.

"So we made a mistake." She tossed them back in the bin where she'd found them. "We'll find the right ones."

"Claire," he said, grabbing her hand when she reached for a different one. "You don't use brushes to paint a wall. You use rollers."

She tried to tug her hand from his grasp. His fingers tightened around hers for a moment, then he smoothed his thumb over her palm and let go.

She shoved her suddenly far-too-sensitive hand into her pocket and shrugged "Fine. We'll use rollers."

He glanced over at Nick and shot him a conspiratorial grin. "I'll bet she doesn't even know what a roller is. What do you think, Kendall?"

Nick looked uneasily from her to Tucker. She could read his thoughts too easily. *Were the adults making fun of him?*

"Nick knows what we need," she said, her voice firm. She grabbed her nephew's arm and pulled him toward what she assumed were rollers. "Thanks, though," she tossed over her shoulder.

Tucker followed them down the aisle. "What are we going to do with her, Kendall?" he asked. He was standing too close to her. "Doesn't she know these projects are best left to the men to handle?"

Nick shot Tucker a startled look, then stood taller and started to grin before he caught himself. "Uh, yeah. Right."

A lump lodged in Claire's throat when she saw the happiness on Nick's face, making it impossible to speak. That was the only reason she didn't cut Tucker down to size for that macho, sexist remark. Her gaze went from Tucker to Nick, who'd moved away from her and casually aligned himself next to Tucker.

She turned to look at a nearby shelf so he wouldn't notice her eyes reddening. "All right, macho men. What do we need?"

They spent the next half hour loading up the shopping cart with rollers, pans, dropcloths, several small brushes and the paint. Tucker consulted Nick before choosing each item, and by the time they wheeled the cart out of the store, Nick's face was as bright as the sun.

"Let's put this stuff in my truck," Tucker said, glancing at her sleek luxury sedan. "That city car would keel over in a faint if you asked it to do real work."

She eyed his pickup truck with a sniff. "And that truck of yours is too big and too loud."

Nick grinned. "I think Coach's truck is awesome."

"That's right, Kendall. Manly men drive pickups." Tucker clapped him on the back, making Nick stagger. His grin grew even wider.

"Why don't you manly men load this stuff into the manly truck so we can get to work," Claire said, her heart swelling as she watched Nick. How could she not be touched by Tucker's care with her nephew?

"Is she always this much of a slave driver?" Tucker asked Nick. Her nephew shrugged, then shot her a careful glance, as if to make sure she wasn't angry.

"Go put the cart away, Kendall," Tucker said, latching the gate of the truck.

As soon as Nick was out of earshot, he turned to her. "Just give me the word if you want me to get lost," he said softly. "The other day you said you wanted to bond with Nick over paint chips. If I'm in the way, tell me."

"Nick would be devastated if I told you to get lost, and you know it," she said, her voice dry. "You're going to have to wiggle out of this one yourself."

"Who said I wanted to wiggle out of it?"

"Come on, Tucker. You don't want to spend the day painting our house."

"It's true I can think of better ways of spending a Saturday," he said, his eyes gleaming with sudden heat. "But if you're determined to paint, I'll give you a hand."

"Why?" she asked.

One side of his mouth curled into a grin. "Anyone ever tell you that you're the suspicious type?"

"Thank you. I worked very hard to develop my suspicious nature. And you still haven't told me why you want to help us paint."

He shrugged. "It seems like the thing to do," he said, his grin widening. "If nothing else, I'm sure it will be good for some laughs."

She looked over at her nephew, whose eyes sparkled as he walked toward them. "Thank you," she said, surrendering. "Nick will love that."

"What about Nick's aunt?"

"I'll be grateful for the help."

He watched her for a moment, then nodded. "Good. I'll follow you back to your house."

"All right," she said, wondering what she'd gotten herself into.

NICK WAS STARVING to death.

His hand cramped and his neck sore, he set the roller back into the pan. "Are we done here?" he asked hopefully.

"Looks like it," his aunt said. She slowly turned, looking at the freshly painted living room walls. "What a difference. What do you think, Nick?"

She looked as if she really cared what he thought, he realized with a jolt of surprise. "I like it, I guess."

She smiled. "Me, too."

"My mom was going to paint the house," he said, feeling like a traitor for enjoying painting with his aunt and Coach. "We talked about it a lot. But she was distracted by all the sh—stuff going on at work."

"Janice would have done a great job fixing up the house," his aunt said quietly. "She just didn't get a chance."

The tenderness in her eyes made him squirm. "So, like, can we eat now?" he said, trying to sound bored.

"Not so fast, buddy," Coach Hall said. "We're not finished until everything's cleaned up," he said.

"Aw, man, I'm *starving,*" Nick answered without thinking. Then he shot a worried look over at Coach Hall. He didn't want his coach to think he was whining.

"Yeah, I'm pretty hungry, too," Coach said. "But we have to get this paint cleaned up before it hardens."

"Right." Nick grabbed the paint tray and the rollers and headed toward the laundry room.

"You did a good job, Kendall," Coach said as they stood side by side at the laundry tub, rinsing out the paint rollers. "You learn real fast."

"It wasn't so hard," Nick said nonchalantly. He glanced over at Coach, watching the way he rubbed the paint out of the roller, then did the same with his roller. "Thanks for helping us."

"You're welcome." Coach pressed the water out of his roller, set it on the counter and picked up another. "You've got a load of responsibility here, Kendall. Your aunt is going to need a lot of help with this place."

"No one asked her to fix it up," he said, sudden emptiness making him feel hollow. He'd be alone after his aunt left. Trying to ignore the panic that clutched at his gut, he rapped the roller against the side of the sink the way Coach had. "She's not staying, so what does it matter?"

"Whether she stays or goes doesn't matter. The house still needs a lot of work," Coach said.

"Why does she bother? She doesn't care what happens to it," he said, anger and sadness warring inside him.

"She worked on the painting pretty hard today for someone who doesn't care about this house." Coach looked at him out of the corner of his eye. "Maybe you need to give your aunt a chance."

"It won't matter," he muttered. "She's just going to leave anyway."

"You really think she'd leave you behind?" Coach asked.

"Why wouldn't she? She doesn't want a kid hanging around." Nick clenched his jaws together to prevent his mouth from trembling.

"She didn't have to come here at all," Coach said.

"The police made her come," he mumbled.

"I don't think anyone makes your aunt do anything."

When Nick glanced over at him, Coach had a funny smile on his face.

Was Coach making fun of him? "It's not your business, anyway," he sneered. He sneaked a look at Coach out of the corner of his eye. If he said something like that at practice, he'd be running laps for sure.

But instead of yelling at him, Coach shrugged. "You're right. It's between you and your aunt. It's your choice, Kendall. You can act like a kid, or you can act like a man. Take your pick."

Coach squeezed the water from the second roller and set it on the counter beside the first. "How about we order pizza?" he asked. "I'm starving."

"Yeah, okay, whatever." He watched Coach to see if he was making fun of him again, but Coach was drying his hands. Then he clapped Nick on the back.

"Let's go, Kendall. We'll let your aunt finish cleaning up while we go pick up the pizza."

"Are we taking your truck?" Nick asked, forgetting his sulk in the excitement of riding in the awesome pickup.

Coach snorted. "You think I'm going to drive that sissy car of your aunt's?"

"Cool!" he said happily.

Forty-five minutes later, they all sat in the kitchen, eating pizza. Nick glanced at Coach again, still awestruck that Coach was hanging out with him, acting like it was no big deal to be there. Nick shoved another piece of pizza into his mouth as he watched the coach. Acting like he wanted to be there.

The phone rang and his aunt picked it up. She said hello, then glanced over at him. "It's for you."

He grabbed the phone. "Hey, Nick, this is Booger," the voice said. "You want to hang out tonight? I just got a new game for my PlayStation. Tony and Jeff are coming over, too."

His hand tightened around the phone. "Sure. Hold on a minute."

He looked up at his aunt. "Some guys from the team

are hanging out tonight. Can I go over to Booger's house?"

"Are his parents going to be there?" his aunt asked.

He scowled. Booger was going to think he was a baby if he asked that. But his aunt just waited, so finally he looked away.

"Are your parents going to be there?" he muttered.

"Yeah, they'll be here." Booger didn't act like it was a weird question and Nick relaxed a little.

"Yeah," he told his aunt.

"Then yes, you can go," his aunt said to him.

"Yeah, I can go," he told Booger.

"See ya," Booger said as he hung up the phone.

His aunt cleared her throat. "Will you need a ride?"

"Nah," he said. "Booger lives a couple of blocks away." He jumped up from the table and turned to go, remembering at the last minute to pick up his plate and put it in the dishwasher. "Is it okay if I go now?"

"Write down his phone number. And be home by eleven o'clock," his aunt said.

He scribbled the information on a piece of paper, then headed for the back door. "So long," he said over his shoulder.

"Be careful walking over to his house," his aunt said as the door banged closed behind him.

Man, she sounded like she was his mother, Nick thought as he headed down the sidewalk.

The thought brought a funny lump to his throat. Aunt Claire wasn't his mother, and she never would be. He didn't need her or anyone else.

But as he turned the corner, he glanced back over his

shoulder and looked at the house, warm light shining from the windows. It was familiar and reassuring. It was his house. And his aunt would be waiting there for him when he got home.

He supposed that wasn't the end of the world.

TUCKER TILTED BACK in his chair and watched Claire jump up from the table. She grabbed their plates and stuck them into the dishwasher, the silverware rattling against each other, the china clinking together. An objective observer might think the cool Ms. Kendall was nervous.

God, he hoped she was nervous. Because his nerves were killing him.

"Let me give you a hand," he said, standing up.

"Thanks, but there's nothing to do." She didn't look at him as she wiped the table. "I'll just wrap the leftovers and we're done." She flashed a smile in his direction.

"Okay."

He leaned against the wall, watching her. The shorts she'd worn to paint in were baggy and shapeless, and the old, faded T-shirt that covered them was now spattered with paint. He'd noticed a tiny hole in the material beneath her arm when she lifted the roller to the wall, and it had driven him crazy all day. He wanted to burrow into that hole, touch her skin. Feel her nerves jump.

"Well." Her voice was artificially bright. "We've managed to take up your whole day. I'm sorry you didn't get your own painting done."

"It can wait," he said easily. "I enjoyed myself."

Closing the refrigerator door, she glanced over her

shoulder and rolled her eyes. "Right. Tell me another one, Hall. Do you really think I'll believe that you wanted to spend your weekend painting my living room?"

"Nah." He moved closer, enjoying the jittery look she gave him as he approached. She *was* nervous. He liked that.

"This isn't how I wanted to spend my weekend," he murmured, stopping an arm's length away from her.

"I didn't think so." Her voice was breathy.

"None of my fantasies included paint, rollers or drop-cloths," he continued. He was close enough to see her eyes darken, close enough to smell her sweet female scent.

She gave him a shaky smile and slipped past him to stand in the doorway between the kitchen and the living room, to what she probably considered a safe distance. "Of course not. You had your own plans for the weekend."

He kept his eyes on hers, delighting in the way her eyes widened, the way heat flared in them as she held his gaze. "On the other hand, maybe I haven't given enough thought to paint rollers," he said, moving a step closer to her. "I can think of some interesting uses for a roller and melted chocolate."

She lifted her eyebrows. "You keep talking like that, you're going to make me think you arranged for that phone call," she said.

He loved that she maintained her composure even though he could see she was rattled. It roused all of his competitive instincts. "Honey, you can't plan for things like that phone call. They just fall into your lap." He grinned. "I think of Booger's call as divine intervention."

"I think of it as a graceful end to the day. You can leave without disappointing Nick."

"And what about Nick's aunt?" he murmured. "Will I be disappointing her if I leave?"

"Not in the least."

"Maybe we should test that theory."

Only a thin sliver of space separated them now. He closed his hands around her arms, feeling her muscles quiver, feeling her breath hitch in her throat.

But when he bent his head to hers, she didn't back away.

CHAPTER TEN

CLAIRE STUMBLED backward as Tucker bent his mouth to hers, but his arms came around her and pulled her against him. For a moment, resting against his broad chest, cradled in his arms, she felt safe and protected.

Then he touched his mouth to hers, and safety vanished in a searing blast of heat.

She knew the heat rocketed through him, as well—his muscles tensed and his heart slammed against hers. But he held himself in check as he tasted her, nibbling on her mouth and brushing his lips across hers.

His hands moved on her back, skimming down to her hips, then up again, brushing over her with a featherlight touch. Then he combed his fingers into her hair, cradling her head, holding her mouth against his.

He was being careful with her, being careful not to use his size to overwhelm her. Instead of grabbing, he was offering and waiting for her to respond. Tenderness welled up inside her, along with desire.

She would have resisted his strength, would have refused to be dominated. She had no defenses against his consideration.

When he traced her mouth with his tongue, another

spear of desire slashed through her. She murmured his name and opened to him, yearning for more of his heat and strength.

He tightened his arms around her, holding her against him, devouring her mouth. Then he nibbled his way down to her neck, splaying his hands on her back, pressing her more intimately against him. He touched her as if she were delicate and fragile, as if she would break in two if he weren't careful.

Who would have guessed that a man like Tucker, a man with his size and strength, could be so gentle?

"I've been trying to imagine how you would taste," he whispered against her neck. His breath heated her skin and made her shiver. "Imagination doesn't even come close."

She turned her head, searching blindly for his mouth. The taste of him melted into her, hot and dark and male. Struggling to free her hands from against his chest, she wrapped her arms around his neck and pulled him closer.

He trembled against her, his muscles hard as iron against hers. She felt him struggle with control, felt the tension that vibrated through him. He stood perfectly still, but his hands roamed restlessly across her back and down her sides.

"You've been driving me wild all day," he whispered, nipping at her earlobe. "Do you know you have a hole in your shirt? Right here?"

He tightened his hand on her side, and she felt the faintest touch of his finger against her skin.

"I haven't been able to think of anything but this hole all day."

He rested his hand against her side, his palm pressing against her breast, and eased one finger through the tiny tear in the material. When he smoothed the pad of his finger over her skin, sensation shot straight to her belly.

"I knew you'd feel like warm silk," he murmured into her ear. His finger traced an arc over her skin, dragging fire with it.

The touch of his finger was hypnotic. She sagged against him, completely lost in the light brush of his finger against her skin, the slight roughness of his fingertip incredibly arousing.

When he reached her bra he hesitated, and she caught her breath, waiting for him to touch her. Longing for him to touch her. When he slid his finger out of the hole in her shirt, frustration swirled through her.

Along with a return to sanity.

What was she doing? She eased away from him, moving out of reach. What did she really know about Tucker, about his past? She knew he had no plans to leave Monroe. And she had no plans to stay.

And here she was, trembling and aroused in his arms, her senses swamped with the taste and feel of him. Her caution and common sense had vanished without a trace.

"What's wrong?" Tucker asked. His eyes were dark with desire, his face flushed and tight.

"I'm… This…" She shoved a hand through her hair. "I don't know what I was thinking, Tucker."

A devil danced in his eyes. "Want me to explain?"

She felt her face burn. "You know what I mean. I can't do this. I can't be attracted to you. I'm not staying in Monroe."

He reached out and tucked a strand of hair behind her ear. "You think you can control that, Claire? Who you're attracted to?" He trailed a finger down her cheek to her neck, slid it lightly across her collarbone. "If you think that, your hormones will make a fool of you every time."

"I can control my hormones," she told him, but her voice was breathy and too soft.

"Yeah, but why would you want to?" He placed his cupped hand on her cheek and brushed his mouth over hers.

She wanted to press her cheek into his hand. Instead she took a step back. "I don't do casual sex."

His eyes darkened even more. "Casual sex? You and me? Honey, there would be nothing casual about it."

Her breath caught in her throat. "It doesn't matter how good the sex would be. I'm leaving Monroe in a few months. Not coming back. We have no future," she said. A sharp spear of regret stabbed her and she pushed it away.

He brushed his knuckle over her cheek again. "I'm attracted to you. And I think you're attracted to me. We could have a good time for the next few months, Claire."

"I'm not interested in a 'good time'" She drew in a shaky breath, tried to smile. Tried to convince herself she meant it.

He watched her with eyes that were far too knowing. "What are you interested in?"

"I'm interested in developing my relationship with Nick. I'm interested in getting my work done, trying to run my business as an absentee owner. I'm interested in getting this house fixed up."

"So you can sell it and go back to Chicago," he said.

"Yes." She lifted her chin. "That's the plan."

"Sometimes things happen that aren't part of the plan," he said. A shadow crossed his eyes, was quickly banished. "What happens then?"

"Then you reassess the plan and figure out how to make it happen."

He skimmed his finger down her neck. "Sometimes those little detours are the best part of life, Claire. You miss those detours if you keep the blinders on. Are you sure that's what you want to do?"

She wasn't sure of anything right now. No, that wasn't right. She was sure she wanted to take Tucker up on his offer of a good time. She was sure she wanted to step into his arms, to feel his mouth and hands on her again.

And she was sure it would be a mistake.

"Is that how you ended up in Monroe?" she asked. "By way of a detour?"

"I grew up in a small town in southern Georgia. I had a rough childhood and football was my escape. I couldn't wait to get out." He took her hand, stared at it while he played with her fingers. "I had a plan, too. And it worked." He looked up at her with a wry smile. "I'm the classic example of 'be careful what you wish for.' But I was damn lucky. When my plan exploded, I found the detour to Monroe."

"Why did your plan explode?"

His hand tightened on hers, then he smoothed his finger over her knuckles. "Some things happened that made me realize I needed to get out of football."

"What kind of things?" she asked.

His eyes went dark, and she saw both grief and pain in them. Then he bent his head and kissed her palm, shielding his eyes from her. "It doesn't matter because I'm not that person anymore. I'm what you see, a small-town high school teacher and football coach. Nothing more."

She wanted to press him, to find out what had happened before he came to Monroe, what put that pain in his eyes. She wanted to know everything about him, but she didn't have the right to ask. Or worse, to dig for details behind his back. She wasn't willing to tell him all the ugly details of her childhood in Monroe, or her marriage and divorce from Roger Vernon.

So she couldn't ask him to strip naked, either.

Instead, she asked, "Do you ever regret what you gave up to get here?"

"Sometimes." He gave her another wry smile. "A small town in central Illinois is a long way from the bright lights and the big city."

She tilted her head. "I guess playing professional football and teaching high school in a small town are at opposite ends of the universe."

He watched her for a moment, then let her hand drop and shoved his hands into his pocket. "Not really," he said. "Football players are lucky if they manage a few years in the pros. You have to be ready for life afterward." He shrugged. "This is the life I chose."

"And the life I chose is in Chicago," she said. To her shock, she heard regret in her voice.

"Yeah, Claire. I know."

He reached out and pulled her close. With his mouth poised above hers, he gave her a wicked smile. "That doesn't mean I can't change your mind about having a good time while you're here."

"You can try," she answered.

He brushed his mouth against hers, lingered. She felt his lips curve on hers. "That sounds like a dare to me," he said. "Have I got this right? A beautiful woman is daring me to seduce her?"

His low voice shivered through her, quickening her pulse. "That's no dare, Hall. That's just fact. I'm immune to charm."

"Oh, honey," he said, his voice humming with laughter and heat. "That was just purely the wrong thing to say. I'm going to play so dirty."

"Give it your best shot."

His hand tightened on her head for a moment, then he stepped back. His eyes sparkled down at her. "You have no idea how much I like a challenge," he said.

"You have no idea how stubborn I am."

He picked up her hand, pressed a kiss into her palm, then blew softly against it. "Stubborn is my specialty."

He tried to draw her near, but she slipped out of his arms, shooed him toward the door. "Get out of here, Hall."

He trailed a finger down her throat until it hooked in her shirt. He tugged her close, brushed his mouth over hers, then let her go. "We'll call it a strategic retreat."

He tossed her a wicked grin over his shoulder on his way out the door and her heart jumped wildly in response.

She was going to have to reach deep for reserves of stubborn she wasn't sure she had.

ON MONDAY MORNING, Claire looked at the pile of faxes on her desk, the stack of mail waiting to be answered, and sighed. It was going to be a very long day.

She and Nick had continued painting on Sunday. They'd worked well together, but it wasn't the same as it had been on Saturday. It wasn't nearly as much fun.

Before they started, Nick had asked hopefully, "Is Coach coming over to help us?"

"Not today. He has his own work to do."

Nick's shoulders had slumped, and she'd told herself it was just as well. The regret that washed through her had been a little too sharp, a little too intense.

It was time to work. This work was her life, she reminded herself.

So why wasn't she diving in?

She was distracted and disorganized. It was because she'd spent the weekend working on the house, she told herself. Tucker Hall and his teasing, his sweet, seductive kisses, had nothing to do with it.

Putting Tucker firmly out of her mind, she sat down and began to make her way through the stack of faxes.

She'd barely made it through half of them when the doorbell chimed. She glanced at her watch and frowned. Who could be at her door at nine o'clock in the morning?

When she pulled the door open, the chief of police stood on her porch. He nodded to her. "Good morning, Ms. Kendall."

"Chief Broderick," she said, shocked to see him standing there. For a moment her mind flashed back fifteen years, to one of the rare appearances of Fred Denton at their door. Her father had been arrested for drunken driving and it had meant nothing but trouble for them.

"May I come in?" he asked with a hint of impatience.

"Of course. I'm sorry." She stepped aside.

"I have some information for you," he said, staring down at her. She couldn't read his eyes.

"Thank you for coming by," she said. "Can I get you something to drink?"

"No thanks," he said. He wandered over to the front windows, examined them. "These locks are pretty flimsy," he said. "You should replace them."

"I'm working on renovating the house," she said, her voice stiff. Her face burned at the reminder of how her mother had neglected the property.

Broderick turned around, gave her an apologetic smile. "Sorry. Once a cop, always a cop, I guess. Just tell me to mind my own business."

Her embarrassment eased at the rueful look on his face. "No problem," she said. "Thanks for the tip."

He looked around the room, and Claire imagined he was assessing the locks on the front door. Suddenly amused rather than offended, she smiled at him. "Don't tell me. The locks on the door are worthless, too."

He grinned at her, and a dimple flashed in one cheek. "Sorry. Force of habit."

More at ease with him, she nodded at the couch. "Please sit down."

"I've talked to Officer Downey," he said. "He's the one who spoke to your nephew on the night of the accident."

His mouth tightened. "He admitted that your nephew

said something to him about his mother getting a phone call. Downey said he thought the kid was just upset."

"Of course he was upset," she said sharply. "He'd been told his mother was dead."

Broderick's eyes flashed, but he merely gave her a curt nod. "Downey understands that it wasn't his job to make those assumptions. He knows he should have followed up on your nephew's information."

"Thank you," Claire said, taking a deep breath, surprised at his words. She'd been sure that Broderick would defend his officer. "What now?"

"I've asked the phone company for a list of all calls into and out of your house the day of the accident and several days before that. It'll take them a while to get it to me. Once we get a look at the numbers and see who called your sister, we'll start asking some questions."

"I appreciate this," Claire said, studying the chief of police. "A lot of people wouldn't bother with such a long shot. A lot of people would say Janice's death was an accident and leave it at that."

The chief's features softened. "The Monroe Police Department has changed since you moved away. I'd like to think we're more responsive to the people we serve."

He clearly knew her history with the department. Heat swept up her neck and into her face. Why was she surprised? He would have found out everything he could about her after her visit to his office.

"I can see that," she said. As she met his steady gaze and saw nothing but sympathetic understanding in his eyes, her embarrassment receded. "It looks like a lot has changed in the department."

"I hope so," he said quietly. "I'll let you know as soon as we have any information."

"Thank you, Chief Broderick." She smiled as she watched him stand up. Another one of her assumptions about Monroe shot down. "I appreciate this."

"Most people in Monroe call me Seth. And you're welcome. I'm just doing my job."

"I know. That's why I'm thanking you."

He nodded once, his eyes steady. "You call me anytime," he said as he walked out the door.

"I will."

He climbed into a black-and-white SUV and drove off, but Claire stared after him for a long time, astonishment and an unfamiliar longing tangling inside her. The people in Monroe continued to surprise her. Maybe things in Monroe really had changed. Maybe it was no longer the place that starred in her nightmares.

Maybe living in Monroe wouldn't be the end of the world.

She had barely gotten started working again when the phone rang. She needed caller ID, she told herself as she reached for the phone. Right now, she couldn't ignore any calls, knowing they could be from her office.

Or from Nick's school.

Judging by the time of day, it was undoubtedly another crisis at the office, she thought wearily as she picked up the phone.

"Claire Kendall."

"This is Roger Vernon."

Her hand froze on the telephone. Had Roger somehow found out that she'd spoken to Andrea?

"Claire?" His voice held the same note of irritation at her inattention that she remembered so well.

"Yes. What can I do for you?" She was proud of the steadiness of her voice, proud of her calm professional demeanor.

"I've been retained by a client to represent him in a custody suit. My client is Nicholas Kendall's natural father and he will be seeking custody of the boy."

CHAPTER ELEVEN

ROGER'S WORDS SLAMMED into Claire's gut. "What?" she managed to say.

"I think you heard me." There was vindictive satisfaction in Roger's voice. "Your nephew's father wants custody of his son."

Claire closed her eyes, fighting off the stunned shock threatening to swamp her. "I didn't expect this, even from you, Roger."

"This isn't personal, Claire. This is business." A sly, gloating note of triumph underlined his words. "You never were able to tell the difference."

Ten years ago, the condescending superiority in Roger's voice would have made her flinch. Now it made her angry. "I know the difference, Roger," she said sharply. "I've been running my own business for several years now."

He paused a beat too long. "Your own business? What kind of business?"

"I don't think that's relevant." She closed her eyes, struggling to control her emotions. She'd defeated Roger ten years ago. He had no power over her. "What do you want, Roger?"

"I told you. My client wants custody—"

"I heard that part," she interrupted. "What do *you* want? Besides humiliating me, I mean."

There was silence at the other end of the phone. Then Roger said, "You always did exaggerate, Claire. I see that hasn't changed."

"What do you want, Roger?" she repeated.

"We need to meet," he said. "I'll stop by your house later this morning."

"No, you won't," she answered in a pleasant, businesslike voice. "I'll come to your office. I can spare you some time at…" She flipped some pages, as if checking a schedule. "I can come by at eleven o'clock."

There was a pause. Then Roger said, "Fine," in a sulky voice.

"I'll see you then," Claire answered, hanging up the phone without waiting for a response.

She wiped her damp hands on her shorts and took a deep breath, trying to calm her racing heart. Roger was merely trying to cause trouble, she told herself. He had no idea who Nick's father was. No one did.

But she knew Roger well enough to recognize that gleeful tone in his voice. He was very certain that he'd outwitted her.

Was it possible he'd discovered who Nick's father was?

There was only one way to find out.

AT ONE MINUTE before eleven, Claire adjusted the jacket of her best black business suit and opened the door to Roger's office. An older woman sat at the reception desk, looking at a magazine. When Claire walked in, she tilted her head.

"May I help you?"

The receptionist's gaze was cool and assessing, but there was no spark of recognition in her eyes. Claire gave her an impersonal smile. "I'm here to see Roger. I have an appointment at eleven."

The woman gazed down at her appointment book and frowned. "I don't see anyone down for eleven o'clock."

"Roger must have forgotten to tell you," Claire said, sitting down and reaching for a magazine. She began reading without having any idea of what the words meant.

"I'll check," the woman said after a moment.

She disappeared into Roger's office and reappeared a few minutes later. "He'll be right with you."

"Fine," Claire murmured, knowing Roger would make her wait at least fifteen minutes. "I can spare five minutes."

When six minutes had passed, Claire stood up and smoothed her skirt. The receptionist looked up, startled.

"Tell Roger to call me for another appointment. I had to squeeze this one in, and I can't wait any longer."

"Wait a minute." The receptionist jumped to her feet. "Let me check with him before you leave."

Moments later Roger appeared in his office door, a brittle smile on his face. "Come on in, Claire," he said. "I'm glad you could come by."

"You're lucky I had an opening in my schedule."

Roger stood at the door, his eyes narrowing as he studied her. She smiled inside at the shock in his eyes. She'd dressed very carefully for this meeting.

The blue shirt beneath the black silk Armani suit she wore fit her like a glove, and her shoes cost more than she used to make in a week. Her employees called the outfit her close-the-deal suit.

Roger scowled and closed the door behind her a little too hard. "Have a seat," he muttered.

She sat and watched him, a polite smile on her face.

He met her eyes once, looking away quickly when she didn't blink or back down.

"What is this about, Roger?" she asked.

"I told you on the phone. Your nephew's father wants custody of him."

"And how do you know this man is Nick's father?"

He flashed a superior smile. "I assure you, he is."

"I'm sure you don't expect me to take your word for it. He has proof, I assume?" She crossed her legs and raised her eyebrows.

His smile faltered. "We'll be requesting DNA tests."

"So he has no proof. Who is he?"

"I'm not authorized to reveal his name at this time."

"Really?" She held Roger's gaze with her own. "He's claiming to be Nick's father but he won't tell us his name?"

"He's waiting for proof before he comes forward."

"So he's not sure he's Nick's father, either."

Roger glanced down at the papers on his desk. "He thinks there's a strong possibility."

"There's a strong possibility that a lot of men could be Nick's father," she said. Her voice was blunt. "And I'm sure he knows that."

His grip tightened on his pen. "I'm surprised you'd

talk about your sister that way. But you never did have any loyalty, did you, Claire?"

"That depends on how you define loyalty," she said. She leaned forward, locking her gaze on his. "I define it this way. I'm not going to allow you to hurt my nephew. Or use my nephew to punish me. I'll do whatever it takes to prevent that."

"Are you threatening me, Claire?"

"No, I'm just telling you the way it is." She raised her eyebrows. "Why would I threaten you? Have you done something you shouldn't have done?"

"You've changed," he said, staring at her.

"You mean because I won't let you bully me?" She gave him a thin smile. "I grew up a long time ago. You can't hurt me, Roger. Think very carefully before you try to get at me by hurting Nick. I won't allow it."

While Roger stared at her, she reached into her purse. "I'll contact my attorney and have him get in touch with you." She laid a business card on the desk, watched Roger's eyes widen when he read the name on the card. Even in Monroe, Roger would have heard of Paul J. Caputo. He was one of the most powerful attorneys in Chicago.

"I'll expect to receive all the information you have, including this man's name and the basis of his claim to be Nick's father. Have it ready when Paul calls you."

She swept out of the office and didn't pause until she was on the sidewalk. Her hand shook as she reached in her purse for her sunglasses.

"You won," she said as she drove away from the office. "You didn't let him bully you. You didn't back down."

But she was still shaking when she walked into her house a few minutes later.

CLAIRE GLANCED OVER at Nick as they cleaned up after dinner that night. Their lives had fallen into a comfortable rhythm. During dinner, she'd ask Nick about his day. He still didn't say much, but he'd begun to tell her bits and pieces. Mostly about football practice, she admitted, but that was better than the strained silence that had accompanied their first meals together.

The angry, sullen boy was still there, but he didn't appear quite as often. There were times when Nick seemed almost happy, enjoying the football team, making friends with his teammates. The phone had begun to ring for Nick, and judging by the blush that flooded his face once in a while, some of the callers were girls.

Nick was regaining some of his balance. Staying in Monroe had been the right thing to do, she admitted. And the therapist Nick visited once a week had helped, too.

What would happen if she told him about the man claiming to be his father?

She had no idea. But it wasn't hard to imagine the emotional storm it would cause. She needed to talk to someone, needed some advice. Someone who would have more insights into a fifteen-year-old boy.

Tucker. She wanted to talk to Tucker.

Warning signs flashed madly in her brain, but she ignored them. Tucker had been a fifteen-year-old boy once. And he dealt with them every day. He was the perfect person to ask, she told herself. Much more logical than Judy Johnson, a woman she barely knew. Much more logical than Nick's therapist, a man she didn't know at all. Much more logical than anyone she could think of.

A part of her said she just wanted to see him again. She ignored that mocking voice and tried to focus on what was best for Nick. She had no idea, she realized. No idea what would be the best thing for him.

"I'm going to do my homework," Nick said as he hung the dish towel on the rack. "If I get it finished in time, can I watch *The Simpsons?*"

"Yes, you can," she said, giving him a quick smile. "Anything you need help with on your homework?"

"Nah. I have to write a stupid essay."

"About what?"

"About the guys who wrote the Constitution. We have to write about why they did it and if it was smart or not."

"That's for Coach Hall's class, isn't it?"

"Yeah." Nick scowled.

"I thought you liked Coach Hall."

Nick kicked at the table leg. "I said he was a good coach. I didn't say anything about his class."

"It sounds like an interesting topic," she said, suppressing a smile. She remembered all too well how much she'd disliked writing essays in high school. She also knew that the information in those essays was what she remembered most vividly.

Nick snorted as he headed up the stairs. After he'd disappeared into his room, she wandered out into the backyard and sat on the porch steps, wishing Tucker were sitting next to her. And it wasn't just because she was attracted to him, she realized.

Beneath the teasing, lighthearted exterior was an intensely caring man. A man who noticed everything. A man who'd struggled with his own demons, if the shadows she'd seen in his eyes were any indication.

A man she trusted. She could ask his advice about Nick's father, and he would give her a thoughtful, honest answer.

Before she could lose her nerve, she grabbed her cell phone and punched in his number. He'd given it to all the players on his team, as well as their parents, and she'd programmed it into her phone.

For emergencies, she'd told herself.

His phone rang three times before he picked it up. "Hall," he said. His voice was abrupt.

"Hi, Tucker. This is Claire. Claire Kendall. Am I disturbing you?"

"Hello, Claire." His voice lowered. "Hell, yes, you're disturbing me. I've been…disturbed since I left your house on Saturday night."

Her heart jolted in her chest and she almost said, "Me, too." Instead she cleared her throat. "Um, I meant are you busy right now?"

"Not at all." His voice sharpened. "Are you all right? Is Nick okay?"

"We're both fine, but I need…I need to talk to someone. About Nick. And I thought of you."

"I'll be right there."

Before she could answer, he hung up. She snapped her phone closed, rubbing her damp palms on her shorts. She'd called him on impulse, and uneasiness congealed into a hard ball in her stomach. What had happened to the woman who didn't take chances, the woman who thought everything out logically before she acted?

That woman didn't call men on an impulse.

But Tucker Hall was on his way over to her house, and she'd have to face him in just a few minutes.

In far too short a time, she heard the crunch of his tires turning into her driveway. She hurried to the front of the house before he could ring the doorbell and alert Nick to his presence.

"Thank you for coming," she said. She was breathless from hurrying, she told herself.

He took her hand. "I'm glad you called. What's going on?"

"Let's go around back." She glanced up at Nick's bedroom window. "I don't want Nick to know you're here."

He nodded and walked around the side of the house, but he didn't let go of her hand. When they reached the back porch, he drew her down on the step next to him.

"What's up?" he asked, studying her face.

She took a deep, trembling breath and closed her eyes, trying to figure out the best way to tell him. "I got a phone call today," she began, opening her eyes to watch his face. "From Roger Vernon."

"What did he want?" Tucker asked with a frown.

"He told me…" She swallowed a hard lump of fear. "He told me he was representing a man who claims to be Nick's father. He wants custody of Nick."

"What? Doesn't Nick know who his father is?"

"No, no one does. Janice never told anyone, as far as I know."

"Including her family?"

"Especially her family." She glanced down at their clasped hands and drew hers away. "Janice ran off after she got pregnant."

"Do you think she told Nick's father?"

Claire shrugged. "I have no idea. But I'd guess not. Janice was pretty wild. And very stubborn."

Tucker slipped a strand of hair behind her ear, let his fingers linger on her cheek. Then he reached for her hands again. "Do you believe Vernon?" he asked.

She bit her lip. Why didn't she see this coming? She had to tell Tucker. She'd asked for his advice, and her history with Roger was relevant.

She didn't want to expose herself that way. She didn't want Tucker to know about her past.

This was what happened when you gave into impulse, she told herself grimly.

"I'm not sure," she said slowly. "He acted as though he was certain, but he didn't have any proof. And he wouldn't, or couldn't, give me the man's name."

"Based on the way you look, I'm wondering if Vernon has another agenda," he said softly.

"Yes," she said. "He does."

He didn't say a thing. Instead he shifted closer to her.

She stared down at the porch, focusing on a nail in one of the boards that had loosened. "He's doing it to strike at me. To punish me."

She felt him tense next to her. "Why would he want to punish you?"

Here it was. The part of her past she wanted to hide from Tucker. The part of her past that still shamed her. "I was married to him ten years ago."

"What?"

She heard the shock in his voice and fisted her hands in the material of her shirt. "We were married for two years. I divorced him before I left Monroe."

"You were married to Vernon? That pimple on the backside of humanity?"

"I was young," she said, her voice barely above a whisper. "There were problems with my family. I thought Roger could give me what was missing from my life."

"So he wants to punish you because you divorced him?"

She nodded. "Roger doesn't take losing well."

"I know."

She looked at him, hearing the bitterness that reverberated through his voice. "What did he do to you?"

"I got onto the wrong foot with him even before I moved here. Apparently he considers himself the most important citizen of Monroe. He didn't like the fact that an outsider wanted to buy my house. Especially an outsider with a little bit of celebrity." Derision filled his eyes. "My house had been vacant for years, but when he heard I'd put in a bid for it, he went to the Realtor and told her that the house was part of Monroe's history and should be sold to someone who was a part of the town. When she told him that my bid had already been accepted, he got angry." His mouth thinned. "He found some information about me and spread it to anyone in Monroe who would listen."

"I'm sorry," she said, laying her hand on his arm. "That sounds exactly like Roger. He always wants the best toy and gets angry and vindictive if he doesn't get it."

"Now he wants to use Nick to punish you." Tucker picked up her hand, massaged her fingers.

"Yes." She swallowed, trying to concentrate on her dilemma with Nick instead of the feel of Tucker's hand rubbing hers. "But what if he's right? What if he somehow found out who Nick's father is? Nick has a right to know. But he's so fragile right now. I don't know how to tell him, or even if I *should* tell him."

"Hell," Tucker muttered, bringing her hand to his mouth and kissing her palm. "You don't ask easy questions, do you?" He gave her a wry smile, kissed her palm again. "And here I was hoping you wanted advice on a lingerie problem."

"I wish it was that simple," she said, feeling her throat swell.

He wrapped his arm around her shoulders and pulled her close. "I'm sorry," he whispered. "I shouldn't tease you. That was my lame attempt to make you laugh."

He tightened his arms and she leaned against him, comforted by his size, his warmth, the steady sound of his heartbeat next to her ear. "I don't know what to do, Tucker," she whispered into his chest.

"Neither do I," he admitted. "But I'll help you figure it out."

She didn't show her vulnerabilities to men. She stayed in control, she guarded her emotions, she kept a careful distance. Most of all, she didn't confide in them.

She would never allow herself to be that weak. She wouldn't be a victim again.

Tucker Hall, a man who'd lived with violence for years, had managed to get her to break all of her rules.

The thought terrified her.

She eased away from him, away from his comfort. "Tell me what you see with Nick."

"He's doing better," Tucker answered. "At football, he acts just like any other kid. He works hard, he goofs around, he seems happy to be on the team. In school?"

He stroked her hair in long, easy caresses that both soothed and stirred her. "In school he's still pretty quiet. He doesn't volunteer much in class. But I've seen him talking to other kids. I put them in work groups the other day, and I watched him. He contributed as much as anyone else. But bottom line? He still has a lot of things to deal with."

He continued to caress her, his warm fingers brushing the nape of her neck, moving to the top of her head again. He had no idea how much his touch was affecting her.

She allowed herself to relax against him a bit more. "I know. Everything feels so brittle right now. I have no idea how he'd react if I told him someone had stepped up and said he was his father." She swallowed again, fear tightening her throat as she reached blindly for his shirt. "And how do I tell him this man wants custody? He's having a hard time accepting me in his life. How would he feel about a perfect stranger?"

"No court is going to force a fifteen-year-old boy to live with a stranger," Tucker said. "Vernon was trying to yank your chain. But if the guy really is his father, he has a right to get to know his son."

"I don't care about some stranger's rights," she said fiercely. "I care about Nick and what's best for him."

His other arm came around her. "Nick is lucky to have you," he murmured into her hair. "He's lucky to have someone who cares so much."

Had Tucker missed that growing up? He said he'd had a tough childhood. Suddenly she wanted to know with an intensity that alarmed her.

"You didn't, did you?" she whispered.

"No. My father took off and my mother stopped caring about anything, including me. I was a wild trouble-maker until my high school football coach took me in. He saved me from myself." He brushed his mouth over hers. "Nick will never have that problem. Not with you in his life."

When she tried to move away, he tightened his arm. "You stood up for Nick from the very beginning. Do you know how rare that is? Do you know how important that is for Nick?"

"Nick is my nephew. I love him."

"Not everyone would be willing to take on a troubled teenager. That makes you very special."

He spoke softly, intimately, and his breath tickled her ear. He nuzzled her neck and she closed her eyes, sinking into the sensation of being surrounded by him.

She struggled to focus on Nick, to ignore the yearning for Tucker that washed through her. "This isn't about me. This is about Nick."

He brushed a kiss across the top of her head. "Do you have an attorney?"

She nodded against his chest, relieved at the businesslike question. "I gave Roger his name and phone number, told him to deal with Paul."

"Then you're legally covered." He stroked his hand down her back, making her feel steadier. But his touch wasn't soothing. His hand lit small fires wherever it lingered. "So the question becomes, what would be best for Nick? Telling him now, or later?"

"I want more time with him," she said in a low voice, trying to ignore Tucker's hand. "More time to forge a bond. We're making progress, but it's slow going."

"Is there any reason Nick has to know immediately?"

"I can't think of one," she said. "So I'll wait." She lifted her face to look at him. "I don't want to upset Nick when I'm not even sure what information Roger has."

He nodded. "I agree. Vernon might be blowing smoke."

She eased out of his arms and stood up, signaling that his visit was over. She wanted to move back into Tucker's embrace, but instead stepped farther away from him. "Thank you," she murmured, "for coming over so quickly."

"Anytime, Claire." He stood up next to her, rocked back on his heels and gave her a lazy grin. "Now that we've solved that problem, are you sure you don't need help with any lingerie dilemmas?"

"Positive," she said firmly, but her mouth curved in an answering smile. "But I'll keep you in mind if one comes up."

"You do that." His voice was relaxed, but his eyes gleamed with sudden energy. "I'm available anytime, day or night."

"Thank you," she said, her voice mock-serious. "That's very generous."

"I try."

He grinned at her again as they walked back around the house. At the truck, he smoothed his hand down her arm. "Besides lingerie, call me if you need help with anything. Even if you just want to talk about Nick and his father."

"Thank you," she said. "I will."

Before Tucker could get into the cab, the front door slammed. When she turned around, she saw Nick charging down the stairs.

The residual glow from Tucker's visit vanished when she saw the anger on her nephew's face.

CHAPTER TWELVE

"WHAT'S HE DOING HERE?" Nick demanded. Running at them, he clenched and unclenched his fists. "I heard you. I was in the kitchen, getting a glass of milk."

He stood too close, towered over her. Rage and humiliation swirled in his eyes. "Were you talking to Coach about my father?"

"Nick, take it easy." Tucker stepped forward, put a hand on Nick's arm.

Nick shook his hand off. "It's none of your business! She had no right to talk to you about it. No right! It's *my* private business." He turned to Claire. "You never asked *me* about my father."

"Do you know anything about your father?" Claire asked, trying to keep her voice steady, refusing to back away from the anger in her nephew's eyes. That anger frightened her. For just a moment, it brought back ugly memories of another angry man who had lived in this house.

"My father is none of your business," he shouted.

Tucker stepped forward, grasped Nick's shoulders, and moved him away from Claire. "Settle down, son. This isn't the way you solve problems."

Nick shook him off. "Don't call me son."

Tucker nodded slowly. "You're right, and I apologize. My Southern roots showing again." He shoved his
hands into his pockets, but Claire noticed that he'd angled himself between Nick and her. Although Tucker's
instinctive protectiveness warmed her, she refused to
hide behind him.

Claire stepped around Tucker and reached for Nick.
He recoiled. "Nick, I'm sorry. I was just asking Tucker's advice."

"On what?" Nick sneered. "How you can get rid of
me and go back to Chicago?"

She sucked in a shocked breath. "Of course not.
That's the last thing I want. I wouldn't think of leaving
you." She touched his arm. "I want us to be a family."

"Yeah, right. You want to dump me on my old man.
A guy who never wanted me *or* my mother."

"Nick, I haven't been looking for your father. I
promise."

"That's bullsh—"

"Enough," Tucker said. "Watch yourself, Nick."

Anger raged in Nick's eyes, a shocking contrast to
the gentle buzz of bees in the garden.

How could she make him understand? "I'll be hon-
est with you, Nick. You know I don't have any children.
I haven't spent much time around teenagers. Sometimes
I need help figuring stuff out."

"You could try asking me," he said, lifting his chin
again.

Tucker laid his hand on Nick's shoulder again, and
again Nick shrugged it off. "Listen, Kendall," Tucker

said, ignoring Nick's gesture. "Fifteen-year-olds don't always know what's best for them."

"She should have asked me," Nick said, hunching his shoulders. "Not you."

Claire saw tears glittering in Nick's eyes, and suddenly understood. Nick was struggling to become a man. He didn't want Tucker to see him as a child.

"I asked Tucker because he's my friend," she said softly. "Because he knows you. He spends time with you every day." She glanced at Tucker, was warmed by the encouragement she saw in his eyes. "Because he was a fifteen-year-old boy once, too."

"Hard as it may be to believe, Kendall," Tucker said, "I was a snotty punk with an attitude once myself."

Claire whipped her head around to look at Tucker. But Tucker winked at Nick, and some of the anger faded from Nick's eyes.

Nick liked being called a snotty punk?

Clearly she didn't understand men at all.

"Can we sit down on the porch and talk?" Claire asked, watching her nephew.

He shrugged. "I guess."

She turned to Tucker, who gave her a small shake of his head. "I'll see you at school tomorrow," he said to Nick. "Punk," he added with a grin.

"Yeah, whatever," Nick mumbled.

They stood and watched as Tucker drove away. Claire turned and dropped self-consciously onto one of the wooden porch steps. Still warm from the sun's rays, it eased the chill inside her. After a moment, Nick sat down below her.

"Do you know anything about your father, Nick?" she asked.

"Not much." He used the toe of his running shoe to move a pebble around on the step. "Mom just told me she cared about him. And that he cared about her."

His eyes were tear-blurred. "That was a lie. If he cared about her, how come he didn't marry her? Or at least give her money to take care of me. Fathers have to do that. I know about child support." He kicked the pebble off the porch, watched it tumble down the sidewalk. "Mom just said that so I wouldn't feel bad. He never wanted me."

"Maybe he didn't know about you. Your mom ran away after she got pregnant, you know. She probably didn't tell your father."

Nick's weary, cynical glance cut at her heart. "Yeah, right," he said.

She had to tell him. She had to ease some of the pain in his eyes. There was nothing worse than knowing your parents didn't want you.

She knew how that felt.

"I want to tell you why I needed to talk to Tucker, why I wanted his advice." She reached for his hand, held it in hers. When he tried to pull away, she tightened her grip. "A man has come forward and said he's your father."

He whipped his head around to stare at her, scowling with disbelief. But beneath the doubt she saw wild hope. "That's crap. Why would someone say that now?"

"I don't know, Nick. I haven't talked to him. I don't even know who he is. He contacted a lawyer."

"How do you know he's telling the truth?"

"I don't." She leaned closer, searched Nick's eyes. "That's why I wanted to talk to Tucker. I didn't want to get your hopes up."

"So it may all be a lie?"

How did she tell him about Roger? "The lawyer is Roger Vernon, that lawyer we saw in town. I used to be married to him and our divorce was ugly."

"You were married to that guy?"

"For two years."

She could see Nick thinking. "So this Vernon guy might be lying because he's still mad at you."

"Yes." She smiled at Nick through the tears clogging her throat. "You're a smart kid, Nick."

He looked away, but not before she saw the sheen of tears in his eyes. "That's a crappy thing to do."

"Yes, it is. That's why I didn't want to tell you right away."

Nick used his shoe to draw circles in the dust on the stair. "What if he is my father? Do you want to get rid of me?"

"No! That's the last thing I want." She took a deep breath, laid her hand on his shoulder. "I love you, Nick. I'll fight like hell if he tries to take you away from me."

He gave her a sidelong look. "Yeah?"

"Yeah." She gave him a mock-fierce look. "And I can kick some major butt."

A smile curved one side of his mouth for a half second, then disappeared. He moved his toe back and forth in the dust, back and forth. "Do I have to decide now?"

"Of course not. This is a lot to think about. And it's your decision."

"What do you think I should do?"

"Right now? Let's wait until we have more information. But if this man is your father, the decision is yours." She wrapped her arm around his shoulders and squeezed. He hunched his shoulders, but he didn't shake off her hand. "I can't tell you to meet your father or not. You're fifteen years old. You're closer to an adult than a child. You have the right to make this decision."

"I don't know what to do," he muttered.

"It's not an easy thing to decide," she said. She stood up and brushed off the seat of her shorts. "It's going to take a lot of thought. I'm here if you want to talk about it. But no one expects you to figure it out this minute."

She put a tentative hand on his arm. "Hey, how about some ice cream? Want to walk into town?"

She expected him to refuse. She was surprised when he shrugged. "Yeah, okay, whatever."

As they walked toward downtown Monroe, the bewildered look on his face made her wind her arm through his, hug him to her side.

Instead of pulling away, Nick leaned a little closer.

FOUR DAYS LATER, Claire stood at the door to the Dog House, the refreshment stand at the high school football field. Judy Johnson had called earlier that day and asked if she could work during the game.

Taking a deep breath, Claire knocked on the door. Judy welcomed her with a smile. "Hey, Claire, come on in."

The scent of hot dogs turning on a grill wafted out the door, mixed with the buttery, salty smell of fresh popcorn. A growling bulldog decorated Judy's apron. Ketchup covered the dog's legs.

Judy followed her gaze and laughed. "A minor kitchen disaster," she said. "Thanks so much for helping out."

"I'm glad you called," Claire replied. And she was. She liked Judy Johnson and looked forward to getting to know her better.

"Do you remember Lucy Groves? She was at the pasta dinner." Judy nodded at the woman in front of the popcorn machine.

"Hi, Claire," Lucy said with a smile. "Welcome to Friday night madness, also known as working the concession stand at a football game."

"Are you trying to scare me off?" Guilt slid through Claire. She should have volunteered to work the games.

"Just try to walk out that door and see what happens," Judy said with a grin. "It won't be pretty."

"What do you want me to do?" Claire asked.

Judy tilted her head. "I think we'll put you at the counter until after the game starts." She led Claire over to the front of the stand. "Here are the prices and here's the cash box. You take the orders and make the change, and Lucy and I will fill them. After the game starts, it'll slow down and we'll show you where everything is."

"I think I can handle that."

A girl whose head barely reached the top of the counter laid a crumpled dollar bill on the counter. "Could I have a licorice rope, please?"

"Sure," Claire said, looking over at the candy display. Red licorice ropes dangled down the side of a box, and she carefully extracted one. Glancing at the price list, she handed the child her change. "Enjoy it."

"Thank you," the girl said, smiling shyly at Claire. She was missing her front teeth, and Claire imagined her sliding the licorice through the gap.

The next person wanted a bottle of Gatorade, and the person after that asked for nachos and a hot dog. A group of high school girls giggled as they bought popcorn and candy. Claire called out the orders, made change and quickly got into the rhythm of the work.

A referee blew a whistle, the game started, and their customers melted away. Judy and Lucy came to the front of the stand and leaned on the counter.

"That wasn't so bad," Claire said. "The way you talked, I pictured a mob scene."

"Wait until halftime," Judy advised darkly. "That's when it gets ugly."

"So we just stand around here until then?"

Lucy rolled her eyes. "We have to get enough hot dogs ready to feed the Russian Army, and enough popcorn to go along with it. And we have to make sure the coolers are stocked with soda and Gatorade."

"But that's not our most important job," Judy said, her eyes twinkling.

"What's that?" Claire asked.

"We have to catch up on all the Monroe gossip. That's number one in our job description."

"Then you shouldn't have asked me to work," Claire said with a laugh. "I don't know any of the gossip."

Lucy grinned. "You will by the time you're finished working tonight."

Before Claire could answer, Judy tugged on her sleeve. "Nick is punting," she said. "Look."

Nick caught the ball and kicked it into the air. Claire watched it sail through the air, a spot of bright brown against the midnight blue of the sky.

"Nice job," Judy said. She turned to Claire. "He got some good distance on that."

Claire watched Nick run off the field to receive a high five from Tucker. Her throat swelled. Even from the other side of the field, she could see Nick's joy.

"Hello, ladies," a voice said in front of them, and Claire jerked her attention away from Nick and Tucker. Mayor Denton stood in front of the stand.

"Hi, Fred," Judy said. "What can we get for you?"

"A cup of coffee and some popcorn." His smile was too friendly. "I've heard you make the best popcorn in town, Lucy."

"We try," Lucy murmured, as she headed toward the grill.

"That will be a dollar seventy-five, Mayor," Claire said, her voice expressionless.

The mayor laid a twenty-dollar bill on the counter, and Claire picked it up to make change. Judy stopped her.

"Fred, don't be an ass," she said. "Give me two singles or a bunch of change. I can't break a twenty this early in the evening."

The mayor's eyes flashed, but he picked up the twenty and rooted around in his wallet. "Here," he said, throwing a five on the counter. "This is the smallest I have."

Claire handed him his change, along with the popcorn and coffee. Judy snorted as he walked away.

"Blowhard," she said, shaking her head. "The idiot thinks we'll be impressed by seeing him flashing a wad of money. 'This is the smallest I have,'" she mocked, her voice wickedly skewering the mayor.

Claire turned to Lucy. "It sounded as if Mayor Denton was hitting on you," she said, sickened by the thought.

Lucy grimaced. "The old coot thinks he's God's gift. Prepare yourself. If you're a single female in Monroe, sooner or later he'll hit on you."

"He's married!" Claire said.

Judy rolled her eyes. "That's a great big 'duh.' And you don't have to be single to get Fred's attention. He'll hit on anything female that moves."

"If he's such a hound dog, how did he get elected mayor?"

Judy sighed. "The Monroe movers and shakers are pragmatists. The mayor has to do a lot of schmoozing with the state legislature, and Fred is good at extracting money from them."

Claire leaned against the counter as Lucy and Judy talked about people she knew. She was enjoying herself, she realized. Cool night air brushed against her skin and the cheers from the crowded bleachers swelled and faded with the plays on the field. Judy giggled at something Lucy said, and suddenly all three of them were laughing.

"I'm glad you're here tonight," Judy said after a moment.

"I'm glad you called," Claire answered. "I'm having a great time."

Lucy smiled. "Who knew that working the refreshment stand at a football game was so much fun?" she said. "Welcome to small-town life."

"You both enjoy living here, don't you?"

"I sure do," said Judy. "I didn't expect to like it. I loved living in the city. Jim had to drag me here, kicking and screaming. But Monroe suits me now. And it's been good for Booger." She gave Claire a rueful smile. "If you had told me before we moved to Monroe that I'd be calling Tim 'Booger,' I would have said you were completely nuts. But I can't imagine living anywhere else."

"My perspective on Monroe comes from my childhood," Claire admitted.

"A lot of things look different from an adult point of view," Judy pointed out. She flashed a sympathetic smile. "I'm not sure I'd want to go back and live in the town where I grew up."

"Sometimes you don't have a choice," Claire said.

"Even when you don't, sometimes it ends up better than you ever could have expected," Lucy added.

She walked to the back of the booth. "Time to gear up for the halftime rush. Claire, you can start with the hot dogs."

Before Claire could follow her, a blond man who looked familiar stopped at the counter. "Hello, Claire," he said.

Embarrassed that she didn't remember his name, she gave him an impersonal smile. "Hi. Can I help you?"

Annoyance flashed in his eyes. Because she didn't remember his name? It vanished as quickly as it appeared, making her wonder if she'd imagined it.

"I'm Derek Joiner. We spoke at the first football game. Your sister worked with me at city hall."

"Of course. I'm sorry I didn't remember your name."

"Don't worry about it," he said with a smooth smile. "You have a lot to concentrate on." He leaned over the counter. "I still have Janice's things at the office. Would you like me to bring them to your house?"

"No, thanks," Claire said quickly. How did Joiner know where she lived? "I'll stop by city hall next week and pick them up."

"No hurry," he said. "I figured you'd been busy, wrapping things up here." He winked. "Not that I'm in a hurry to see you leave Monroe. We can always use more beautiful women in town."

"Thanks, Derek," Claire said. "I'll see you when I stop by city hall."

"I'm looking forward to it," he said with a pleasant smile. He nodded to all three women as he walked away.

"Pretty smooth, isn't he?" Judy said.

"If you like his type," Lucy added.

Claire glanced over at them. "Another one who thinks he's a lady-killer?"

Lucy grimaced. "Way too slick for me," she said.

Claire grinned. "Maybe I'll work here at the concession stand with you two every Friday night. I'll know everything there is to know about Monroe by the end of the football season."

"Stick with us, baby," Judy said with a laugh. "We'll let you in on all Monroe's deep, dark secrets."

"But not at the concession stand." Lucy shuddered. "Once a season is enough for me."

"Speaking of which, brace yourselves," Judy said. "The halftime buzzer just went off."

AN HOUR AND A HALF LATER, after a disappointing loss, most of the fans had filed out of the stadium and the three women were cleaning the booth and putting away the food. Claire was washing the coffeepot when Lucy shrieked. Popcorn cascaded onto the floor in a yellow-white stream as she stared helplessly at the mess. Lucy had been having trouble with the popcorn machine all night.

The three women slipped on popcorn as they struggled to turn off the machine, their giggles escalating to helpless laughter as it regurgitated kernels. Popcorn crunching beneath her feet, Claire staggered back against the counter, waving a dustpan and brush.

"Smack it with the broom," she called between hoots of laughter. "Don't let it bully you, Lucy. You have to show it who's boss."

"And here I thought you ladies were so brave, volunteering to work the concessions at the games. You're having way too much fun to be working."

Claire spun around to find Tucker grinning at her from the other side of the counter. The khaki pants, blue dress shirt and tie he wore to Friday night games were slightly rumpled-looking, but they only emphasized his wide shoulders and long legs. The faint tang of clean sweat clung to him.

"Hi, Tucker," she said.

"Hi, yourself." He nodded at the mess on the floor, his lips twitching. "I guess it wouldn't be smart to ask for popcorn."

"Not if you value your life. We just beat that machine into submission."

"Then I guess I'll settle for a Gatorade."

"I'll go grab one."

She headed for the small storage area and crouched down to retrieve a cold bottle. When she turned around to stand up, Tucker was right behind her.

"The door was open," he said. "I thought I'd save you some steps."

He was so close that she couldn't help brushing the front of his body as she stood up. Her legs bumped against his and her breasts were less than an inch from his chest. The breeze through the open door was chilly, but heat rolled off Tucker's body and seeped into hers.

"Here you go," she said brightly, handing him the bottle. When she tried to back up, she bumped into the stacked cases of Gatorade.

"Thanks, Claire," he said. Without taking his eyes off her, he unscrewed the cap and gulped it down. She couldn't tear her gaze away from his throat muscles, contracting rhythmically inches away from her.

He finished the drink and tossed the bottle into the trash can. "I've been thinking about the Dog House all night," he said in a low voice. "I had such a craving…" He gave her a slow, intimate smile. "For a Gatorade."

"We have plenty of that," she managed to say.

"So I see."

"I should finish cleaning up here," she said, her hands scrabbling for a hold on the boxes behind her as she eased away from him. "Nick will be waiting for me."

"He asked me to tell you he's going to Sparky's with a couple of the guys," Tucker said. "Take your time."

His eyes gleamed as they settled on her lips. For a breathless moment, she was sure he intended to kiss her. Then he moved away.

"Thanks for the drink," he said. "I'll wait and make sure you ladies get to your cars safely."

"You don't have to do that," she protested.

"Oh, it's my pleasure, Claire," he said.

With a smile that held a promise, he disappeared out the door.

When Claire turned around, she saw Judy and Lucy watching with frank interest. "Looks like you have something to contribute to Monroe gossip after all, Claire," Judy said with a wicked grin.

Claire felt her face flush bright red. "Tucker wanted some Gatorade," she said. "I guess he was thirsty after the game."

"Oh, he wanted something, all right," Judy said. "But it wasn't a sports drink."

"You have a dirty mind, Judy Johnson," Lucy said, laughing.

"It doesn't take a dirty mind to understand that look on a man's face," Judy shot back. "Tucker might have said he wanted a Gatorade, but he wants Claire for dessert."

"I have no idea what you're talking about," Claire said, grabbing desperately for dignity.

Judy snorted. "You didn't expect to keep this a secret, did you?" Her eyes crinkled with laughter. "And I thought you grew up in Monroe."

"There are no secrets in a small town," Lucy said.

But that wasn't true, Claire thought. Everyone had them. Life wasn't black-and-white anymore, the way it had been when she was younger. Now everyone's life was shades of gray, an amalgam of choices made and roads taken.

Claire looked at the other two women, women who were her friends. No one emerged from their childhood unscathed.

Maybe the people in Monroe weren't so different from people everywhere else.

Maybe they were more like her than she thought.

Maybe she was the one who needed to change her thinking about Monroe.

CHAPTER THIRTEEN

TUCKER LEANED against Claire's car and watched Claire, Judy Johnson and Lucy Groves walk out of the concession stand toward the parking lot. His heart sped up as Claire smiled at something Judy said, then turned to Lucy and laughed.

"Down, boy," he murmured to himself. But he tensed in anticipation as she said goodbye to the other women and headed toward him.

"You didn't have to wait for me," she said, stopping a careful distance from him. "I think I'm safe in the high school parking lot of a small town like Monroe."

"You never know." He moved toward her. "Someone thinking wicked thoughts could be waiting for you."

"Really?" she said, her voice light. "In Monroe?" Excitement leaped in her eyes.

"You wouldn't believe the wicked thoughts in the air tonight," he said, heat rushing through his veins. He reached out and drew her close, wedging her against him, hip to chest.

She looked up at him, her green eyes dark. "Try me," she whispered.

The urgent drumbeat of desire pulsed through him as

he bent his head. When he kissed her, she clung to him and kissed him back, opening her mouth to him. Need obliterated common sense. Crowding her against the car, shadows surrounding them, he slipped his hand between their bodies and cupped it around her breast.

Her gasp turned into a moan, and he drank it in. He deepened the kiss, and she wrapped her arms around him and melted into him.

Tires crunched in the gravel behind him and a car horn honked. He jerked back. How had he forgotten where they were?

"See what I mean?" he whispered. "Monroe is a hot-bed of wickedness."

"I must be losing my mind," she murmured, staring at him.

"Did I offend you completely by kissing you in public?"

"Maybe not completely." She smiled, touching his lips with her fingertips, and heat surged through him again. "I think it's a good thing we're in public. I see what you mean about those wicked thoughts."

"I can fix the public part," he said. Her arms were silky smooth and cool against his hands. He wanted to touch her everywhere.

Moonlight highlighted the lines of regret on her face. "Nick is waiting for me."

"Tomorrow then."

Sadness filled her eyes. "Not tomorrow."

"What's wrong, sweetheart?"

Her eyes softened at the endearment. "Nick and I are driving over to Bakersfield tomorrow to look at Janice's car," she said. "We want to make sure there's no evidence that she had help going off the road."

Definitely not the time for seduction. His hands gentled, slid down her arms to twine with hers. "You want some company?" he asked.

She sighed. "This isn't going to be a fun trip."

"I know," he said quietly. "Maybe I can help."

She searched his face. Finally she nodded, relief seeping into her eyes. "I'm taking advantage of you, but if you're sure you don't mind, I'd like that. Nick would enjoy your company."

He asked the now familiar question. "What about Nick's aunt?"

She smiled at him. "Nick's aunt would enjoy your company, too."

It wasn't a declaration of undying passion, but he'd take it for now. "I'll be there. What time do you want to leave?"

"I hate to wake Nick early. How about noon?"

"Noon it is. I'll see you then."

He felt her gaze on his back as he walked away and anticipation hummed through him. He'd made it clear he was attracted to Claire. He knew she was attracted to him. Her reluctance to give in to the attraction that smoldered between them aroused all his competitive instincts.

Tucker wasn't used to losing. At anything. And he didn't intend to lose this time, either.

"THIS IS IT." The junkyard owner gestured with a tattooed arm at the twisted mass of metal and plastic that had been Janice's car. "This is how it looked when it came in. We don't get much call for parts from a '91 Escort." He smoothed his hand over his bandanna-covered head and gave Claire an apologetic look, as if he was embarrassed for her.

He stood next to the wreck of the car, his arms folded across his massive chest, oddly protective of the ruined shell. The windows were gone and the roof had been peeled away to expose the interior. The torn vinyl seats, carefully patched with duct tape, were a silent reminder of her sister's poverty.

And her failure to help Janice.

"Thank you," Claire said. She looked at him, trying to keep the tears from spilling out of her eyes. "Can we look at it for a few minutes?"

"Sure." The owner gave her a kind smile that transformed his hard face. "Take all the time you want. I'll be in the office when you're done if you have any questions."

He disappeared down one of the narrow aisles, leaving them alone with the car. The car that had killed her sister.

Without thinking she wrapped her arm around Nick's shoulders and pulled him close. He edged closer to her, seeking comfort. He sniffled once, then swiped his arm across his face.

Tucker stood off to the side, studying the car. Trying to give them a little privacy, she realized with a flutter of her heart. She and Nick huddled together as Claire tried not to picture her sister as the car sank below the surface of the lake, struggling to free herself.

Janice had been dead before the car hit the lake, she told herself sharply. That was what Chief Broderick had said. She'd died almost instantly.

"Why…why is it so smashed up?" Nick asked, his voice barely above a whisper. "I thought it went into the lake."

She tightened her hold on her nephew. "Chief Broderick said the car bounced down the embankment before it got to the lake." She hesitated. "He told me your mother died instantly. She didn't suffer."

Nick sniffled again.

Tucker knelt by the left side of the car, studying the rear wheel. "Come and take a look here, Nick," he said.

Nick moved away from her and knelt next to Tucker. She squatted on Tucker's other side.

"Had your mom had an accident lately?" Tucker asked.

"I don't think so," Nick answered. "She didn't say anything about one."

"Are you sure? Look at this." Tucker pointed to a deep indentation in the panel behind the wheel.

Nick shook his head. "That wasn't there, at least not two days before the accident." His lip quivered. "I know because I washed the car. Mom was going to take me out driving. To practice before I started driver's ed."

Tucker looked at Nick. "Yeah? How did you do?"

Nick shrugged. "Okay, I guess." His eyes filled with tears. "We just drove around the church parking lot, but Mom said I did a good job."

"I bet you did," Tucker answered. He gave Nick an encouraging smile. "You have good judgment and good reflexes. You're going to be a fine driver."

Nick stared at the ground, blinking furiously. "That's what Mom said."

"Once you get your permit, I can take you out to

practice," he said. He glanced over at Claire. "Unless you want to learn on that sissy car of your aunt's."

"Really? You'll take me driving? In your truck?" Nick looked at Tucker. His eyes, drenched with tears, were suddenly full of stunned hope.

"Sure. Every guy needs to learn to drive a truck." Tucker gently punched his shoulder. "Take a look at the back of the car, Nick. See if there are any new dents since you washed the car."

Nick stood up, then moved to the rear of the car and bent to study it.

"Thank you," Claire said to Tucker in a low voice. "Thank you for distracting him." Her throat thickened and she stopped talking. Finally she managed to say, "I knew this would be hard for him."

"And for you." He stroked her face with a featherlight touch, gently brushing away a tear. "Do you want me to take you driving, too?"

She gave him a shaky smile. "Thanks, but I'll stick to my sissy car."

He took her hand, brought it to his mouth and pressed a kiss to her palm. "Take a look here." He outlined the dent in the fender. "It makes me think Nick might be right, that Janice's death wasn't accidental."

"What?" Ice congealed in her veins. She wanted to make sure Nick knew she wasn't dismissing him, but she hadn't really believed there was anything to his fears.

"See these scrape marks?" He pointed to an ugly gouge in the metal. "There's some red paint in these scrapes. Like another car bumped her."

Claire stared at the marks, her brain frozen, unable to believe what Tucker was saying.

He stood up. "You find anything in the back of the car?" he asked Nick.

"I don't know." Nick sounded bewildered. "There's a dent back here, too."

"Let's see."

Tucker went to the back of the car, squatted next to Nick. He was careful not to touch the metal. "More scrapes. And more red paint."

Nick stared at him. "You think I'm right? You think someone pushed Mom off the road?"

"I have no idea, Nick," Tucker said, standing up. "But I think we should let Chief Broderick know about these dents. I think he'll want to follow up with this."

"WHAT DO WE DO NOW?" Nick asked, turning to her with an expectant look as they headed back to Monroe.

Wedged between Tucker and Nick on the bench seat of Tucker's truck, Claire gratefully turned to Nick. She was far too aware of Tucker's thigh brushing against hers as he drove, the nudge of his elbow against her breast when he turned the steering wheel.

"I'm going to talk to Chief Broderick on Monday," she said. "I'm sure he'll want to have a look at the car."

"We should go talk to him today," Nick said, his voice raw with urgency. "What if something happens to the car?"

"The man at the junkyard promised he'd take care of the car," she reminded him. "He'll put it inside and keep an eye on it until he hears from Chief Broderick."

Nick's shoulders slumped and her heart twisted. "How about if I call the station when we get home and find out if he's there?" she said.

"I guess." He looked at her out of the corner of his eye. "What else are we going to do?"

"I'm going to talk to the people Janice worked with. I saw Derek Joiner at the game last night. I told him I'd come by to pick up Janice's things."

Nick scowled. "Is he that slick-looking blond dude?"

"You could describe him that way," she answered cautiously. "Do you know him?"

"Not really. He came by the house a couple of times."

"Was your mother dating him?"

"I don't know. Maybe." Nick turned to look out the window. "I didn't like him."

"Why not?" Tucker asked.

"He tried to suck up to me. Acting like he was my best friend." Nick scowled again. "Trying to be so cool."

"If he was dating your mother, naturally he'd want you to like him," Tucker said in a neutral voice.

"Yeah, well, I didn't." Nick slumped in the seat, staring out the windshield. Suddenly he looked over at Tucker. "My mom and I didn't need him," he burst out. "I heard him talking to her. He wanted to help her. We didn't need any help. We were just fine on our own."

"I guess that's the last time I get to paint with you guys, then, huh?" Tucker drawled.

Nick flushed a bright red. "That's different," he muttered. "You wanted to help us." He gave Tucker a sidelong glance. "Didn't you?"

"You bet." Tucker gave him a lazy grin. "Watching your aunt with a paint roller was quite the sight."

"Yeah, well, Mr. Joiner didn't really want to help us. I could tell by his fake smile."

Claire glanced at Nick, wondering what to say. "I'll go to your mom's office on Monday," she said. "I'll talk to the people she worked with."

"Like they're going to know anything?"

"You never know. People who work together know a lot about each other."

"Whatever."

Nick looked out the window, but not before she saw the bright sheen of tears in his eyes again. She reached for his hand and gave it a squeeze.

After a moment, Nick squeezed back. She stared straight ahead, holding on to Nick's hand, her vision suddenly blurred by her own tears.

"I DON'T RIGHTLY KNOW what Janice was doing." The older woman sitting behind the desk in city hall on Monday morning gave her a doubtful look. "None of us worked for anyone special," she said. "We all did for everyone."

Claire glanced at her name tag. "Was anything different about Janice in the last week or two, Ms. Shelton?"

"You can call me Annamae, hon," the woman said. "And no, Janice didn't seem any different than usual."

"I'm sorry," Claire said. "It must seem odd, asking all these questions about my sister. But Nick, her son, misses her terribly." She lowered her voice. "I thought if I could tell him what she was doing, how important her job was, he'd feel a little better."

And since Chief Broderick wasn't in the office and wouldn't be until tomorrow, she needed to have something to tell Nick.

Annamae melted with sympathy, as Claire had hoped. "Oh, hon, you tell him that his mom was the best worker here. Why, even the mayor always looked for her first when he had a job for us."

"Really? The mayor?"

"Yes, indeed. Mayor Denton was very pleased with your sister's work. Of course, it didn't hurt that Janice was a fine-looking woman. The mayor has an eye for the ladies." Annamae's mouth curled into a faintly disapproving frown.

"Mr. Joiner spoke to me at the football game last week," Claire said. "He seemed to think a lot of Janice, too. Did she do a lot of work for him?"

Annamae gave her a sly smile. "We thought Derek had more in mind for Janice than work," she said. "He was always sniffing around her. And she didn't seem to mind."

Claire looked around, as if to make sure they wouldn't be overheard, then leaned closer. "Do you think they might have been involved?"

Annamae's eyes sparkled. "Janice was a good woman. Derek could have done a lot worse."

"So Janice wasn't upset about anything right before her accident?"

"Oh, my, no," the woman responded. "If anything, she seemed excited about something." She winked. "That's why I wondered about her and Derek." Annamae studied Claire, her eyes sympathetic. "That accident was a real tragedy."

"Yes." Claire struggled to maintain her composure. "There were some marks on the car we don't understand. Almost as if Janice crashed into something before her car left the road. That's why I'm asking if she was upset about anything."

"Just the opposite of upset," Annamae assured her. "Like she had big news and couldn't tell anyone."

Someone touched Claire's arm and she spun around. Derek Joiner stood behind her, a little too close.

"Hello, Claire," he said, a tight smile on his face. "You've come for Janice's things?"

"Yes," she said, turning back to the woman in front of her. "Excuse me, Annamae."

Derek placed his hand in the small of her back and steered her toward an office along the wall. "I have her things in here. I put them aside after I spoke to you."

The sleek, modern furnishings of his office felt out of place in the ornate old building. An area rug that was a bold slash of color covered the glowing patina of the hardwood floors, and a painting of geometric patterns in black and white hung on the wall. A cardboard box was the only thing on the surface of his desk.

Claire looked down at the box that held Janice's belongings. How easy it was to wipe away all traces of her from the office where she'd worked. "Thank you for taking the time to get her things together."

"We all miss Janice," he said.

Claire studied him. "Did Janice have any particular friends here? Anyone she might have confided in?"

Derek smiled, but his eyes were wary. "Janice was

friendly to everyone." He looked over at the door, and relief flashed across his face. "Isn't that right, Mayor?"

Fred Denton stood in the doorway, watching Claire and Derek. "She sure was," he said. He smiled, but his eyes were flat. "Everyone liked Janice."

Claire's heart jumped. She lifted the box and clutched it to her chest, forcing herself to acknowledge the mayor. Tension shivered in the air of the office, closed around her chest like a vise. If these walls could talk, could they tell her what had happened to her sister?

Her hands tightened on the box. "Thank you, Derek, for gathering her things for me."

The younger man's smile didn't reach his eyes. "If you have any questions about Janice's work, I'll be happy to answer them for you."

"I'll keep that in mind." Claire edged out of the office, leaning back to avoid brushing against the mayor. She could feel both men's eyes on her as she walked away.

She paused at Annamae Shelton's desk. "Thanks for your help, Annamae. Will you call me if you think of anything else I can tell her son?"

"Of course I will, honey." She reached out and patted Claire's hand. "You tell that boy of hers that his mama talked about him all the time. She was so proud of him that she like to burst the buttons on her blouse."

"Thank you," Claire whispered, her chest tightening. "He'll appreciate hearing that."

"And I'll ask the others if Janice said anything to them."

"Thanks." Seeing the avid curiosity in the other woman's face, Claire knew everyone in the office would hear about her visit. "It was nice meeting you, Annamae."

"Likewise." She studied Claire. "Janice said her sister had a big job in the city. You look like a city girl."

Claire nodded, not sure if that was a compliment or an insult. "I'll be talking to you."

"You take care, honey." Annamae's voice trailed her out of the office. Claire stepped out into the sunshine and took a deep, trembling breath of fresh air.

Her conversation with Annamae Shelton had gone just as she'd hoped. Claire couldn't question all the women in the secretarial pool, but Annamae would do that for her. If anything unusual had been going on with Janice in the weeks before she died, Claire was confident she'd hear about it.

As she headed away from city hall a shiver crawled up her spine, as if someone was watching her. She spun around, but the street was deserted. The flat, gray light from the cloudy sky turned the windows of city hall into a mirror, obscuring her view into the building.

Feeling oddly unsettled, she walked to her car and slid inside. She glanced at the police station as she drove past, disappointed she hadn't been able to talk to Chief Broderick. She wanted to tell him about Janice's car.

Just when she was becoming more comfortable in Monroe, she had to consider the possibility that someone in the town had murdered her sister. Sick at heart, she held the steering wheel tightly as she drove back to the house.

In spite of her growing friendship with Judy Johnson, in spite of Nick's devotion to the football team and his determination to stay, they were leaving Monroe when the football season was over.

Tucker drifted into her mind, giving her a lazy smile,

teasing her in his slow drawl. Regret was sharp and deep. She would miss Tucker. And so would Nick.

That was just another reason to leave. There was no future for her and Tucker. They wanted different things out of life, had different goals and dreams. Still, his presence in their lives was becoming addictive.

Not to mention his kisses.

It had been a mistake to allow him to become so involved. Better to leave soon, before she had the chance to get more deeply involved with him. Better to break it off cleanly, before she had time to make another mistake.

Better to protect her heart, even if she had to run away to do it.

Running away was the coward's way out, a small voice murmured.

She ignored it. Running away was the sensible thing to do.

She knew how to run away. She was an expert at it.

CHAPTER FOURTEEN

A DARK SENSE OF DANGER CLUNG to Claire as she turned into her driveway after her visit to city hall. The midday streets were deserted, the town silent as she stepped onto the front porch. Suddenly her skin prickled and the hairs on the back of her neck rose. She whirled around.

There was no one on the quiet street, no cars in the road. She was alone. She shook her head and walked into the cool quiet of the house. Since they'd found the paint scratches in Janice's car on Saturday, her imagination was running wild. Suddenly there was menace everywhere.

Which just proved how tightly wound she'd become. She'd always prided herself on her pragmatic view of life. Never before had her imagination spun far-fetched tales of murder and conspiracy or built wildly improbable stories from a few tiny scraps of information.

She sat down at her desk and tried to concentrate on her work, but the numbers on the pages swam in front of her. Another pot of coffee did nothing to help.

Getting up from her desk, she prowled through the house, looking for something to distract her, something to take her mind off the fear that had her in its grip.

She stopped at the front window of the house. An aura of menace waiting, poised to strike, sent a chill shivering through her. The sky was a dull gray, the air thick and heavy, weighted down with the ominous still-ness that came before a violent thunderstorm. She wanted Nick at home, safe in the house with her.

Football practice wouldn't be over for more than an hour. Restless and too edgy to work, she slipped on her gardening gloves and headed into the yard.

An hour later she was digging up canna tubers when Nick appeared out of the woods at the back of their property. He froze when he saw her.

"Hi, Nick," she said, standing up and pulling off her gloves. "Why are you coming that way?"

He shrugged and didn't meet her gaze. "I dunno."

"Did someone give you a ride home?"

"Yeah," he said, nodding hard and shuffling his feet. "One of the seniors lives on the other side of the woods. He gave me a ride." His gaze met hers then skittered away.

Fear rushed through her. What was wrong? What was Nick trying to hide? "Come and have a snack while I make dinner," she said, forcing herself to smile.

"No, thanks. I'll wait for dinner," he muttered.

As soon as he stepped into the house he hurried up the stairs to his room, grabbing the phone on the way. She could hear his low voice, speaking urgently to someone, before the door to his room closed.

When she called him down to dinner a half hour later, he slid into his chair without looking at her. He shoveled food into his mouth and gave short, monosyl-labic answers to her questions. He'd barely swallowed the last bite of food before he pushed away from the table with a muttered "excuse me."

She watched him leave, worried and afraid.

She'd barely finished putting the food away when Nick came clattering down the stairs. "I'm going over to Booger's house," he announced without looking her in the eye. "We have to work on a project for English class."

"All right," she said, struggling to keep her voice calm. "Make sure you're home by nine o'clock."

He nodded and hurried through the front door, clutching a notebook to his chest. She watched as he hurried down the sidewalk and disappeared from sight.

Minutes later, a low roll of thunder rumbled through the air. When she looked outside, she saw the sky was dark with angry clouds. A few fat drops of rain hit the sidewalk, lightning flashed, then the heavens opened.

Nick shouldn't be outside walking in a thunderstorm. She grabbed her car keys and ran out the door. By the time she slid into the car, she was soaking wet.

She drove to the Johnsons' house but didn't see him. He must have started running as soon as the first raindrops fell, she thought uneasily. But what if he didn't go to Booger's? What if he never intended to go to Booger's? The memory of his hunched shoulders, and inability to meet her gaze, filled her head. Nick was hiding something.

Maybe Judy would know. Bright flashes of lightning crashed across the sky, illuminating the Johnsons' house with each strike. Lights flickered in the house, then steadied. Claire dialed Judy's number, worry dampening her palms and tightening her chest.

When Judy assured her that Nick and Booger had arrived moments earlier, Claire thanked her and closed the phone, staring at the curtain of rain outside the car window. Maybe Nick had just had a bad day at school.

Rain drummed on the roof of her car and water sheeted down the windshield. Claire closed her eyes, wondering what to do. She didn't want to make a misstep, didn't want to destroy the fragile relationship she and Nick had started to build. But she didn't want to ignore possible signs of trouble, either.

"Tell me what to do, Janice," she whispered. "Tell me about your boy. Tell me how to help him."

The rain eased and she started the car. But instead of returning home, she impulsively drove in the other direction. In minutes she was past the town, driving through the twilight toward the lake where Janice died.

It had been raining that night, too. Claire needed to see the road for herself, feel how slippery it was on the curve where Janice had gone through the guardrail. She needed to stand at the place where Janice died, to see if any part of Janice lingered there.

It wasn't hard to find the exact spot where Janice's car had broken through the guardrail. That part of the low barrier was shiny and new. The rest of the rail was a weathered pewter gray.

She drove past slowly, her heartbeat speeding up as she looked down the incline at the black waters of the lake. Once she was past the lake, she turned around and backtracked.

Another turn brought her to the replaced section of guardrail. The car rolled to a stop on the soft shoulder as she stared at the guardrail. Its newness stood out against the dirt and grass like a fresh wound. Finally she got out of the car and walked to the spot where Janice had died.

Thunder rumbled far in the distance and the rain had almost stopped, but a chilly wind whipped her hair around her face and plastered her clothes to her body. Still wet from her earlier dash to the car, she shivered as she stood next to the flimsy barrier.

One car, then another sped by on the opposite side of the road. Then there was nothing but the moaning of the wind and the splash of the waves against the rocks. The shoulder of the road dropped off steeply, and the embankment was rocky and uneven. In the gathering darkness she saw fresh scars on the dark gray rocks, mute witnesses to Janice's plunge into the lake.

Horrible images crowded her mind. Janice, trapped in her car, bouncing down the rocks to the lake. The crack of noise like a gunshot as the car hit the water, the splash of the waves as they rose into the stormy sky. Then the car disappearing silently beneath the black surface of the water, leaving the lake smooth again, swallowing Janice and her car as if they'd never existed.

Had Chief Broderick been telling her the truth, or was he merely trying to spare her pain? Had Janice really been dead when her car went into the water? Had she been aware of what was happening? Was she afraid? Or in pain?

She couldn't bear to think of her sister's life being snuffed out so easily, so quickly. Claire turned away. This had been a mistake. There were no answers here. Nothing of Janice lingered at this desolate, dark place.

The headlights of an approaching car bore down on her, blinding her in their glare. She raised her hand to shield her eyes. As she watched, the car swerved onto the shoulder of the road and surged forward.

Straight for her. For a stunned moment she stared at the oncoming vehicle, unable to move. At the last moment she dove over the guardrail.

The air from the car's wake swirled around her as she tumbled down the embankment. She slammed into a rock and her side screamed in pain. Another rock gouged her hip and something sharp scraped her leg. She scrabbled frantically for a handhold.

Her fingers closed around the branch of a bush, yanking it out of the ground as she continued to tumble down the slope. But the flimsy bush slowed her progress, and she dug her heels into the rocky mud. Sliding on her stomach, she saw a thick root to her right and grabbed at it. It stretched as her hand closed around it and her body jerked against it, but it held.

For a long moment she hung there, her toes searching for a hold, her hand burning from the effort of holding on to the root. Desperately she reached her other hand to the root and managed to grab on. At the same time, her feet found a narrow ledge of rock to cling to.

The rain began again, the warm splatter of water almost comforting. But the mud beneath her hands was cold and slimy and her feet skidded off the slippery ledge.

She looked down as she struggled to regain her footing. The black water of the lake waited below her, the waves churning in the wind like a hungry mouth ready to devour her. Waiting for her to fall.

She would *not* die here and leave Nick alone again. Shaking her wet, muddy hair out of her eyes, she saw a thin branch above her and reached for it.

After testing her weight against it, she dragged herself a few inches higher. Refusing to look down, refusing to accept the possibility of falling, she moved up the embankment inch by inch. Her feet skidded in the mud, her hands slipped off the branches and rocks in her way, but she continued to crawl up the slope.

Finally the guardrail was within reach, and she hauled herself up the last foot. As she crawled beneath the rail, she collapsed onto the shoulder.

Her hands burned, her body ached and the heavy, earthy smell of mud filled her mouth and nose. She struggled to her hands and knees, then used the guardrail to pull herself upright.

Her legs wobbled, but she staggered to the car. Her hand shook so badly with the cold she could barely open the car door.

It was barely warmer inside the car. She huddled on the seat, wracked with convulsive shivers. She managed to start the car but couldn't put it into gear.

Remembering a blanket she kept in the trunk, she hobbled through the rain to get it. She wrapped it around herself, but it was no help against the bone-deep cold.

She had to get home. She had to get warm and cleaned up. And she had to do it before Nick got back.

The thought of Nick seeing her like this, muddy, bruised and bloody, gave her the strength to put the car in gear. Holding grimly to the steering wheel, she pressed on the accelerator and turned the wheel.

Nothing happened.

The engine revved and the tires screamed, but the car didn't move. When she stumbled into the rain again, she saw that two tires were mired deep in the mud.

She sagged against the car, her frozen brain working slowly through her options. The garage in town was closed. She could call a tow truck from Bakersfield, but it could be hours before they arrived. Hours she didn't have.

She had no family besides Nick to call. And Nick wasn't an option.

Tucker.

She could call Tucker. He'd help her.

His image floated in her mind like a lifeline. Fumbling for her cell phone, she punched in his number with trembling fingers.

"Hello." His voice warmed her, and she closed her eyes.

"Tucker?" she said, steadying her voice. "This is Claire. Can you pick me up?"

"What's wrong?" he asked, his voice sharp. "Claire, what happened?"

"Car's stuck. Out by the lake. Where Janice died."

"On Route 32?"

"Yes." Thank goodness he understood.

"I'll be right there."

The phone clicked in her ear, and she closed her cell phone. She tried to drop it back in her purse, but her hand was still shaking so it ended up on the passenger seat.

Tucker was coming. He'd help her. She held that thought in her head and closed her eyes.

CHAPTER FIFTEEN

RAIN SPATTERED against the windshield of Tucker's truck as he sped along the road to the lake. Anxiety hummed through him as he watched for Claire's car. What the hell was she doing out here at this time of night?

Finally he saw a white blur on the side of the road in front of him and he rolled to a stop behind the car. Even before he got out of his truck he could see what had happened. The car listed heavily to the right, the tires almost buried in the mud.

Climbing out of the truck, he hunched his shoulders against the rain as he ran to her door. Yanking it open, he said, "Hurry and get into the tru—"

He stopped abruptly when he looked at her.

"My God," he finally managed to say.

He barely recognized Claire. Her face and hair were smeared with mud, which had begun to dry and harden like a mask. Droplets of brown water dripped on the blanket she'd wrapped around her shoulders, and her hands trembled as she held the ends together in front of her.

Smears of blood mixed with the mud coating her hands. She was hurt.

He reached for her blindly, dragging her into his arms.

The chill from her wet clothes seeped through the blanket, dampening his shirt and jeans. Her convulsive shivering tore at his composure and he tightened his hold on her. "I'll call an ambulance. Where are you hurt?"

"No ambulance," she said, her teeth chattering. "Just cold and wet. Need to get home."

"You're damn well more than cold and wet. Look at your hands." He peeled one of her hands away from the blanket and stared at the ugly network of scratches. He used the blanket to wipe the mud off her palm, then noticed the scrapes on her arms. "What the hell happened, Claire?"

She closed her eyes and drew a deep, shaky breath. "I fell off the edge of the road, but I'm okay. Really. I couldn't drive home because my car is stuck."

He studied her, noting the stubborn set to her jaw. And the way she trembled uncontrollably with the cold.

"All right. No ambulance. Let's get you warmed up."

He swept her into his arms and she curled into him, trusting him to help her. He wouldn't let her down.

She held on to him when he slid her into the passenger seat of the truck, clutched him as he buckled her in right next to him.

He needed her there, needed to feel her pressed against him and know she was safe. She leaned into him and he wrapped his arm around her.

He drove as fast as he dared on the dark, winding road. Her arm felt small and delicate beneath his hand, far too delicate to survive a tumble down that steep embankment. A surge of fierce protectiveness rose up inside him. Glancing down at her, he said,

"You want to tell me what the hell happened back there, sweetheart?"

She squeezed his hand. "I wanted to see the place where Janice died," she said in a low voice. "I was standing there, looking at the lake, when a car veered onto the shoulder of the road. It looked like it was coming right at me. I jumped over the guardrail to get out of the way."

"Did it hit you?" he asked, swerving the car to the shoulder and slamming on the brakes. He grabbed her upper arms and held on tightly, examining her. "Is that why you're so beat up?"

"No. I rolled down the hill. The mud was slippery and it took a while to get back up to my car."

His hands tightened on her arms. "My God, Claire! You could have been killed!" He wrapped his arms around her, and she burrowed into him.

"I know," she whispered.

He felt her hands grabbing desperately at his T-shirt, as if she needed to hold on to something solid.

"God!" As he closed his eyes, picturing the car coming at her, picturing her diving over the guardrail, a killing rage welled up inside him. He wanted to get his hands on the driver of that car and rip him apart.

When she flinched, he realized he'd been holding her too tightly. Appalled, he eased his grip.

He'd worked so hard to control his temper. The struggle had been the driving force of his life since he'd retired from football. Now Claire had made him forget all the lessons he'd learned so painfully.

He was horrified at how quickly he'd forgotten, terrified at how he'd slipped into the old patterns.

His hand shook when he brushed strands of wet, muddy hair from her face. "Let's get you someplace warm."

"Wait," she said, holding onto his arms. "Nick is at the Johnsons' with Booger. I need to call Judy and ask her to keep Nick there for a while. I don't want him to see me like this, so soon after his mother's accident."

"I'll call her."

He pulled his cell phone out of his pocket with one hand, keeping the other wrapped around Claire. It only took a moment for Judy to answer her phone.

"Judy, this is Tucker. Is Nick still with Booger?"

"They're up in his room. Do you need to talk to him?"

"No. But could you keep him over there for a while? Maybe two, three hours?" He looked at Claire and she nodded. "Claire had a little accident and she wants to get cleaned up before Nick sees her."

"Of course Nick can stay. What happened? Is Claire okay?"

"She's fine. Just cold, wet and a little shaken up. She'll tell you about it later. Thanks, Judy."

He snapped the phone closed before Judy could ask anything more, and turned to Claire. "Judy will keep him for a couple of hours. Okay?"

She nodded, shivering violently, and he eased the truck into gear again. When he reached his own house, he made a quick decision and swung into the driveway. Claire needed to be warmed up fast. And her house was still some minutes away.

He pulled her off the seat and into his arms, then carried her up the steps and into the house. Kicking the door closed behind him, he headed for the stairs.

Claire raised her mud-smeared face and looked around. "Why are we at your house? What are you doing?"

"My house was closer than yours. And you need to get warmed up as quickly as possible."

"I could have waited a few more minutes," she said, her arms tensing around his neck.

"Yeah, but I couldn't have. I want to make sure you're all right."

"I'm fine," she insisted. "Just cold."

He looked down at her mud-smeared face. "You can't always be in control, Claire. Sometimes you have to let go. And this is one of those times."

Her gaze shifted away from him. "I don't like to feel helpless," she muttered.

"Tell me something I don't know." He brushed his lips over the top of her head. "Figure that you're doing me a favor. You're giving me a chance to show off my muscles."

"You're an idiot, Hall," she said, but he got a weak smile out of her.

He swung toward the bathroom at the top of the stairs. Maneuvering Claire through the door, he stood in the middle of the room, reluctant to let her go. He glanced at the whirlpool tub, big enough for two, and looked away.

"Shower or bath?" His arms tightened around her.

"Shower."

He set her down on the floor but held her close to his side. He could hear her teeth rattling together.

"Shower it is." He turned on the water in the shower stall, then crouched in front of her. "Do you need help?"

She gave him a halfhearted grin. "I think I can manage to undress myself."

"Darn it," he said, rubbing her hand between his. "I was hoping this would be one of those lingerie assistance occasions we talked about the other day."

"Don't you ever give up, Hall?"

"Nope. I'm relentless. That's why you might as well give in now."

"Are you trying to take advantage of my weakened condition?" she asked with a half smile.

"Absolutely. I warned you that I play dirty."

"I can see that." She rubbed at a smear of mud on his T-shirt, then pressed her hand against it. "Thank you, Tucker. For rescuing me." Her smile wobbled. "For making me laugh and forget how dirty and wet and cold I am."

"You rescued yourself," he said, using his thumbs to brush dried mud off her face. "I just came in at the end and hogged all the credit."

Her hand trembled against his chest. "I was so scared," she whispered. "I thought I was going to fall into the lake."

The blanket fell away as he gathered her in his arms, held her close. "I was terrified when I saw you," he said, burying his face in her hair. Beneath the stench of mud and fear he could smell the essence of Claire and he focused desperately on that. "But I have you now."

Her arms tightened around him and she pressed her face into his neck. "Don't let me go," she whispered.

"Not a chance of that, sweetheart."

He held her tightly, feeling her heart beating in rhythm with his, feeling her shivering lessen as she soaked up his warmth. The wet chill of her clothes seeped into him, but he didn't notice the cold as her heart bumped against his. It began to race, and her hands slid into his hair.

He set her away from him, feeling as if he had ripped off one of his limbs. "Take your shower," he said, his voice hoarse. "You need to warm up."

And he needed to leave if he wasn't going to take advantage of her. He wanted Claire to come to him freely, not because she was shaken and scared.

"Okay." She gave him a shaky smile. "Can I borrow some clean clothes?"

"I'll find you something warm," he said.

"Thank you." She touched him, pulled her hand back. "I won't be long."

"Stay in there until you're warmed up."

"I will."

Just before he closed the door, he stuck his head back in the room. "You sure you don't need help washing your back? That's one of my specialties."

Longing flashed in her eyes, but she shook her head. "You don't need to be dirty, too."

"Call if you need me."

She nodded slowly. "I will."

His hand shook as he closed the door.

CLAIRE LISTENED to the click of the door closing behind Tucker and shut her eyes. It was only because she was tired, sore and scared that she'd almost asked him to stay. To keep holding her like he'd never let her go.

She adjusted the water with a quick flick of her wrist.

She'd be fine once she cleaned up and got warm. She'd regain her balance and her sanity.

She tried not to visualize Tucker standing in the shower with her, holding her close as the warm water sluiced down their joined bodies. When her body softened and heated, she caught herself and yanked her mind back to reality.

Rivulets of brown water swirled down the drain as she stood beneath the shower, letting the warm water soothe her aching muscles and sore limbs. By the time she warmed up and washed away all the mud and blood, the water was cool.

Her hands burned as she rubbed at her hair with a towel. Angry scratches crisscrossed her palms and fingers. It was all right, she told herself. They weren't serious. They'd heal soon.

So would the scratches on her arms and legs and the ugly purple bruise on her side. She touched it and moved experimentally, encouraged when it didn't hurt too badly. All her injuries were superficial and soon mended.

If only her fears were as easily banished.

When she closed her eyes, she saw the car bearing down on her, accelerating as it got closer. Felt the sweep of air as it rushed past, smelled its exhaust as she tumbled down the embankment.

She wasn't fanciful, she reminded herself. She was far more grounded than that. She didn't allow her imagination to run wild.

But her hands shook as she picked up the clothes Tucker had set on the floor just inside the door.

His boxers rode low on her hips and hung almost to her knees. The sweatpants she drew over them bagged just as much, and she rolled up the legs of the pants so they wouldn't drag on the ground. His sweatshirt drooped off one shoulder and hung halfway down her thighs.

She didn't care. The clothes were warm, and they covered her. She didn't bother to look in the mirror before opening the door and rushing downstairs. To Tucker.

He stood staring out the kitchen window into the night, his hands braced against the counter. He turned around when she walked into the kitchen.

"Feeling better?" he asked with a strained smile. But darkness hovered in his eyes and was etched into the grim lines around his mouth.

"Tucker? What's wrong?" She reached for him, needing to comfort him as he'd comforted her.

He held her at a distance with one hand as he studied her. Finally he folded her into his arms.

"Nothing's wrong now," he said. He pressed a kiss into her damp hair, skimmed his mouth down her cheek to her throat.

"Are you sure?" She leaned back to search his face. "You look so grim. So fierce."

He closed his eyes, then pulled her against him. "I'm fine. Just thinking about what I'd like to do with the idiot driving that car."

"It's okay," she murmured. "I'm not hurt."

"Not hurt?" He gave her an incredulous look, pushed up the sleeves of the sweatshirt to reveal her scratched arms. "What do you call this?"

"That's nothing," she said, giving him what she hoped was a nonchalant shrug. "Just scratches."

"Just scratches." He stared at her arms for a while, and when he raised his head, something dangerous flared in his eyes. "What other 'nothings' do you have?"

"Not much. My hands and arms got the worst of it."

"Is that so?" He studied her for a moment, warmth gradually returning to his eyes. Finally he gave her a faintly teasing smile. "I'm a teacher, you know. I have a very finely tuned BS meter."

"Really," she insisted. "I'm fine. If you'll make me a cup of tea, I'll be back to normal." She nodded at a glass-fronted cabinet. "I'll get a mug."

She reached for the cabinet and froze as the bruise on her side screamed in protest.

"What?" Tucker asked, his voice sharp.

"I'm okay," she told him, lowering her arm carefully. "Just a little more sore than I realized."

"Like hell you're okay." He grabbed the hem of the sweatshirt and yanked it up. He sucked in a sharp breath when he saw the purple bruising on her side.

She was naked beneath the sweatshirt. Although her breasts were still covered, her nipples tightened in the cool air. Too aware of Tucker's hand hovering dangerously close, she tried to back away from him. With effortless strength, he caught her hands in one of his and held her steady as he studied the ugly bruise.

His eyes were dark with anger when he looked at her again. "You didn't tell me about this. You said you were all right."

"I am. It looks a lot worse than it feels."

"You should have X rays. You might have a cracked rib."

"I don't. I've had cracked ribs before and I know how it feels."

He skimmed his hand lightly over the bruise and her skin tingled. Feeling vulnerable and exposed, she stepped back and tugged the sweatshirt down.

"I'm fine," she repeated. "A cup of tea, a good night's sleep and I'll be back to normal."

He reached up for a mug, looked over his shoulder at her. "It's not a crime to admit you need help, Claire."

"Fine. I need help getting a mug off the shelf."

He set it down on the table in front of her. "Was that so tough?"

"Yes," she said, her mouth curving in a smile as she watched him scowl.

"You are a piece of work," he said, but his eyes finally thawed and a smile hovered on his mouth. "No wonder I'm crazy about you."

Her heart pounded in her chest and she busied herself making the tea. A comment like that, she decided, was best ignored.

"I should probably get going once I have my tea," she said, her voice bright.

He came up behind her and ran his hands down her arms, making her nerves jump. "Sorry, sweetheart," his voice rumbled in her ear. "Wrong answer. The correct answer is, 'I'm crazy about you, too, darling.'"

"I'm glad to see you don't have an ego problem, Hall."

"I already admitted I have a large ego." He paused for a beat. "It fits right in with the rest of me."

She turned around, grinning. "Okay, you win. You managed to make me laugh tonight, and I didn't think that was possible. I *am* crazy about you."

His smile faded as his eyes darkened, heated. "Some things I don't joke about. I'm not teasing you now, Claire," he said in a low voice.

"Neither am I," she whispered. Her heart banged against her chest and desire swelled inside her, sucking all the oxygen out of the bright kitchen. She couldn't breathe.

If Tucker could make her forget the horrors of her fall down the embankment, if he could tease her into laughter just an hour later, she was in deep trouble.

Their gazes caught, held. Tucker didn't try to hide the need in his eyes. Raw and urgent, it wrapped around her and brought her up against him.

He closed his eyes, pressing against her from chest to thighs as if he could absorb her into himself. Finally he eased away.

When she reached for him, drew him back, he stiffened. "Don't, Claire," he said, his hands tense at his sides, his voice hoarse. Hunger throbbed in the air around them. "Not tonight. I don't want to take advantage of you."

The horror of her fall, the fear that had consumed her, disappeared in a rush of heat and passion. She was alive. She wanted Tucker. And he wanted her.

She lifted her arms to his neck, wriggled closer against him. "That's too bad. Because I want to take advantage of you."

He groaned, but he didn't pull away from her. "You're hurt, sweetheart."

Her mouth curved. "Make me forget that."

He leaned his forehead against hers. "One last chance, Claire. Let me take you home right now."

"I don't want to go home." She reached up, brushed her mouth across his. "Are you going to make me beg?"

"God, no." He wrapped his arms around her, held her as gently as if she was made of paper-thin glass. "But I don't want you to regret anything."

"I couldn't," she whispered. "I want to make love with you, Tucker."

He closed his eyes and she could feel him trembling. Then he swept her up in his arms again, fusing his mouth to hers. She tasted his strength, his hunger, the knife-sharp edge of his control as he ascended the stairs, never lifting his mouth from hers.

In moments he stood in his bedroom and took his mouth from hers as if tearing off a piece of himself. An enormous bed dominated the room, a skylight splashing the silvery light of the moon across it.

Suddenly nervous, overwhelmed by what she'd set in motion, she plucked at the baggy sweatshirt and sweatpants she wore. "I'm sorry this won't be a lingerie moment for you."

His eyes gleamed in the dim light. "Believe me, I'll survive." He swept his hand slowly down her chest, trailed over her belly, stopped just above the junction of her thighs. "You can save the fancy lingerie for another time."

He gripped her hips, drew her against him and took her mouth again. The hard length of his erection burned into her. Her knees wobbled and she wrapped one leg around his.

He groaned into her mouth and swept the sweatpants down her legs. His eyes darkened even more when he saw the boxers, riding low and clinging to her hips.

"Oh, yeah," he said, his voice hoarse. "I can make do without the fancy lingerie."

He slid the shorts down her legs, pausing to kiss her belly just above the dark swell of hair. Then he drew the sweatshirt over her head and tossed it aside, and she stood naked in front of him.

"Don't move," he whispered. He drank her in as he pulled off his shirt and began to unbutton his jeans. "I want to memorize the way you look right now."

Her self-consciousness disappeared as she devoured his body with her eyes. His chest was broad and covered with dark-blond hair, which narrowed down his belly and disappeared into the waistband of his boxers. When he ripped off the boxers, she swallowed at the sight of him.

He scooped her up and laid her down on the bed. "I don't want to hurt you," he said.

"You won't."

He kissed her again and swept his hand down her body. He lingered at her breasts, cupping them gently, brushing his finger across her nipples. When she groaned and arched her back, he lowered his head and drew one nipple into his mouth.

She closed her arms around him, desperate to be joined to him. But instead of pressing her down into the mattress, he reached out, fumbled in the drawer of the night table next to his bed and pulled out a condom. After sliding it in place, he rolled over so she lay on top of him.

He was trying to be careful, trying not to hurt her. A rush of tenderness swept over her, making her forget everything but her need for him. She shifted her hips, slid on top of him.

He groaned and surged into her, his hands bracketing her hips. Passion held in check too long exploded, and she shattered above him. His hands tightened on her hips and he poured himself into her.

She wasn't sure how long she drifted, her mind empty, her body draped over his. He wrapped his arms around her, held her tightly against him as his heart slowed next to her ear. After a long time, he lifted his head and brushed the hair away from her face.

"Are you all right?" he asked. "Did I hurt you?"

"I'm wonderful," she said.

He brushed his hand over the bruise on her side with a featherlight touch. "Is this okay?"

"It's fine," she murmured. "I'm fine. I'm more than fine."

She felt his mouth curve against her throat. "That's good," he said. "Because I'm feeling pretty fine myself." He shifted his hips against her, making it obvious he was aroused again. He lifted his head, and she saw him examine the clock. "We have another hour," he said. "I don't intend to waste a minute of it."

CHAPTER SIXTEEN

IGNORING HER ACHING MUSCLES, Claire stirred in bed the next morning and reached for Tucker.

She found nothing but the cold sheet. Suddenly completely awake, she rolled onto her back and stared at the ceiling. The dream dissolved in front of her. Tucker wasn't lying beside her. He'd never been in her bed.

She'd shared his for only a couple of stolen hours.

Longing sliced through her, sharp and painful. But when she heard Nick moving around in the bathroom, she pushed it away and struggled out of bed. Her muscles screamed in protest but she ignored them. She didn't want to alarm Nick.

Twenty minutes later, while she was bagging Nick's lunch, he said, "What happened to your arms and your hands, Aunt Claire?"

Claire glanced down at the angry red lines snaking up her arms. "I took a little fall yesterday," she said lightly. "Into some bushes."

"Yeah? You okay?"

"I'm fine, Nick. But thanks for asking." A few weeks ago he wouldn't have bothered to ask.

He got up from the table. "I'll see you after school."

"I'm picking you up at practice, remember?" she said. "So we can go shopping."

"Yeah," he tossed over his shoulder as he galloped out the door. "I've got to go. I'm late."

She glanced at the clock, frowning. It was much earlier than he normally left. He must have something going on before school.

For the rest of the day, no matter what she was doing, Tucker crowded her thoughts. If she closed her eyes she felt his touch and smelled his scent, heard his murmured words of endearment. When she licked her lips she tasted his kisses, dark and potent and seductive.

Too distracted to work, she finally gave up and drove to the high school early to pick up Nick from football practice. She told herself she wanted to watch her nephew, but her gaze kept straying to Tucker.

He wore shorts and a polo shirt, and his golden hair lifted in the breeze. As he moved from one group of boys to another, showing them what he wanted to do, watching them do it, she drank in the sight of him. He smiled frequently, his body language encouraging all of them. When he slapped a boy on the back, the boy invariably gave him a huge grin in return.

Obviously, these boys adored Tucker.

She knew how they felt.

Edgy and unsettled, she moved restlessly on the leather seat. Then the boys were heading toward the locker room and Tucker was heading toward her car.

She gripped the steering wheel tightly, then relaxed her fingers and rolled down her window.

"Hello, gorgeous," Tucker said, resting his forearms on the edge of the door. "How was your day?"

"Too long," she muttered.

He grinned at her. "Didn't get much work done?" He ran a finger down her cheek. "What a coincidence. My mind sure wasn't in the classroom."

Her heart fluttered. She leaned into his hand, turned her head and pressed a kiss into his palm.

What had happened to her? If Tucker's slightest touch could make her heart leap in her chest, if a smile could make her legs feel weak, she was in trouble.

She didn't care. She'd never been so happy.

"What are you doing tonight?" he murmured.

"Nick and I have to go shopping," she said, reaching for his hand, twining her fingers with his. "He's growing out of all his clothes." She gave him a teasing grin. "Want to come along?"

He brushed a kiss across her mouth, gave a mock shudder. "No, thanks. Maybe I'll stop by later."

She should tell him no. She should give herself a breather, try to ground herself. But all she could do was smile as her heart bounded in her chest. "Okay."

He touched her cheek, then stood up reluctantly. "Here comes Nick. I'll see you later."

She was still smiling when her nephew got into the car. "Hi, Nick. How was school today?"

"It was okay," he said, sliding down in the seat. "Are we going straight home?"

"We're going shopping." She glanced over at him. "That's why I picked you up. Remember?"

"Do we have to go shopping?" he asked, giving her

a sideways glance. "I'd rather get home and do my homework."

"Are you sure? A few days ago, when we planned this trip, you told me you didn't have any clothes that fit."

He shrugged. "I don't want to go shopping."

"All right," she said, puzzled but pleased that he was so conscientious about his homework. "Maybe we'll go shopping this weekend."

"Cool."

Apparently Nick was serious about his homework, because he ran up to his room as soon as they got home, emerging only to wolf down his dinner, then ran back upstairs. A half hour later, while she tried to finish the work she'd neglected that day, Nick tiptoed behind her into the kitchen. The refrigerator door opened quietly, as if he was trying to muffle the sound.

Curious, she looked in the kitchen door, just in time to see Nick shove a carton of milk beneath his sweatshirt.

"Nick? What are you doing?"

Guilt and fear flashed across his face, and for a moment he looked like a child caught stealing a candy bar from a store. "I wanted a glass of milk. Okay?"

"Sure." She nodded at the bulge beneath his sweatshirt. "But you don't have to sneak around with the carton beneath your shirt. What's going on?"

He looked around wildly, as if searching for an escape. For a moment she thought he'd bolt out the door. Finally he collapsed into a chair and set the carton of milk on the table.

"So am I in trouble for stealing milk?" He gave her

what he probably thought was a tough look. But she could see the anxiety beneath his scowl. And the desperation.

Two months ago, his defiance would have pushed all her buttons. Now she understood that was the reaction Nick wanted. "You can't steal what's already yours," she said, praying she was handling this properly. "You've been acting odd since yesterday. I want to know why."

His face filled with stubborn bravado and he opened his mouth, no doubt to give her an angry answer. But when she continued to watch him calmly, not saying a word, he seemed to deflate.

Staring at the carton of milk on the table, he pushed it from one side to the other. Finally he looked at her. "I found a cat," he blurted. "I think it's sick. I've been feeding it, and Booger's been helping me."

"You found a cat?" She stared at him, shocked. It was absolutely the last thing she expected him to say.

"Yeah. I was cutting through the woods to Booger's. It kind of followed me."

"And you've been bringing it food?"

He nodded and she asked, "Why didn't you tell me, Nick?"

"I was afraid you'd make me take it to the humane society," he mumbled. "You know what they do with sick animals there."

She took his hand. "Don't you know me better than that?" she asked with a stab of sadness. "Did you think I wouldn't care about a sick animal?"

He shrugged. "You never talked about pets. I assumed you didn't want any."

"I didn't know you did," she said quietly. Her heart

ached at the raw need in his eyes. "Can we go see your cat? Maybe there's something we can do for it."

"Really? You want to see it?" He looked up at her with a blaze of hope.

"Of course I do," she said. "Let me get my jacket."

Moments later they were walking down a faint path through the woods. It looked like the same one she and Janice had used when they were children. Nick finally stopped at what looked like a random pile of twigs and branches. But when he squatted next to them, she saw that although the branches had mostly fallen, at one time they'd been arranged to make a tiny shelter.

It was the fort she and Janice had made.

Her throat swelled as she looked at the old branches, now gray and smooth with age. They'd absorbed so many tears, so much pain. They'd been a needed refuge. Their fort had survived all these years, a mute monument to the bond she shared with Janice.

Did you lead your boy to our old fort, Jan?

She wiped the back of her hand across her eyes as Nick knelt in the dirt and pushed the branches aside. Immediately she heard a plaintive meow, and a small gray head poked out of the shelter.

The cat butted its head against Nick's hand as he petted her, and with a shamefaced glance back at Claire, Nick pulled something out of his pocket. It was a piece of the chicken they'd had for dinner, and the cat inhaled it.

"He doesn't look too sick to me," she said softly.

"He hardly moves at all," Nick replied. "When I found him, he was just lying in some leaves. He followed me for a while, then he lay down again. I'm afraid he's hurt."

"Can you coax him out of the shelter?" she asked.

Nick nodded. "He comes when I call his name."

"You named him?" Her heart twisted in her chest.

"Yeah. I call him Joe."

Joe was a gray tiger cat. When he emerged from the shelter and plopped down on the ground next to Nick, she saw that he had an enormous belly. "Are you sure it's a he?" she asked softly.

"What do you mean?" Nick glanced at her, confused.

"It could be pregnant."

"Is that why he's so fat?"

"It's possible. I have no idea how to tell." She shifted on her knees and reached out a tentative hand to the cat, allowing it to sniff her fingers. When she ran a hand over its side, the cat began to purr.

"He does that a lot," Nick said.

"This isn't a wild cat," Claire said as the cat arched into her hand. "This cat belongs to someone."

"What should we do with him, Aunt Claire?"

Claire blinked as her eyes burned again. Nick rarely called her "Aunt Claire." "Let's take him back to the house, to begin with. A sick cat doesn't belong outside."

"Okay." Nick scooped up the cat, cradling it tenderly in his arms. The animal seemed perfectly happy.

Once they were home, Joe explored the house, sniffing at everything, weaving around the legs of the table, finally plopping onto the floor and meowing plaintively.

"I think Joe is hungry," Claire said.

"That's why I was bringing him some milk."

"I think he needs more than milk. Why don't we go to the grocery store and get him some food?"

"Can we?" The hope on Nick's face was almost painful.

"Sure. Let me grab my purse."

"Do you think he'll be okay while we're gone?"

She looked at the cat lying in the middle of the kitchen floor. He looked perfectly content, gazing around like a king surveying his kingdom. "I think he'll be fine," she answered. "But if you're worried that he's going to be scared, we can put him in the bathroom."

"Okay." Nick picked up the cat, murmuring to it in a low voice. After he closed the bathroom door, he bounced to his feet. "Hurry. I don't want to leave him alone for long."

Forty-five minutes later they walked back into the house, carrying litter, a litter pan and several different kinds of cat food. Her eyes had prickled with tears as she watched Nick choose everything with great care.

When they closed the door behind them, Joe started crying in the bathroom. Nick dropped his bags on the floor and flung open the door. The cat crawled into his arms.

Claire watched them, bemused. Nick cuddled the cat next to his chest, crooning something to him. And the cat seemed perfectly happy to be there.

"Which kind of food do you want to give him to-night?" she asked.

Nick looked up and shrugged. "Whatever you think."

She opened a can of food, and Joe jumped out of Nick's arms. Scooping the contents into a bowl, she handed it to Nick. "Here, you should be the one who feeds him."

Nick set the bowl on the floor, then hovered as Joe

wolfed it down. In less than two minutes the food was gone and Joe was licking the bowl.

"I think he's still hungry," Nick said.

"He probably is," Claire agreed. "But I think we should wait a while to feed him again. If he eats too much, he might get sick."

Claire set up the litter pan in the bathroom, then watched as the cat followed Nick around the house like a shadow. Finally, she said to him, "Are you finished with your homework?"

"I have a little more to do."

"Why don't you get started? You can take Joe up to your room with you if you like. Just leave the door open in case he needs to use the litter pan."

"Okay."

Nick's face glowed with happiness as he scooped up the cat and hurried up the stairs. She heard him talking to Joe in a low voice and her eyes burned again. Why hadn't she thought about a pet for Nick before now?

Because a pet was another complication she didn't want to think about. Her condo in Chicago had a no-pets rule. They wouldn't be able to bring Joe, or any other animal, back to Chicago with them.

Part of her wanted to warn Nick not to get too attached to the cat. Even without the issue of her condo, someone was likely to claim Joe. He was too sweet-natured to be feral.

But right now she just wanted to enjoy this side of her nephew, a side of him she'd never seen before. Maybe a pet, even if he was temporary, was just the thing Nick needed.

Maybe Joe could be the anchor Nick needed in his unsettled life. She wanted her nephew to revel in the uncomplicated love of a pet. And maybe Joe could help Nick express the love she knew was hiding inside him.

NICK LOOKED at Joe again, but the cat was still sleeping on his bed, his head tucked into his chest. He'd been there ever since they came upstairs. As he watched the cat sleep, it looked like Joe's belly began to move.

"Aunt Claire," he yelled. "Come quick."

His aunt ran up the stairs. "What's wrong?"

"I think Joe has worms." He stared at Joe's belly, which had stopped moving.

Aunt Claire shrank away from the cat. "How come? Did you see one?"

"No! But his belly was moving like it was full of worms."

"Ewww." Aunt Claire backed away from the cat. "Take him off your bed."

"It's not his fault," Nick protested. "He can't help it if he has worms."

"I know it's not his fault. But I don't want him on your bed if he has worms."

Nick didn't like the idea very much either, so he picked Joe up and held him close. "What should we do?"

"I'll call the veterinarian," Aunt Claire said. "Maybe we can take Joe to the clinic and have someone look at him."

A few minutes later she called up the stairs, "They can see us right away. Let's go, Nick."

It didn't take long to drive to the clinic. Nick clutched Joe, worried about what the vet would say.

The receptionist asked them a bunch of questions. Then she put them in a room and said Dr. Burns would be right in.

A few minutes later a woman walked in. Aunt Claire stood up. "Molly? Molly Burns?" she asked.

"Hi, Claire. Welcome back to Monroe," the vet said. She gave his aunt a smile. "I'd heard you were back in town. I've been meaning to call."

"This is my nephew, Nick. Janice's son."

"Hi, Nick," the vet said.

"You moved away in high school," Aunt Claire said. "When did you move back here?"

"A couple of years ago." The vet looked sad for a moment. "I came back with my daughter after my husband passed away."

"You have a daughter?" Aunt Claire asked.

"Her name is Caitlyn. She's fourteen. We didn't change her name after I got married."

Nick tightened his grip on Joe and the cat meowed. The vet was Caitlyn Burns's mom?

"What do you have here, Nick?"

"This is Joe. We think he might have worms."

"Let's take a look at him."

Caitlyn's mom poked at Joe and looked at his ears, his mouth and beneath his tail. Then she pushed at his belly.

"I think you're going to have to come up with a different name for Joe," she finally said with a smile. "Josephine might be a better choice. Joe's a female. And she's very pregnant."

Aunt Claire put her hand on Joe's belly. "So that's why her belly was moving. We thought she had worms."

"She might, but what you saw was her kittens."

"What do we do?" Aunt Claire asked.

"I'll give her medicine for worms today."

"No, I mean about the kittens."

"You don't have to do a thing." Dr. Burns smiled and petted Joe. "You can give her a box with towels, but she'll have the kittens when and where she feels like it."

After more questions about taking care of Joe, his aunt said to Mrs. Burns, "We should get together, Molly."

Caitlyn's mom smiled. "I'd love to, Claire. Give me a call."

Nick watched the two adults, wondering what they would talk about. Maybe Aunt Claire would tell Dr. Burns about seeing Caitlyn in the ice cream shop. His face burned as he remembered what a dork he'd been.

"Call me if you have any more questions," Dr. Burns said as she held the door open for them.

Joe purred the whole way home. Nick watched his aunt's face, wondering what she was thinking.

"I'll take care of Joe," he finally said, desperate to keep the cat. "I'll feed her and clean up after her and everything. You won't have to do a thing."

His aunt glanced over at him. "You know her real owner might show up," she said. Nick couldn't believe she actually sounded sad about it. "We'll have to put up signs in case someone is looking for her."

"What if no one wants her? Can I keep her?" He held his breath, waiting for her answer.

"Of course." His aunt smiled at him. "I've always wanted a cat."

"Then how come you don't have one?"

A shadow crossed her face. "My condo in Chicago doesn't allow pets."

That sick feeling in his stomach came back, the one he hadn't felt for a while. "Then I guess she'll have to stay here with me when you go home."

She shot him a look, but said only, "We'll figure something out."

Nick was still worrying about it when they turned into the driveway and saw Coach Hall's truck. Another fear gripped him. Was Coach here to tell his aunt about the grade he'd gotten on his essay, the one he'd blown off because he needed to take care of Joe?

"Hey, Nick. Hi, Claire," Coach called as he got out of his truck. "I just stopped by to see how you were doing."

Coach went up to his aunt and took her hand, and Nick narrowed his eyes. What was going on?

"I'm fine," Aunt Claire said. She gave him a sappy smile. "Thanks for checking on me."

"I told you I'd stop by."

Aunt Claire smiled at Nick. "Show Tucker why we weren't home," she said.

He climbed out of the car, holding Joe in his arms. Coach came over and petted the cat. "Who is this?"

"This is Joe," Nick said. "She's our new cat." He glanced over at Aunt Claire.

"Looks like you're going to have more than one new cat pretty soon." He touched Joe's belly and smiled at Nick.

"Nick found her." Aunt Claire came over and put her

arm around his shoulders. "He's been taking care of her in the woods for a few days."

She actually sounded proud of him! Surprised, he studied her face. She was looking at Coach.

"Yeah?" Coach grinned at him. "I wondered why you took off from practice the last few days like your hair was on fire."

Both Coach and Aunt Claire smiled at him, as if he'd done something cool. Nick squirmed, his ears burning. "I thought she was sick. I was worried about her."

"Good job, Nick," Coach said. Nick held Joe more tightly.

Coach petted her again. "Is it okay if I stop by again to see how she's doing?"

Nick shrugged. "Sure."

Coach turned to Aunt Claire. "You sure you're all right?" He touched her side. "How are your ribs?"

"I'm fine," she said.

Nick frowned as he watched the two adults look at each other. Something *was* going on. Aunt Claire had that sappy smile on her face again.

"See you at practice tomorrow, Nick," he said as he swung into his truck.

Nick watched the truck disappear down the street, then turned to Aunt Claire. "What's up with you and Coach?"

CHAPTER SEVENTEEN

CLAIRE STARED at Nick, not sure what to say. She should have realized this was coming. Sooner or later, Nick was bound to realize that she and Tucker were…what? Flirting? Involved? In lust?

Please, God, don't let him figure out that she and Tucker were sleeping together. She *so* did not know how to talk about sex with a teenage boy.

"I'm not sure yet what's going on," she said, opting for complete honesty. "I like him and he likes me."

He gave her an uncertain look. "Are you going out with him?"

"We haven't actually been on a date, no," she hedged.

"Are you gonna go out with him?"

"Yes, I am." She shoved her hands into the pockets of her shorts, suddenly nervous and self-conscious. "Do you have a problem with that?"

He shifted the cat in his arms. "I don't know. I think it would be kind of weird."

"I guess it could be." She gave her nephew a strained smile and plucked at a loose string inside her pocket.

"If you go out with him, are you gonna make him go with you when you leave?" he demanded. "'Cause

Coach likes it here. And the guys on the team would be mad if he wasn't their coach anymore."

"Coach Hall isn't going anywhere," she told him. "He's staying in Monroe."

"You sure?"

"Positive." It was the one certainty in the whole situation. Tucker wasn't about to leave Monroe.

"Then I guess it doesn't matter, does it? If you go out with him, I mean. 'Cause you're not going to be here that much longer."

Nick clutched the cat more tightly and brushed past her to walk into the house.

Claire watched him go. Was that disappointment on his face? For the first time, she felt a pang of loss at the thought of leaving Monroe. For the first time, the thought of going back to Chicago didn't fill her with yearning. It left her with the cold ashes of regret in her mouth.

LATE TUESDAY NIGHT of the next week, Claire rolled over on the couch, startled awake from an uneasy sleep while she waited for Nick. She glanced at her watch. He'd gone to the homecoming week bonfire at school, and he was late getting home.

She sat up, brushing her hair out of her eyes as she heard footsteps pounding through the kitchen.

"Aunt Claire! Aunt Claire, there's a fire in the backyard."

Nick's voice.

"What?" She stumbled to her feet as Nick skidded to a stop in front of the couch. "A fire? In the backyard?"

"Get out of the house! I'm going to get some water."

"I'll call 9-1-1," she said as she ran into the kitchen. She watched bright orange flames flicker in the window as she waited for someone to answer the phone.

Moments later, after giving the dispatcher her name and address, she ran out the door. The flames licked at the old wooden porch. If it caught fire, it would burn quickly.

And so would the house.

"Nick!" she called, frantic to find him.

"I'm trying to get the hose," he yelled, and she ran around the side of the house.

Nick tugged on the hose, but it refused to budge, twisted around the wheels of the cart that held it. She kicked the cart over and reached to untangle it. Nick staggered backward as it came loose, then recovered and yanked a length of it free. She turned on the water as he ran toward the fire.

Sirens grew louder, swelling to fill the air and drown out even the crackle of the flames. As Nick stood with the hose trained on the fire, three firefighters ran around the corner of the house, hauling a thick fire hose.

"Get back!" one of them yelled, waving to her and Nick. The firefighter turned a valve and water gushed on the fire, a thick stream that extinguished it in seconds. Gray smoke filled the air, making the yard look surreal and otherworldly.

As she and Nick stood to the side and watched, the firefighters examined the porch carefully to make sure it wasn't smoldering, then spread out through the yard. One of them unbuckled his breathing apparatus and squatted next to the smoking pile of what looked like firewood.

"That looks like a pile of logs," Claire said.

The firefighter didn't answer. He stood up, kicked at the charred and blackened wood, then squatted in front of it again. Finally he stood up, a grim look on his face.

"Did you start this fire, young man?" he asked Nick.

"No!" Nick stared at him, and Claire saw the confusion in his eyes. "It was burning when I got home."

"Is that right?" The firefighter narrowed his eyes as he watched Nick, obviously skeptical.

"Nick didn't do this," Claire said, putting her arm around her nephew's shoulder.

"Someone started it. I can smell lighter fluid, and the scorch marks prove that an accelerant was used."

"It wasn't Nick. It's ridiculous to even think he would start a fire in his own yard."

The firefighter pushed his helmet to the back of his head and sighed. "Tonight was the bonfire at the high school," he said. He glanced over at Nick. "Maybe your nephew thought it would be fun to have his own bonfire."

"He said he didn't do it and I believe him."

The firefighter shrugged. "It wouldn't be the first time a kid came home from the bonfire at school and started one of his own."

He trudged off, leaving the pile of logs smoking on the lawn. She tightened her arm around Nick's shoulders. "I don't think for a moment that you did this."

"He's a jerk," Nick answered. "Why would I set my own house on fire?"

"Exactly." She kept her arm around Nick, and he leaned closer as they stood there, watching the smoke curling off the logs and drifting across the yard.

Multiple doors slammed in front of the house, and the fire truck rumbled away. A few moments later, Tucker ran into the backyard.

"Are you guys all right?" he asked.

Nick slid out from beneath her arm. "Someone tried to set our house on fire," he said, gesturing at the smoldering pile of logs.

"What?" Tucker grabbed Nick's shoulders, looked over at Claire. "Are you hurt?"

"Nah," Nick said, shrugging. "Aunt Claire and I almost had it out by the time the firefighters got here. Jerks."

"They asked me if Nick might have started the fire," Claire explained in response to Tucker's questioning look.

Tucker scanned Nick quickly, then let him go and turned to her. His face tightened when he saw her hands. "You said you weren't hurt."

"I'm not."

He turned her hands over, his touch featherlight. Blood smeared her palms and she stared at them, bewildered. "I must have torn off the scabs when we dragged the hose over here. I didn't feel a thing."

"You're bleeding, Aunt Claire," Nick said, staring at her hands.

"It's not a big deal," she said, curling her fingers into her palms.

"We need to get her cleaned up, Nick. Do you know where all the first-aid stuff is?" Tucker asked.

"Yeah, I think so." He seemed to stand taller, and Claire silently blessed Tucker for deferring to him. All Tucker's instincts, she was beginning to realize, demanded that he protect and defend.

But he was remarkably sensitive to Nick, a boy whose own sense of belonging, of being needed, was heartbreakingly fragile right now.

Nick ran ahead of them and clattered up the stairs. When she and Tucker reached the brightly lit kitchen, Tucker cupped his hands around her face.

"Are you sure you're all right?" he murmured, raw fear in his eyes.

"I'm fine. Really. Nick found the fire and called me in time."

"God," he said, laying his forehead on hers. "I was terrified when Judy Johnson called and told me the fire trucks were here."

His breath feathered on her cheek, and his hands were warm against her face. Suddenly shaky with delayed reaction, she leaned against his solid strength and wrapped her arms around his waist. "I didn't have time to be scared," she whispered. "But I'm glad you're here now."

"I'm staying the night," he said. "In case whoever started the fire comes back."

Pleasure rippled through her. Almost as quickly, reason reared its head. "We can't do that," she whispered. "Not with Nick in the house."

He raised his head, his eyes darkening to indigo. "I didn't mean I'd be spending the night in your bed," he murmured. "Although that's where I want to be."

"Me, too," she whispered.

Nick came running down the stairs, and Tucker stepped away from her. "I'll take a rain check on that," he said, his eyes full of seductive promise.

He smoothed one finger down her throat, caught the

edge of her T-shirt and gave it a playful tug. She caught her breath, and his eyes darkened even further as he let his gaze linger on her breasts.

He'd moved away from her by the time Nick rushed into the kitchen. "I didn't know what we'd need, so I brought everything I could find."

Tucker looked at the armful of bandages, ointments and bottles. "Good Lord, Kendall. You've got enough stuff here to patch up the whole football team."

He gave Nick's shoulder a light punch. "That was thinking ahead. I guess you know your aunt pretty well. She's going to fight us like a wildcat, probably ruin a bunch of that stuff." He winked at Nick, and her nephew grinned back at him. "You want to hold her down, or should I?"

"You can hold her down," Nick said happily. "I'll fix her hands."

"Yeah, give me the tough job," Tucker said. He pulled out a chair, sat down and eased her onto his lap. When Nick turned away to set up his supplies on the kitchen counter, Tucker picked up her hand and kissed it.

His erection pressed heavily into her backside, and she drew in a sharp breath. Watching Nick, she slid off Tucker's lap. "I'm too heavy for you," she said, her voice breathless.

"Yeah, you're an armful, all right," he said, sliding out from beneath her and moving to stand behind her chair. "You about ready there, Nick?"

"Yeah," Nick answered. He turned around and bent over her hands. His touch was surprisingly gentle as he washed away the blood and applied ointment and bandages.

"Thanks, Nick. Nice job," she said, standing up and kissing his cheek. "With hands like those, you ought to be a doctor."

Nick flushed. "Yeah, right."

"Someone should stay down here tonight, make sure whoever did this doesn't come back," Tucker said.

Before he could offer to stay, Nick nodded. "I'll sleep in the living room."

She didn't want her nephew staying down here if there was a chance the person who started the fire would be back. She opened her mouth to tell him so, then stopped.

Nick needed to do this. She saw it in his eyes. He needed to be the one to protect her, to protect his house. "All right," she said slowly. "But keep the phone close by. If you hear anything, you call the police."

"I'll get my blankets and pillow," Nick said, bounding up the stairs again.

As soon as he'd disappeared, Claire leaned into Tucker. "Thanks for coming over to check on us," she said.

"It was my pleasure." His eyes gleamed as he bent his head, took her mouth.

Need swept through her, making her tremble. When he stepped back, she was shaking all over.

"I'll see you soon, Claire." He smiled as he stepped out the door, stuck his head back inside. "And I *will* be cashing in that rain check."

THE NEXT MORNING, Claire stared down at the charred pile of logs so perilously close to the porch, wondering who had started the fire.

Had it really been kids coming home from the bon-fire? A chill ran down her spine.

She desperately wanted to believe it was kids.

She didn't think it was.

It was past time to talk to Chief Broderick.

Hurrying to the phone, she confirmed he was in the office, then got in her car and drove downtown. In minutes she was standing in his office.

"Have a seat, Ms. Kendall," he said.

"Please, call me Claire."

"Claire. Thanks for stopping by. I heard about the fire last night."

Claire clasped her hands together in her lap. "The firefighters think it was one of the high school kids who started it. I'm not so sure."

"Was it your nephew?" he asked.

"No! I'm sure it wasn't Nick."

Seth Broderick eased back in his chair. "He's had a lot to deal with. Sometimes good kids do stupid things when they're overwhelmed."

"Nick didn't do it," she said. "I'm sure of it."

"Okay. You know him better than I do. I'll send an officer over to take a look, ask some questions."

"Thank you." She pressed her fingers together more tightly. "Have you found anything else in your investigation of Janice's death?"

"I have, as a matter of fact." He sat up straight in his chair, all business. "I got the phone records I requested for your sister's house. In the weeks before she died, she'd had a number of phone calls. All of them were either from her office or from friends of hers. The friends all have what appear to be solid alibis for the time she died."

"What about right before she left the house that night? Nick said she got a phone call."

Seth nodded. "It was from city hall."

"Who was it from?" She leaned forward.

"That's what's interesting. It was from her own office."

"Her own office? But she was at home when she got the call."

"Exactly. Whoever called used the phone on her desk."

A cold chill rippled over Claire. "Why would someone do that?"

"My guess is, they didn't want anyone to know who made the call."

"Did you get my message about her car?"

"Yes, we've already gone to Bakersfield and picked it up." Seth twirled a pencil on his desk as he watched her. "I saw the paint in the dents you talked about, and we're having it tested." He paused, as if weighing how much to tell her. "The city of Monroe cars are all painted red. I'm beginning to think your nephew may be right. Maybe your sister did have some help driving into the lake."

"My God." Claire leaned back in her chair, shaken, staring at the chief of police. "I didn't really believe Nick, you know. I just wanted to reassure him."

"I never underestimate gut feelings. Your nephew was pretty adamant."

"What next?" Claire asked.

"I've been talking to people over at city hall. I haven't worked through all of them yet, but I will."

Claire's chill deepened. "I was over there last week,"

she whispered. "I talked to Annamae Shelton. She was going to ask around to see if anyone remembered anything unusual." She wrapped her arms around herself. "That night, I went to the lake, to see the place where Janice went off the road. It was raining, just like it was the night Janice died. I'm not even sure why I went there." She shivered. "A car swerved onto the shoulder of the road and almost hit me. I had to jump over the guardrail and I fell down the slope."

"What?" Seth bounced forward in his chair, his eyes hard and intent. "Did you report this?"

"No. I assumed it was just an accident."

"And then someone started a fire in your backyard last night," he said slowly.

"I think they're connected."

"If your house burned down, you'd have to leave Monroe, and that would be the end of the questions. It was quite a coincidence that the car ran you off the road right after you'd been talking to Annamae. I'm not much of a believer in coincidence."

"You think Annamae has something to do with this?" she asked, incredulous.

"I haven't ruled anyone out." He smiled, his mouth a grim line. "I can't see Annamae trying to run you down, but she's the biggest gossip in Monroe. Everyone in city hall would have known about your questions fifteen minutes after you left."

"What should I do?" Claire asked.

"Nothing. This is a police investigation now and you need to stay out of our way." He stood up. "Your job is to keep your nephew safe. Fifteen-year-old boys are impulsive and reckless. Make sure he doesn't do anything stupid."

"I'll try," she said, shaken.

Seth's expression became gentle. "I know you will."

"Thank you," she said as she stood up and shook the police chief's hand. "Thank you for taking me seriously."

His hand tightened on hers. "I told you things are different now in Monroe," he said quietly. "I meant it."

"I can see that," Claire said.

Over the past weeks, she'd let down her guard. She'd allowed herself to become entangled in the fabric of Monroe. Now she felt like an outsider again.

As she drove home, she studied everyone she saw, wondering if one of them was hiding a deadly secret. Had one of them killed her sister?

CHAPTER EIGHTEEN

THE SETTING SUN WASHED downtown Monroe in gold as Claire walked to the garden center. In spite of her fears, she was determined not to hide in her house.

As she passed the tobacco shop, the door opened and Andrea Vernon stepped in front of her.

"Hi, Andrea," she said. "I haven't seen you lately."

Andrea clutched a bag to her chest and looked away from Claire. "I've been busy at work," she said. "I don't get into town very often."

"How are you doing?" Claire asked.

"Fine." Andrea gave her a tight smile. "Just fine."

The young woman still hadn't looked at Claire, and a sick feeling rose up inside her. "Andrea, what's wrong?"

"Nothing. Why would you think anything's wrong?" Andrea's voice sounded brittle, as if each word would shatter if it hit the ground.

Claire moved around Andrea and studied her face. "You're wearing an awful lot of makeup for a trip to the tobacco store," she said softly.

Andrea turned her head away. "I like makeup."

"I used to wear a lot of makeup, too," Claire said, laying her hand on Andrea's arm. The other woman flinched, but Claire didn't let go. "Is that Roger's favorite brand of pipe tobacco?" she asked, nodding at Andrea's bag.

When Andrea didn't answer, Claire moved around to face her head-on. "It's not going to help, Andrea. I used to try and pacify him, too. I'd buy that tobacco for him, or fix his favorite dinner, or rent a movie he wanted to see. It didn't stop him from hitting me."

"I didn't say he was hitting me!"

"You don't have to, Andrea. I was married to him. I know what he is."

"It doesn't matter," Andrea whispered. "I don't have anywhere else to go."

"Yes, you do." Claire fumbled in her purse, held out the card she kept there. "This is the shelter I went to. They helped me get away and reclaim my life, and they can do the same for you."

Andrea stared at the card, hope and fear battling in her eyes. "What would I do if I left Roger?"

"Anything you want." Claire tucked the card into the pocket of Andrea's sweater. "I went to college and eventually started my own business."

Andrea touched her pocket, then let her hands fall to her side. "I'm not smart enough to go to college."

"I know Roger told you that, because it's what he told me, too. He's lying, Andrea. He doesn't want you to go to college because then he'll lose his control over you." Anger sharpened Claire's voice and she struggled to rein it in. The last thing Andrea Vernon needed was another angry person telling her what to do.

Claire saw the indecision and fear in Andrea's eyes and touched her arm again. "I'll drive you to the shelter, Andrea. Call me anytime and I'll pick you up."

"I can't do that," she whispered, touching her face. "Roger would be even more angry if you helped me."

"Then call Seth Broderick. He'll take you to the shelter."

"The police?"

"Yes, the police. What Roger is doing is a crime."

Andrea shoved her hand into her pocket. "I'll think about it."

Claire let her hand drop away from the other woman. "It's not going to get any better," she said, her voice gentle. "You know that."

"I said I'd think about it." She raised her voice and shoved past Claire. "Don't tell me what to do."

Claire watched as Andrea hurried to her car. Had she pushed Andrea too hard? Had she only alienated the young woman?

On the other side of the street, Derek Joiner and two women stood on the steps of City Hall, watching. When they caught her eye, they waved and hurried away. One of the women was Annamae Shelton.

Employees leaving for the day, she thought. *Please don't let Annamae gossip about this,* Claire prayed. Everyone in town knew her marriage to Roger had ended badly. So far, the people she'd talked to had been careful not to mention it, but the small-town grapevine would be quick to let Roger know his wife had been talking to his ex-wife.

She'd done the right thing, she told herself. She

couldn't ignore the abuse. At least Andrea had the card. Maybe she'd gather the courage and strength to use it.

THE FOLLOWING AFTERNOON, Claire sat back on her heels and used the back of her hand to push her hair out of her eyes. The mums she'd bought the evening before at the garden center were almost all planted. But she couldn't enjoy the pungent scent of the flowers or the pleasure of working in the dirt.

She couldn't stop thinking about Andrea, couldn't stop worrying about her. And she couldn't stop her growing anger at Roger from spilling over, painting everything in her life with its toxic brush.

No more. Stripping off her gardening gloves, Claire stood up and strode into the house. Picking up the phone, she dialed her attorney's office.

"This is Claire Kendall," she said when the receptionist answered the phone. "Is Paul available?"

"I'll check, Ms. Kendall."

The music that played while she waited was supposed to be calming. Instead, it just made her tap her foot with impatience. Finally her attorney picked up the phone. "Hello, Claire. What can I do for you?"

"Hi, Paul. You can tell me what's going on with Roger Vernon and the man he says is my nephew's father."

"Hold on while I get the file."

When he came back on the line, her attorney said, "You haven't heard anything more from Vernon?"

"I told him to contact you. I don't want to deal with him."

"I sent him a letter right after I talked to you, asked

him for the information he had, as well as the name of your nephew's father. I haven't heard back from him."

"Is that unusual?"

"Most of the time I'd say no. Delay is one of the favorite tactics of the legal profession." Claire could hear the grin in his voice. "But since he was the one who came to you, it's not what I would expect."

Cold, implacable anger began building inside her. "Do you think it's possible he's made the whole thing up?"

"What would be the point of that?"

She cleared her throat. "I have a history with him. And it's not a pleasant one."

"I suppose it's possible," he said, and Claire could hear him frown. "But it would be an incredibly stupid thing to do. That's the kind of stunt that could get him disbarred. Why don't I give him a call, see what's going on?"

"Thanks, Paul."

"I'll call you back as soon as I talk to him."

Claire was back in the garden twenty minutes later, planting the last of the mums, when the phone rang.

"Hello?"

"It's Paul, Claire. I just spoke to Vernon. After a little gentle persuasion, he admitted that he doesn't have the name of the man he says is your nephew's father."

She sucked in her breath. "That bastard."

"But he says he has a client who knows. This client is supposedly acting as a go-between for Vernon and the father."

"Why go to Vernon? Why not come directly to me?"

"The exact question I asked Vernon. He got all blustery and pompous on me, but I think he sees himself as a big wheel in that little town of yours. When this guy asked him to handle the situation, I suspect his ego got in the way and prevented him from asking why."

"I think I need to have a talk with Vernon," Claire said.

"That's the kind of thing I should handle for you, Claire."

"Not this time. This time I'm fighting my own battles."

And Nick's. She should have done this when Roger had first told her about Nick's father, she thought as she set the phone back in its cradle. Her own issues with Roger didn't matter. Roger was playing a game with Nick's emotions, and it was going to stop today.

An hour later, she walked into a small restaurant in Clinton, the county seat, and spotted Roger talking to a waitress. The woman smiled and blushed at something Roger said, and he leaned forward and took her hand.

Anger for Andrea joined her rage at what he was doing to Nick, and she strode toward Roger's booth.

"Hello, Roger," she said, and the waitress gave her a shocked look. "No, I'm not his wife," she said to the waitress. "She lives in Monroe."

The waitress backed up, her face crimson, and Roger started to slide out of the booth. "What do you think you're doing, Claire?" he snarled.

She leaned toward him. "Sit down, Roger, and I'll tell you exactly what I think I'm doing."

The shock on Roger's face matched the waitress's. Slowly he sank down into the vinyl bench of the booth.

Instead of sitting opposite him, Claire stood, staring down at her ex-husband. "What's going on, Roger? I just talked to my lawyer, and he said you don't know the name of the man who claims to be Nick's father."

"I have a client—" he began, but she interrupted him.

"I know all about your so-called client. And don't tell me about attorney-client privilege. You tell me who your client is, right now."

"I can't do that," he said, regrouping and giving her a superior look. "And even if I could, I wouldn't."

"Is that right?" She kept her gaze on him and felt a vicious tug of satisfaction when he began to squirm. "I'll give you twenty-four hours to think about it. If you haven't given me the name by then, I'll go to Chief Broderick." She narrowed her eyes. "You *do* know he's investigating Janice's death? I think Seth might be very interested in a mysterious man who claims to be her son's father and appears right after she dies."

"Don't be so dramatic, Claire," Roger blustered. "My client is a prominent citizen of Monroe. He couldn't be involved in your sister's death."

"We'll leave that to Seth Broderick to find out," she retorted. "Twenty-four hours, Roger. Or you'll be talking to Seth."

She turned on her heel and walked out of the restaurant, but instead of the triumph she expected, she felt only sadness. It was more than likely there was no man claiming to be Nick's father. She dreaded telling Nick, dreaded the pain she'd see in his face.

Would she be enough for her nephew?

TUCKER JUMPED UP from Claire's porch, paced across the floor again. He'd been waiting for almost an hour, but there was still no sign of Claire.

Frantic worry tangled with building anger inside him. She hadn't even told Nick where she was going.

He'd tried calling her cell phone, but got only her voice mail. He'd driven back to his own house three times, hoping she'd left a message on his machine. And he'd checked his cell phone more times than he could count.

Nothing.

He peered through the front window once more, hoping to find a clue to her whereabouts. But nothing looked different than it had five minutes ago.

As he stared into the window, he heard tires crunching on the driveway behind him. Spinning around, he saw Claire's car roll to a stop.

He ran down the steps and yanked her door open. "Are you all right?" he said, grabbing her wrist.

"I'm fine. Tucker, what's wrong?" She reached out, clutched his shirt. "Is it Nick? Did he get hurt at practice?"

"Nick is fine."

"Then what are you doing here?"

"Nick called me from the Johnsons'. He'd been trying to call you and thought I might know where you were. I got worried when I couldn't get hold of you, either."

"What did Nick need?"

"Apparently a bunch of the guys on the team are sleeping over at the Johnsons' tonight, after the pasta party. He wanted to know if he could stay."

"Oh." She smiled as she climbed out of the car. "I'll call and tell him it's okay."

"Is that all you can say?" The words exploded out of him, and he felt his grip on his temper loosening.

She turned to look at him. "What am I supposed to say? Of course Nick can stay at the Johnsons'."

"I'm not talking about Nick," he said, slashing his hand through the air. "You scared the hell out of me."

"What?" She stared at him, puzzled. "How did I scare you?"

"You disappeared!" Fear and relief swirled through him in a churning, roiling mix. "You took off and didn't tell a soul where you were going. Nick didn't even know."

"Nick was going right over to the Johnsons' after school," she said. "He wouldn't have known the difference if I was home or not."

"You had your cell phone turned off," he shouted, taking a step toward her. "No one could get hold of you."

Fear darkened her eyes for a moment, then she straightened her back. "Why don't you come into the house, Tucker?" she said, her voice stilted. "I don't want to give the neighbors a free show."

The relief that she was unhurt had transformed his worry into anger. He stalked behind her into the house, slammed the door behind them.

She turned on him. "What's this about, Tucker? And don't tell me it's about Nick."

"No, it's not about Nick. Damn it, Claire! You didn't think anyone would worry if you just disappeared?"

"I didn't disappear! I went somewhere for a few

hours." Her eyes darkened. "You think because I slept with you that I'm supposed to report to you before I leave the house?"

"Of course not." He wondered at that shadow of fear, the remembered pain in her eyes. Unease slithered through him as he realized he wanted the right to know her schedule, to know where she was and what she was doing. It scared the hell out of him.

He struggled to control his temper, to rein in his anger. "Nick was worried," he said in a steadier voice. "And so was I."

"I'm sorry," she said, touching his arm. "I didn't mean for you or Nick to worry about me."

"Can I ask where you were?" he said, fighting with the anger that made him want to reach out and punch the wall.

"I went to Clinton to talk to Roger Vernon," she said. "I think he's been lying about knowing who Nick's father is. I haven't figured out how yet, but I think it has something to do with Janice's death."

"What?" he shouted. The wave of fear that swept over him almost brought him to his knees. "You drove to Clinton, by yourself, to confront a man who might be involved with your sister's murder?"

"He wasn't a stranger. I know Roger."

"Claire, have you forgotten about your little slide down the slope at the lake? The fire next to your house? How do you know Vernon isn't involved? I can't believe you went to Clinton, by yourself, without telling anyone, to confront him."

She paled. "I didn't think of that. I was so angry at

Roger that I guess I didn't think at all. When his secretary said he was in Clinton, I just took off."

"Damn it, Claire! Use your head. Don't take chances like that!" he shouted.

She flinched. "Don't yell at me, Tucker."

"Don't tell me not to yell! I've been standing here for the past hour, picturing you dead in a ditch somewhere. I'll damn well yell if I want to yell." Fear churned in his stomach and pounded in his head.

"Fine. Yell all you want. But do it somewhere else. No one screams at me in my own house."

She threw open the door so hard that it bounced off the wall and almost closed again. As she reached out for it, he saw her hand trembling.

His anger drained away, leaving him appalled at himself. He grabbed the door, steadied it and eased it closed. "God, Claire, I'm sorry," he said, pitching his voice low. "I'm sorry I lost my temper." He took a tentative step toward her. The wariness in her eyes twisted a knife in his gut. "I was so worried about you."

He closed his eyes, his throat swelling on the words. When he opened them, he saw a mixture of wariness and astonishment on Claire's face.

"Do you want me to leave?" he managed to say.

"No," she said slowly, tilting her head as she watched him. "I don't."

"Then say something," he begged after a long moment had passed. "I know I was out of line, but you're staring at me as if I'm an alien life-form."

Claire steadied herself against the door. "You're angry with me," she said.

He closed his eyes. "I lost my temper, yes."

"You yelled at me," she said in a low voice. "You're bigger than me."

Acid burned his stomach and ice filled his veins. "Guilty on all counts."

"I didn't back down." She stared at him, satisfaction filling her face.

"No." He gave her a puzzled look. "You didn't back down. You told me to get the hell out. Am I supposed to think that's a good thing?"

"Yes." She nodded. "Yes, it's a good thing." Her mouth trembled as she tried to smile and failed. "A lot of good things have happened today."

As he watched her, he struggled to rein in his temper. It had been a long time since he'd gotten so angry. A long time since he'd almost lost control. And it terrified him.

He took a deep breath. "Why is it a good thing that you didn't back down from me?"

She swallowed and let her gaze wander away from his face. "I hate being yelled at. I hate the sound of anger. I do anything I can to avoid it. I was yelled at every day growing up. Then I married an abuser."

He watched her force herself to continue. "I've been afraid of confrontation all my life. The sound of a man's raised voice terrifies me. Before now, I always handled it by running away." She took a step toward him. "You're everything that I was most afraid of, Tucker. You're a big man. You were angry with me. And you were yelling."

"God, Claire." Tucker closed his eyes as pain lanced

through him. "I'm so sorry. I should never have yelled at you that way. I have trouble with my temper."

"Yes," she said. "And I lost my temper right back. Don't you see? I didn't back down."

"You're not angry that I yelled at you?" He wanted to reach out for her, but he didn't dare. Not yet.

"No. I'm happy that I stood up to you instead of running away. I'm thrilled that I yelled back."

A spark of hope stirred inside him. "You want me to yell some more? So you can practice yelling back at me?"

Finally she smiled. "Yell all you want. You're not going to scare me away."

"Thank God," he whispered. He took a tentative step toward her and she moved into his arms.

"You terrify me, Claire," he said, pressing his mouth into her hair. "I'm nuts about you. I can't think of anything but you. That's why I lost it when I couldn't get hold of you."

He swept his hand down her back, savoring the soft curves of her body. "You said something else good happened today."

She leaned away from him. "I confronted Roger and I wasn't afraid of him. I was only angry about what he was doing to Nick. I'll never be afraid of Roger again."

Anger stirred inside him again at the thought of Roger Vernon intimidating her. He struggled to subdue it as he cupped her face in his hands. "I'm not sure whether to yell some more or make love to you."

"Are you giving me a choice?" she whispered, reaching up to stroke his face.

"You always have a choice."

"Then I choose option number two." She moved closer so their bodies were barely touching. "I didn't want to care about you, Tucker. I didn't want to get involved. But I couldn't help myself."

He bent his head to brush his mouth over hers. "I thought you were a snotty city girl the day we met," he whispered. "But I still wanted you."

"I was a snotty city girl." She nipped at his lower lip, drew it into her mouth.

He inhaled sharply. "I've decided that snotty city girls are my favorite kind."

"Is this where you insert the joke?" She licked his lips and her eyes fluttered closed.

"I told you once before, some things I don't joke about," he whispered against her mouth.

Claire pressed a kiss to Tucker's neck, felt his pulse jump against her mouth. "You? Not joke?" She inhaled the heady male scent of his skin. "I can't imagine that."

He combed his fingers through her hair. The heat of his gaze scorched her. "There are no jokes when I kiss you, Claire. No jokes when I touch you." His mouth possessed hers, claiming her, loving her.

"You're driving me crazy, Claire," he said, his voice rough in her ear. He slid his hands beneath the shirt she wore, swept over her back and around to her abdomen. "You're so soft," he said, pushing her shirt up and bending down to drag his mouth across her skin. "So smooth."

She was barely able to open her eyes. The sight of his blond head moving against her skin, his hands spanning her waist, made her shudder with need. "Tucker," she managed to whisper.

"What?" He circled her belly button with his tongue and liquid heat washed through her.

"I want…"

He lifted his head. "What do you want, sweetheart?"

"Everything." She shuddered. "I want you, Tucker."

"I'm yours, Claire." He kissed her mouth and through a haze of passion she felt his fingers on her chest. A moment later her blouse parted and his hands trembled against her ribs.

"Okay, this is one of those lingerie assistance moments," he said, his voice hoarse as he looked at her lacy bra. "But it's not going to last long. I want this off now."

A moment later her bra fell away. He sucked in a breath as he caressed her, and when his thumbs brushed against her nipples, she couldn't contain her moan of pleasure.

Backing her up against the door, he drew her blouse and bra down her arms and tossed them to the floor. He bent his mouth to her nipple, circling her with his tongue before drawing her into his mouth. She quivered in his arms, barely able to stand. Desire crashed through her, leaving her trembling and aching with need.

She fumbled with the buttons on his shirt, desperate to feel his skin against hers. When she couldn't get the buttons through the hole, he tore it off, throwing it onto the floor.

The hair on his chest gleamed like gold in the evening sunlight. His skin was hot, stretched taut over muscles that trembled. He smelled like the outdoors, like pleasure. Like Tucker.

He lifted her, settling her against the hard ridge of his erection. The stab of pleasure made her cry out.

She pressed her mouth to his chest, greedily tasting him. His hands roamed over her back, down her sides, tugged at the waistband of her jeans.

When she flicked her tongue over his small, taut nipple, he sucked in a breath and eased away from her. His hands shook as he lowered her to the floor.

"Bedroom," he muttered against her mouth. "Now."

He swept her into his arms and started up the stairs.

CHAPTER NINETEEN

TUCKER'S MUSCLES TREMBLED as he laid her on the bed. His hands shook as he drew off her slacks, then yanked at the buttons on his own jeans. Finally he stood next to the bed, his skin dappled with the fading sunlight, his body taut and hard and beautiful.

He knelt on the bed next to her, smoothing his hand down her body from her neck to her toes. "I haven't been able to think about anything but you, anything but this since the last time we made love," he murmured. "But my fantasies are pitiful compared to the real thing."

"Fantasies?" she whispered.

His eyes grew even darker. "Sweetheart, you have no idea."

"Tell me," she said, twining her arms around his neck and urging him down next to her.

He whispered in her ear, his breath caressing her neck. While he told her what he wanted to do to her— with her—his hands worked magic on her body. Finally, he pulled a condom from his jeans. After he sheathed himself, he held her gaze as he filled her. "Claire," he whispered as he began moving inside her. "Claire."

He kissed her again, his mouth urgent and hard against hers. She wrapped her legs around him, trying to melt into him as she came closer and closer to release.

When she reached it, she cried out his name. Moments later he followed her.

Time drifted until Tucker stirred, rolling over and carrying her with him. When she opened her eyes, he was watching her with tenderness and passion in his eyes.

"I love being naked with you."

"Me, too," she murmured. "I'm completely naked, and I'm glad. You know all my secrets."

His eyes clouded and he slid off the bed, pulling on his jeans at the same time.

"What's wrong?" she asked.

"Not a thing," he said, but his smile was strained. "I'm going to get the clothes I ripped off you downstairs. I don't want anyone to come to the door and see your lingerie decorating the floor."

Moments later he returned, carrying their clothes. He deposited them on a chair in her room, then shucked his jeans and slid back into bed next to her. The clouds had disappeared from his eyes, and she wondered if she'd imagined them.

"Now, where were we?" he murmured, as he reached down and kissed her.

Passion roared back, and she forgot about everything but the way he felt in her arms.

CLAIRE SETTLED HERSELF in the stands at the football game the next day, her gaze lingering on Tucker as he talked to the boys on the other side of the field. They'd talked and made love until late into the night. Around three, he'd torn himself away. He didn't want anyone talking about her. And if he stayed at her house all night, people would talk.

Desire stirred as she watched him, and she admitted to herself that she'd fallen in love with him. She'd never wanted to spend every waking and sleeping moment with a man, never wanted to give herself so completely before. And never had she wanted a man to give himself so completely to her.

She'd let down all her barriers with Tucker, and it only made her want to give him more. She was drunk with love for him.

What would happen when she left? a small voice asked.

She ignored the voice. She wasn't going anywhere right now.

Nick ran onto the field and took his place for the kickoff. She could see him searching the stands and she gave him a tiny wave. His mask and helmet hid his face, but she thought he smiled.

Halfway through the second half of the game, Nick kicked a field goal. She jumped up and cheered wildly, her heart swelling as he jumped into the air in celebration. He landed awkwardly on his bad leg, but instead of acting self-conscious, he ran over to Booger Johnson and banged helmets with him.

The team lost the game in spite of Nick's field goal and a touchdown by another boy. As the last few minutes ticked away, a man behind her said, "What's the matter with Hall, anyway? Why isn't he teaching our kids what he knows?" His voice was hard with anger.

She turned to see who had spoken as muttered agreement swept through the parents' section. "We need to talk to him," another voice said.

A woman she didn't recognize spoke up. "We need a team meeting."

"Great idea," someone else agreed.

Uneasiness crept over Claire as she listened to the comments around her. Anger swirled through the stands, dark and ugly. She prayed that the parents would regain their composure before they talked to Tucker.

But at Sparky's, after the game, one father stood up and let out a sharp whistle. The room fell silent as everyone looked at him. "We need to talk to Coach Hall," he said. Everyone looked at Tucker.

He straightened slowly. "Fine. When would you like to get together?"

"How about right now?" another man called.

Tucker looked around the restaurant, at the suddenly tense boys. "I don't think this is the time or place."

"Sparky's has a banquet room. We can go in there while the boys have their pizza," the first man suggested.

Tucker's face tightened. "All right. Let's go."

Claire rose from the table where she'd been talking to Molly Burns, a sick feeling gathering in her stomach. These parents didn't want to compliment Tucker on the fine job he'd been doing.

The parents crowded into the back room, and Tucker jumped up onto the tiny platform that served as a stage. "All right," he said, his voice even. "What's this about?"

"We've lost four games," one of the fathers said. It was the same man who'd stood up in the restaurant.

"Yes, we have," Tucker answered. "But the boys are getting better."

"The other teams are running all over them," the man shouted. "They're getting their butts kicked."

"Your sons are having fun, they're working hard, and they're learning good lessons. Isn't that more important?"

"Why aren't you teaching them how to play football?" another man shouted.

Tucker's eyes flashed. "I *am* teaching them to play football."

The man waved his arm impatiently. "You know what I'm talking about. Teach them how you used to play football. Aggressive. Mean."

Claire could see anger gathering in Tucker's eyes. "Are you saying you want me to teach them to play dirty?" He scanned the crowd, met one person's eyes after another.

Before he'd gone halfway around the room, one man shouted out, "Why not? They need to learn how to compete, how to be their best."

"You think playing dirty is what they need to learn? That that's how they'll be their best?" His voice was low and deadly, a warning that the parents had gone too far.

"I think Coach Hall is doing a fine job," Claire said.

The parents all turned to look at her.

Someone on the other side of the room snickered. "A fine job doing what?" he called. "We're talking about what he's teaching our boys, not what he's teaching you."

Claire flushed as Tucker jumped off the stage and took a step toward the man. Then he stopped, clenching and unclenching his fists. She saw the effort it took for Tucker to tear his gaze away from the heckler, to focus on the other parents.

"This discussion is about the football team. The next person who makes a remark about Ms. Kendall is going to get a very personal lesson on playing dirty."

His gaze swept from one person to the next. The uneasy shuffle of feet was the only sound in the room. "Claire's right," Judy Johnson said into the strained silence. "Tucker is doing a great job. I like what Booger's learned since Tucker has been the coach." She stepped closer to the front of the room, closer to Tucker. "I don't want you to change a thing."

Tucker's gaze relaxed as it rested on Judy for a moment. "Thank you." A muscle jumped in his jaw as he turned back to the others. "I won't teach your sons dirty tricks. I want them to learn how to play football, how to enjoy the game. I want them to learn about good sportsmanship, about keeping wins and losses in perspective. Isn't that what you want them to take away from this season?"

"No," someone shouted from the back of the room. "That's not the way you played. You were tough. That's what we want our kids to be."

"You want your kids to be tough?" Claire heard the anger returning to Tucker's voice. "You want them to play like me? Are you sure?"

He shook his head. "A good man can't make his living playing the game he loves because of the way I played football." He narrowed his eyes as he stared at the man who'd first spoken. "Another man almost died because of my temper. Is that what you want your kids to learn? Is that what you want them to become?"

A muscle twitched in his face, and Tucker whirled and punched the wall. "Goddammit! I'm not going to do it." He spun to face them. "I won't teach your sons to cheat. If that's what you want, you can find someone else to coach them."

Tucker pushed his way through the suddenly silent crowd. The door of the room banged shut behind him, and they all stood there for a moment. Then they slowly shuffled out of the room.

Claire stood frozen in place, Tucker's words pounding at her brain. He'd injured a man playing football, so badly that he couldn't play anymore? A man had almost died because of him?

Her heart shriveled in her chest, compressing to a hard kernel of pain. She'd bared her soul to Tucker, told him all her most intimate secrets. Told him things she was ashamed of, things she'd sworn never to reveal.

And he hadn't shared anything of himself.

Only when all the other parents had left did she walk out the door. Somehow she managed to find Nick in the crowd of kids.

"Nick," she said, swallowing hard, "I need to leave. Do you think you could get a ride home with the Johnsons?"

Nick looked at her, stars still in his eyes from his field goal. "I guess." He punched Booger in the arm. "Can I, Boog?"

"Sure. No problem."

"Thanks, Booger." Claire forced herself to smile. "I'll see you at home."

"Okay."

The smell of tomato sauce and cheese drifted through

the air and the room hummed with conversation as Claire pushed her way through the crowds. Her vision blurred but she refused to blink, refused to let the other parents see her cry.

The air outside was crisp and cool, a perfect autumn night. The stars looked smeared across the deep blue of the sky, and somewhere an owl hooted. She stumbled to her car, but before she could slide in someone touched her arm.

"I need to talk to you, Claire." It was Tucker.

She kept her back turned. She didn't want him to see her crying, either. "It's a little late for talking."

"Don't say that." He tightened his grip on her arm, turned her to face him. "Please, Claire."

She shrugged. "Fine. Talk."

"Not here." He tried to take her in his arms, but she resisted. "Come to my house."

She wanted to refuse, to run home and lick her wounds in private. But he held her gaze, refusing to back down, refusing to let her get away.

"All right. I'll follow you there."

"I don't want you to drive. Come with me. We'll get your car later."

She should tell him no, she thought, but he urged her toward his truck and helped her into the cab. His face looked hard in the moonlight, and she saw weariness and resignation in his eyes.

The streets of Monroe were deserted, and in a few minutes they turned into Tucker's driveway. Once they were out of the truck, he led her around to the backyard.

Crickets chirped in the darkness, and the scent of the

night-blooming flower she'd smelled the last time she was here filled the air. He drew her down beside him on the porch step.

"I'm sorry for what that idiot said about you."

She shrugged. "It's a small town. Everyone knows everyone else's business."

"Yeah," he said, staring out into the darkness. "That's the downside of small-town life. Randy apologized to me afterward. So did some of the others."

After a moment he turned toward her. "I scared you tonight, didn't I?" he asked.

"Scared me?"

"When I lost my temper. Punched the wall." His mouth twisted. "That was an ugly little display, and I saw your face after it happened. You looked devastated."

He swallowed. "You're afraid of me, aren't you?"

"No. I'm not afraid of you." In spite of herself, she leaned toward him. "You would never hurt me."

"I'd rip off my arm before I would hurt you," he said.

"I know that."

"Then what is it?"

He didn't get it. She could see the bewilderment in his eyes, and her heart shriveled a little more.

"That *was* an ugly display at Sparky's," she said, her voice quiet. "But that's not why I'm upset. You were right to be angry. The parents were wrong and out of line."

With a finger on her chin, he turned her to face him. "Then why do you look so sad? So shattered?"

"You don't know?" she asked.

"I thought it was because I frightened you."

"No." She shook her head, moistened her lips. "No, it

wasn't that." She looked up at him. "When were you going to tell me your secrets? When were you going to tell me about the man you injured, the man who almost died?"

She rubbed her eyes with the heels of her hands, trying to rub the pain away. "I stripped my soul naked for you. I told you all the things I'm ashamed of, the things I hide from everyone else. And you didn't tell me a thing about yourself. I thought we knew each other intimately. But I guess intimacy for you stops at your skin."

Silence pulsed between them. After a moment he said in a low voice, "I'm not the same man I was when those things happened. I've changed."

"And you didn't trust me to see the difference."

"Damn it, Claire! I was afraid you wouldn't want anything to do with me if you knew about my past. Especially after you told me you'd had a violent childhood. I didn't want to lose you." He slid his arm around her shoulder.

She wanted to accept the comfort she'd find in his arms. Her heart breaking, she got to her feet.

"I trusted you, Tucker. I told you last night that I wasn't afraid of you. I'll never be afraid of you. But I guess I'll never know you, either."

"Do you want to hear about Ted? About Carl?"

She shook her head. "It's not a gift if it's not freely given. You can't demand intimacy and trust." She swallowed the hard ball of tears in her throat, closed her eyes against the pain. "I need to go home."

After a long moment, Tucker stood and tucked her hand into his. And God help her, she clung to him.

Most cars were gone from the parking lot by the time

they returned to Sparky's. He stopped his truck next to her car. He shifted on the seat, reaching out to unbuckle her seat belt. When he pulled her close, she didn't resist.

His kiss tasted of desperation, of regret. Tears leaked out of her eyes as she pulled away.

He let her go reluctantly. "This isn't over, Claire," he said. "I'm not letting you go."

"Goodbye, Tucker," she whispered.

Without looking back, she climbed out of the truck, got into her car and drove away.

CHAPTER TWENTY

ON SATURDAY MORNING, Claire sat on the front porch of the house, a book in her hand. She wanted to read, to take her mind off Tucker, but she'd chosen the wrong book. Her heart quivered as she set it down. She couldn't read a happily-ever-after book right now. It would only make her cry, and after last night she had no tears left.

She had no idea how she'd managed to hide her grief from Nick, but her nephew had been happily oblivious to her pain. He'd bounded down the stairs that morning, his eyes shining, his face open. While he scraped a can of cat food into Joe's dish, she'd overheard him telling the cat how he'd kicked the field goal the night before.

By the time he flew out the door to play video games with his friends, her face felt brittle and hard, as if one more forced smile would make it crack into pieces. She watched Nick until he'd disappeared around the corner, then sank down onto the top step of the porch. She couldn't bear to stay in the house. The air vibrated with memories of Tucker, memories that made grief claw at her throat and tear at her heart.

Now she sat in the warm autumn sunshine, trying

desperately to find something to make her forget about Tucker. She was just about to head back into the house to look for another book when her cell phone rang.

"Hello?"

Silence stretched at the other end of the line. "Hello?" Claire said again.

This time, she heard a deep, shuddering breath. "Claire? This is Andrea Vernon."

"Andrea?" Claire's hand tightened on the phone. "How are you doing?"

Another pause. "Not so good," the other woman said in a low voice. "Could you come over here?"

"Are you all right?" Claire asked, rushing into the house to grab her car keys. "Are you hurt?"

"I need you to come over here," she repeated.

"I'm on my way." Claire walked out the door and pulled it shut. "Leave the house and start walking toward town, Andrea. I'll be there in just a few minutes."

"I can't leave," she whispered. "You have to come here."

"Is Roger in the house?"

"Hurry."

The phone disconnected with a soft click. Oh, God, Roger had found out Andrea had been talking to her. Claire sprinted for her car.

In less than ten minutes she pulled to the curb in front of the house she'd shared with Roger. Memories washed over her in a rough wave, memories of pain and humiliation and despair.

They didn't matter. She swallowed, forcing down her nausea, then got out of the car and hurried to the door. Roger couldn't hurt her now, Claire thought. But he could hurt Andrea.

The door opened before she could ring the doorbell. Andrea stood in the doorway, her eyes wide with fear, her face bloodless. Two ugly bruises painted the side of her face purple and green.

"Let's go, Andrea," Claire urged.

"No, you have to come in," the other woman said. Her eyes flickered to her left.

Alarm shivered down Claire's spine. "Is Roger standing next to you?"

"Roger isn't here."

Claire hesitated, warning bells clanging in her head. "Then why don't you just step outside?" she asked Andrea.

"You have to help me pack," she blurted, her hand tightening on the door. "I don't know what to bring."

"You don't have to bring anything," Claire answered. "They have whatever you need at the shelter."

Andrea shook her head. "I want my own things."

Claire remembered what it was like to be completely alone and have nothing of her own, not even underwear. "All right," she said, stepping into the house.

The door slammed shut behind her. "Hello, Claire," Derek Joiner said. He held a large black gun in his hand, pointed at her heart. His hand was rock-steady. "I'm happy to see that you're as predictable as I'd thought." He gave her a terrifying smile. "I've seen you talking to Andrea. Since you can't seem to keep your nose out of other people's business, I knew you were sharing stories about Roger's unfortunate habit of beating his wives. I figured a sob story from Andrea would bring you running."

"Damn it!"

Tucker hurled the hammer through the air and grabbed his throbbing thumb. The hammer landed on the asphalt of the driveway with a hollow, clanking sound.

A sound that echoed the emptiness inside him.

He was a damn fool.

All the carpentry projects in the world couldn't distract him from the disaster he'd created. He could pound on nails all day and all night and it wouldn't change a thing. He was the one who needed to be pounded.

The devastation on Claire's face the night before was something he wouldn't soon forget. He'd destroyed the best thing that had ever happened to him.

Fear and regret had eaten at him during the long, lonely hours of the night. Claire had been right. He'd told himself he'd been waiting for the right time to tell her about his past, that he didn't want to upset her, but the truth was, he'd been afraid.

Afraid to trust her, afraid to see scorn and fear on her face. Afraid the warmth would disappear from her eyes, replaced by wariness and caution.

And because he was afraid, he'd screwed up, big-time.

He'd kept part of himself hidden, the part he was ashamed of. And he'd lost her because of it.

No, he hadn't. He wasn't going to let her get away. He'd get her back if he had to crawl to her on his hands and knees. He'd never crawled to a woman, but he would grovel until she forgave him.

And he'd start right now.

He put his tools away, washed his hands and got

into his truck. If Claire thought it was over between them, she hadn't even begun to learn the meaning of stubborn.

As he drove toward her house, he saw Nick walking down the sidewalk, apparently heading for town. He slowed the truck and rolled down the window.

"Hey, Kendall. You need a ride somewhere?"

Nick looked over at him, his face tight with worry. "You want to give me a ride to town?"

"Sure. Hop in."

Tucker turned his truck around and glanced over at Nick. "What's up?"

"Aunt Claire disappeared."

Tucker's stomach clenched with fear. "What?"

"I can't find her. She's not at home and she didn't leave me a note. And she's not answering her cell phone."

"Maybe she just had to run a few errands," Tucker said.

Nick shook his head. "We made a deal—" he said, swallowing "—after that time I wanted to stay overnight at Booger's and couldn't get hold of her. She said that since she always wanted me to tell her where I was, it was only fair if she did the same thing. She said if I wasn't home when she left, she'd leave me a note and have her cell phone on. But she didn't do either one."

"Maybe she just forgot," Tucker said.

Nick gave him a scornful look. "Aunt Claire doesn't forget. If she says she's going to do something, she does it."

"You want to go to the police station?" Tucker asked.

Nick slumped, staring out the window, and Tucker

saw him swallow three times. "Yeah," he finally said. "Let's go to the police station."

"Police. Broderick speaking." Seth sat up and reached for a pencil, waited for the caller to speak.

"Chief Broderick?"

Seth's hand tightened on the receiver. The caller's fear throbbed through the telephone line. "Yes. Who is this, please?"

"This…this is Andrea Vernon," the woman whispered. "Derek Joiner took Claire Kendall away."

"What?"

"He made her get in the car with him. He had a gun."

"Are you sure? Did you see it happen?"

Andrea choked back a sob. "Yes! He was in my house. He made me call Claire and ask her to come over."

"Hold on."

Seth put his hand over the mouthpiece and called out, "Someone run Derek Joiner. I need to know what kind of car he's driving and the plates." He turned back to the phone. "All right, Mrs. Vernon. Tell me exactly what happened."

He heard a sniffle. "Derek came to the house and said he needed to talk to Roger. I told him Roger wasn't home, but he asked me if he could wait. So I let him in." Her voice trembled. "He hit me in the face. He had a gun. He told me to call Claire and get her over to the house." She sobbed. "I had no choice," she said, crying. "He said he would shoot me."

"How long ago did they leave, Mrs. Vernon?"

"I'm not sure. He said I couldn't call you." Her

voice broke. "He said he would tell Roger I'd been talking to Claire."

The pencil snapped in Seth's hand. "I'm going to send an officer over to your house, Mrs. Vernon," he said, struggling to keep his voice calm. "I want you to tell her exactly what happened with Joiner this afternoon." He hesitated, searching for the right words. "The officer will take you anywhere you need to go. All right?"

"Okay." She hung up the phone in the middle of another sob.

Seth walked into the other room and said to the dispatcher, "Get Rohrmann on the radio." When the officer's voice came over the radio, Seth took the microphone from the dispatcher.

"Kinsey, I need you to go over to the Vernon house," he said, giving her the address. "Mrs. Vernon just called and we have a possible abduction from her premises. Take a report." His hand tightened on the microphone. "I suspect there might be a domestic situation with the Vernons. Do what you can to convince Mrs. Vernon to go to the shelter."

"Got it, Chief," the officer said. "I'm on my way."

When he handed the microphone back to the dispatcher, she handed him back a piece of paper with the make and model of Derek Joiner's car and the license plate number.

"Thanks, Josie." He grabbed his hat and headed out the door. "If anything comes in about the Vernons or Claire Kendall or Derek Joiner, patch it through to me."

"Yes, sir." The dispatcher's eyes were wide as she watched him leave.

He drove over to Derek Joiner's house and pulled into the driveway. No one answered the door, and Seth went around to look in the garage window. Joiner's luxury SUV was gone.

Seth checked all the windows and doors, but none of them were unlocked and there was no sign that Joiner was in the house.

He hadn't expected him to be, but you never knew. Criminals did incredibly stupid things all the time. That's how most of them were caught.

Seth drove to Claire's house, made sure Joiner's truck wasn't there. He sped through Monroe, checking any place that could possibly hide a fugitive and his captive, but there was no sign of either of them.

Frustrated and worried, he pulled to the curb in front of the police station. As he got out, he saw Fred Denton leaving city hall.

"Hey, Fred," he called, heading across the street. "Have you seen Derek Joiner today?"

The mayor froze and glanced to either side of him, as if he hoped there was someone else Seth was talking to. By the time Seth reached him, the mayor's face was flushed and beads of sweat were forming on his upper lip.

"How're you doing, Chief," the mayor said, sticking out his hand. When Seth tried to look him in the eye, the mayor's gaze slid away. "Beautiful day, isn't it?"

"Not particularly," Seth said in a hard voice. He caught the mayor's gaze and held it. Denton quivered like a bug impaled by a pin. "Where's Joiner, Fred?"

"How would I know?" The mayor's voice was all bluster. "It's Saturday. He doesn't work on Saturday."

Seth leaned closer. "Joiner is suspected of a serious crime, Denton. If you're withholding information, you'll be charged as well." He paused for a moment, watched the mayor's face sag with fear. "Do you want to answer my question now?"

"I didn't have anything to do with Janice Kendall's accident," the mayor said, his voice shrill. "I never knew it wasn't an accident, until—"

The mayor closed his mouth abruptly, as he realized Seth hadn't said anything about Janice Kendall.

"We'll talk about Janice later, Fred. I promise. Now tell me where I can find Joiner."

"I don't know." The mayor licked his lips. "The last I saw him, he was heading out of town."

"Today?"

Denton nodded. "A little while ago."

"Was he alone in his car?" Seth leaned closer and the mayor drew back.

"No. There was someone with him."

"You going to tell me who it was?" Seth asked.

"I'm not sure who it was."

Seth stared at him until he muttered, "It might have been that Kendall woman."

"Might have been, Denton?" Seth shifted, rested his hand on his gun.

"I'm pretty sure it was her. It's hard to miss that dark red hair of hers," he said with a scowl.

"All right, Denton. As the former police chief, I'm sure you know the drill." His smile was humorless. "Don't leave town."

He was almost in his car when Tucker Hall walked

up to him. Nick Kendall was with him, his face drawn and pinched with worry.

"Nick is afraid that something's happened to his aunt. She's missing," Hall said without greeting him. "Do you have any idea where she is?"

Seth glanced at Nick. "I'm aware of the situation."

"What situation? What do you know?"

Tucker stepped closer, and Seth saw why he'd been feared when he played football. The man oozed menace. "Fred Denton saw her heading out of town with Derek Joiner," he said, his voice carefully neutral.

Hall's eyes darkened. "What was she doing with Joiner?"

"I can't say."

"Goddammit, tell me what's going on."

"Let me handle this," Seth answered. "Take the kid home. I'll call as soon as I know something."

He got into his car and slammed the door. As he pulled out of town, he saw Hall and the kid look at each other. Then they headed for Hall's truck.

He hoped to God they listened to him.

But based on the look on Tucker Hall's face, he didn't think he had a hope in hell of that happening.

Seth accelerated as he left the last houses of Monroe behind him, then switched on the lights and the siren. Now if only he had some idea of where Derek Joiner was headed.

CHAPTER TWENTY-ONE

Nick. And Tucker.

Claire could think of nothing else.

If Derek Joiner killed her, Nick would be alone again. And Tucker would never know how she felt about him. He'd never know that she loved him.

"You're awfully quiet," Derek said. He raised his eyebrows. "Quite the cool one, aren't you?"

"I'm just making all the connections, Derek."

"Is that right?" He looked pleased. "Do you want to tell me how brilliant I was?"

"You're the one who set the fire in our backyard, aren't you?"

He frowned. "You were supposed to think it was the kid. You were supposed to worry about him. I thought it would take your mind off Janice."

"Is that why you told Roger Vernon about the man who claimed to be Nick's father?"

He gave her a startled look. "Vernon told you I was his client?"

"You're not going to deny it, are you? When I realized there wasn't any man who claimed to be Nick's father, I figured the mysterious 'go-between' had to be whoever killed Janice. It was just another effort to distract us."

"You shouldn't have given Vernon that ultimatum. When he called me in a panic, I knew I couldn't wait to stage my next little accident for you." He gave her a sidelong glance. "You have to admit, I had you going for a while."

"You're despicable, Joiner."

He shrugged. "I'm just protecting my interests."

"Why are you doing this?" she asked.

"This whole mess is your own fault, Claire," he said. "You shouldn't have meddled in my business."

"Janice didn't go over the edge of the road on her own, did she?" Claire looked at him. "You pushed her."

"You're a smart woman," Derek said with a smile. "Almost as smart as your sister. Now you're going to have to die, just like Janice did."

"Why did you kill her?"

Joiner's mouth tightened. "She was a nosy bitch." His handsome features twisted, grew ugly. "Just like you. Sticking her nose in my business, trying to make trouble."

He smiled, a cold upturn of his lips that chilled her heart. "She ran to Fred Denton, told him there was a problem with one of the zoning requests in front of the council." His face contorted with anger. "She figured out that there was a sales tax break included with the zoning change. If she hadn't said anything, it would have gone through with no questions. But after she went to Fred, I had to do something about it."

"Fred? Is Fred Denton part of this?"

"Fred and I are partners in a small real estate venture," he said, his voice smug. "We purchased a block of land outside of Monroe, and we have several developers interested. It would be a perfect place for a mall."

"That's what this is about? A shady real estate deal?" Her voice shook. "You killed my sister to make a few lousy dollars?"

"More than a few dollars, Claire. Denton and I both stood to make several million dollars on the deal." He scowled. "As long as we could get the sales tax break through city council."

"And Janice found out."

"She told Fred she was going to go to the local paper. She seemed quite indignant about the whole situation." He shrugged. "It was her own fault that she died. She didn't give me a choice. I had to get rid of her. If the developers found out there was a public uproar, they would have pulled out of the deal. They didn't want their good name dragged through the mud."

Claire looked down at her hands, clenched into fists in her lap, and deliberately relaxed her fingers. Anger wouldn't help her. She had to think.

"I know you called her at home that night," she said, trying to keep her voice conversational. "You used the phone on her desk. How did you get her out of the house?"

"Janice always wanted to work overtime." His mouth curled in a sneer. "Said she was saving for college for her kid. I told her I had papers that had to be picked up in Clinton that night." He flashed Claire a condescending smile. "I promised her double time and she agreed."

"Then you knocked her off the road."

He glanced at her, resentment in his eyes. "It was a tragic accident until you started sniffing around. So now you're going to have an accident, too."

He steered the car onto the shoulder of the road, and Claire saw with a spasm of fear that they were at the place where Janice had died. Where she'd almost died just two weeks earlier.

"You were the one who almost ran into me that night," she said, watching him.

"I didn't think you'd be strong enough to climb back up the embankment," Derek answered. He gave her a cold smile. "This time, I'll make sure you're not."

"You can't possibly think you're going to get away with this," Claire said, her heart slamming against her ribs. "Andrea Vernon saw you take me away."

"Andrea will do what she's told." He gave her an ugly, triumphant smile as he yanked her out of the car. "She knows if she doesn't, I'll tell Roger all about her visits with you."

"You're wrong," Claire said, holding onto the car door as Derek pulled on her other arm. "Andrea will tell Seth Broderick exactly what you did. She'll stand up to Roger."

"I doubt it. But thanks for the warning," Derek said, pulling the gun out of the pocket of his overcoat. "I'll arrange for her to have an accident, too." He gave another vicious pull and ripped her hand away from the car door.

"But first things first, Claire. You're going to take another tumble off the road."

Claire dug her heels into the dirt and gravel on the shoulder of the road as Derek tried to drag her toward the guardrail. His face turned red and he began to swear, ugly words spat out between wheezing breaths. Abruptly he stopped pulling, and she landed on her rear end in the gravel. Derek towered over her, his face twisted with rage. Holding the barrel of his gun, he raised it over his head like a club.

"Say hi to Janice for me," he snarled as he swung it toward her head.

Claire threw herself to the side and the gun smashed onto her forearm. Pain exploded from her arm and dimmed her vision. Her stomach heaved.

The force of his swing made Derek lose his balance and stumble. His gun waved wildly in the air as he flailed his arms, trying to remain upright.

Cradling her injured arm with her other hand, Claire scooted toward him and aimed a kick at his groin. There wasn't a lot of force behind it, but it was enough to make Derek double over.

Claire struggled to her feet and used her good arm to shove Derek. He stumbled backward and she kicked out at him. The guardrail caught him in the back of the legs.

It felt as if she watched in slow motion as Derek tumbled backward over the guardrail and disappeared down the side of the cliff.

Claire staggered over to the guardrail. Derek clung to a ledge below, just above the boulders scattered on the edge of the lake.

As she stared down at him, she heard the sound of a

car roaring up the road. Moments later, it stopped and Seth Broderick ran toward her.

"Are you all right?" he called, stopping in front of her and searching her face. When he saw her cradling her right arm in her left hand, his eyes became cold and hard. "Did he hurt you?"

"My arm," she said. "I think it might be broken." She nodded toward the cliff. "It's Derek Joiner. He's down there."

"I saw what happened." His eyes flashed as he stepped over to the guardrail and looked down at Derek. "He's not going anywhere. Let me call an ambulance, then I'll worry about getting him up here."

"I don't need an ambulance," Claire said, her teeth chattering. When had she gotten so cold? "I'm fine except for my arm."

Before Seth could answer, she heard doors slam on another vehicle. "Aunt Claire! Aunt Claire!"

Nick ran toward her at full speed. He skidded to a stop a foot away from her. "Are you all right?"

"I'm fine," she said, managing a shaky smile.

"We could see what was happening," Nick said, his voice wavering and his mouth trembling. "We knew we couldn't get here in time. I was so scared."

"Oh, Nick." Claire dropped her injured arm and pulled Nick to her with her good arm. "I'm so glad you're here. Thank you for coming to rescue me."

Nick wrapped his arms around her and held on tightly. Her arm screamed with pain, but she gritted her teeth. When Nick buried his face in her neck, she felt the hot burn of tears against her skin.

Clutching him to her, she held on fiercely, both comforting him and drawing comfort for herself.

After a moment Nick wiped his eyes on the sleeve of his jacket. "You were awesome, Aunt Claire," he said in a shaky voice. "We saw you kick that guy over the edge."

"We?" Her nephew's presence so far out of town registered. "How did you get here, Nick?"

She looked behind him and saw Tucker standing several feet away, his gaze devouring her. "Tucker?"

"Yeah, Coach brought me," Nick said.

She hardly heard her nephew as she ran toward Tucker. He folded her into his embrace, being careful not to jostle her injured arm. "My God, Claire," he whispered into her ear. "My God."

When he fastened his mouth to hers, she tasted his fear, his panic, his desperation. She closed her eyes and murmured his name, clinging to him.

Finally, he stepped back and tore his mouth away from hers. "Did he hurt you?" Cold rage chilled his eyes. "Besides your arm?"

"No," she said. "He didn't do anything else to me."

He looked down at her arm, hanging at her side, and ripped off his shirt. He used it to form a makeshift sling. The soft flannel cradled her arm and enfolded her in his scent.

"Let's get an ambulance out here."

"I don't need an ambulance," she said, her teeth chattering. "It's just my arm."

"Like hell you don't need an ambulance." He scowled at her. "Once, just once, let someone take care of you."

"You can take care of me," she said. Her voice broke. "I just want you and Nick. Please." She turned around and used her good arm to pull Nick close.

She felt Tucker behind her, smoothing his hand over her hair. "Nick is the one who realized you were missing," he said. "He's the one who went to the police." He bent and pressed a kiss into her hair. "Nick and I will take you to the hospital."

"Yes," she whispered. "You and Nick."

"In just a moment," he said, moving away from her. "I have one more thing to do here."

She wanted to grab him, to hold him and never let him go. But he was already gone.

He waited until the chief pulled Derek over the guardrail and cuffed his hands behind his back. Then Tucker curled his hand into a fist and drew it back. But instead of punching Joiner, he let his hand drop.

"I want to hit you, Joiner," he said, his voice soft. "I want it real bad. But it might upset Claire," he said as Derek cowered away from him. "You can thank her for saving your ass." He spit on the ground, then turned and walked away.

Tucker hurried back to where Claire stood with her good arm around Nick. He held on to her tightly, clinging to her like a frightened child.

"Let's get going, Nick," Tucker said, urging them toward his truck. "We need to get your aunt to a hospital."

IT WAS EXACTLY twenty-seven steps from one end of the emergency room waiting area to the other. Tucker stopped for a glass of water, then started back in the other direction. Nick sat in a chair with a copy of an old newsmagazine, but Tucker noticed he'd been reading the same page for a long time.

The doctor had let them stay with Claire while he examined her arm and gave her a shot of medication for the pain. When they brought in the mobile X-ray machine and diagnosed a fracture, Nick and Tucker were banished to the waiting room.

Tucker was ready to tear down a wall to get to Claire, but he looked at Nick and forced himself to calm down. The kid was upset enough already. He didn't need Tucker making a scene in the hospital.

After what seemed like years the door swung open and a nurse wheeled Claire out in a wheelchair. Her face was pasty white and her eyes were hollow. Her arm, enclosed in a bright green cast, rested in a sling. She clutched his shirt, the one he'd used for a temporary sling, in her other hand.

Nick jumped off the chair and ran over to his aunt. He reached out and touched her cast with a tentative finger. "Cool cast, Aunt Claire."

"You like it?" She managed a smile. "I wanted to go with the fluorescent pink, but the nurse convinced me it would clash with my hair."

Nick shoved his hands into his pockets. "You okay?"

"I'm a little sore, but otherwise I'm fine," she said, squeezing his arm with her good hand. She looked past Nick, found Tucker. She gave him a shaky smile. "Thanks for bringing me here, and waiting for me."

"Try keeping me away," he said quietly. He never wanted her out of his sight again. His throat tightened as he thought about what could have happened, how he might have lost the chance to tell her how he felt.

"Come on," he said, his voice gruff. "Let's get you home."

As they pulled into Claire's driveway, he saw a crowd of people on her front porch.

Claire straightened. "What's going on?"

Before he could get her out of the truck, the people poured off the porch and headed for the truck. Judy Johnson opened the door.

"Claire! How are you feeling?"

Claire stared at Judy, then looked past her at the crowd of people behind her. "I'm okay," she said, staring at the faces. "What are you doing here?"

"We heard what happened. Everyone wanted to make sure you were all right."

Tucker saw that most of the parents from the football team were there, as well as Molly Burns and her daughter and the neighbors from the houses around Claire's. Most of them held a dish in their hands.

"We heard you broke your arm." Judy gestured to the people behind her. "It's going to be hard to cook for a while, so we figured you could use some help."

Claire stared at the crowd, apparently speechless. Finally she slid out of the truck and awkwardly embraced Judy. "Thank you," she whispered. She stepped away from Judy and looked from one face to another.

"How can I thank you all?" she asked. "This is…this is overwhelming."

"No thanks necessary," one of the mothers said. "You'll bring a dish next time someone is sick."

Molly Burns embraced her. "We're all neighbors," she said. "Neighbors take care of each other."

Claire sniffled as she clung to Molly. "Thank you." She swallowed hard. "I don't know what to say."

"You'll be saying plenty when you're eating lasagna for the tenth time in the next two weeks," someone joked.

Tucker came around the truck and wrapped his arm around her shoulders. When she leaned into him, his arm tightened and he drew her closer.

Judy stepped forward and addressed the crowd. "Why don't you bring your dishes in the house, and Molly and I will make sure they get put away. Claire looks like she needs to sit down."

Tucker glanced down at her face. It was pinched and white, and she had dark circles under her eyes. He scooped her up into his arms and headed toward the front door.

"She's a little wobbly," he told the crowd as he wove through them. Fear clutched at him when she closed her eyes and laid her head on his shoulder. "I think it's the pain medication." He hoped it was nothing more than the pain medication. He wanted his feisty Claire back.

He set her down on the couch, then crouched in front of her as a stream of people walked through into the kitchen. "What can I get you?" he asked in a low voice.

"Nothing," she said, groping for his hand without opening her eyes. "Can you stay for a while?"

"You couldn't blast me out of here with a stick of dynamite," he told her.

"Thanks, Tucker," she said, leaning her head against the back of the couch.

He wanted to snatch her close, to hold her so tightly that she'd become part of him. Instead he eased himself onto the couch and gently pulled her close. She nestled into his side as people began to leave. Out of the corner of his eye, he spotted Nick standing off to the side, talking to Caitlyn Burns. The kid's face was bright red, but his eyes were shining. Tucker relaxed a little. Some things, at least, were back to normal.

After everyone had left, including Molly Burns and a reluctant Caitlyn, Judy Johnson came out of the kitchen. "Hey, guys, how about if I pick you up a pizza?"

Nick looked up from where he was talking to Booger. "That would be awesome." He gave Claire a guilty look. "If that's okay with you, Aunt Claire?"

"That's fine," she said without opening her eyes.

"Nick, why don't you come with me and Booger to get the pizza?" She shot Tucker a significant look. "Your aunt could probably use a few minutes to herself."

"Sure," Nick said. Moments later, Nick and the Johnsons left and silence settled on the house.

Claire opened her eyes. "I need to talk to you, Tucker."

His gut clenched. "Yeah, I need to talk to you, too." He jumped off the couch. "Let me get you a glass of water first. You're supposed to take a pain pill."

When he came back into the living room a few minutes later, Claire was asleep. Tucker stared down at her. He wanted to talk to her, needed to tell her how he felt. Apologies, pleas for forgiveness, explanations crowded his throat. But he wouldn't wake her up to satisfy his need for confession.

Gently lifting her into his arms, he carried her up the stairs and into the bedroom. When he'd removed enough of her clothing so she'd be comfortable, he sat down in the chair next to her bed and watched her sleep.

He wouldn't wake her up. But he wouldn't leave her alone, either.

CHAPTER TWENTY-TWO

"AUNT CLAIRE?"

Claire struggled to clear away the cotton around her brain. Opening her eyes with an effort, she saw Nick standing in the doorway of her room.

Her nephew cleared his throat. "How are you feeling?"

How was she feeling? Why would Nick ask her that?

Claire struggled to sit up and smacked herself with a cast. She looked down at her arm, confused. Then the events of the day before slid into her memory.

Joiner. Andrea Vernon. Her arm.

Tucker and Nick racing to her rescue.

She clutched the blanket and looked around the room, happiness blossoming inside her. Last night, Tucker said he would stay with her.

He was nowhere in sight.

She swung her legs onto the floor. Her arm screamed in protest, but the pain in her heart was far worse.

"Aunt Claire?" Nick's forehead creased with a worried frown. "Are you all right?"

"My arm is a little sore," she told him. Her smile wobbled. "And banging myself with this cast didn't help."

Nick relaxed. "Coach said I should make you breakfast in bed."

"He did?" She straightened, wild hope coursing through her.

Nick nodded. "He left a couple of hours ago." Nick paused and his chest seemed to swell. "He said I'd take good care of you. So, do you want breakfast in bed?"

"I'd rather come downstairs," she said. "Was Tucker here all night?"

"Yeah." Nick gave her an uncertain look. "I told him I'd stay with you, but he said that I needed to get some sleep so I could take care of you today."

Disappointment that he hadn't stayed sliced through her. She told herself he'd needed to get some sleep, but her throat swelled with tears as she blindly reached for her robe.

"Is it okay that I let him stay all night?" Nick asked, uncertainty in his voice.

"Of course, Nick," she answered, hugging him. Instead of pulling away, he gave her a fierce hug in return.

"I, ah, thought it would be okay. Since you kissed him and everything." Nick's face turned red.

His words pinched her heart. "You did just the right thing," she managed to say.

As they headed downstairs, Nick chattered about the many people who'd called to check on her. Then his face turned red again. "Mrs. Burns and Caitlyn came by. She said they'd come back later."

"That was thoughtful of Molly." She remembered seeing Nick talking to Caitlyn the day before. "Maybe you can help me straighten up the house before they come back."

"Sure."

Nick sat at the table and watched her as she ate, jumping up to refill her coffee whenever she took a sip. Clearly Tucker had told him exactly what to do to help her. Her heart swelled with love for both the men in her life.

"Thanks, Nick," she said, reaching for his hand. "You're pampering me." Who would have thought, a couple of months ago, that Nick making her breakfast would make her feel as if she'd won the lottery.

Nick shrugged, but his eyes lit up. "Coach and me talked about what you'd need. He helped me make the coffee." He shot her a sidelong glance. "He said he figured you'd need coffee this morning."

"I guess he knows me pretty well," she said, giving Nick a smile as her eyes filled with tears. Tucker knew Nick pretty well, too. He knew her nephew needed to feel useful, needed to take care of her.

The doorbell rang and her pulse quickened. Was it Tucker?

Moments later, Seth Broderick walked into the kitchen. Claire forced down the disappointment.

"Good morning, Seth," she said.

He took her hand, studied her. "Hey, Claire. How are you feeling this morning?"

"Sore but very lucky," she said. "I'm glad you got there when you did."

The police chief smiled. "It looked like you had things under control."

He dragged the chair closer to the table, fixed her with his penetrating gaze. "Do you feel up to giving me your statement?"

For the next half hour, she described what happened

the day before. After she finished, he began asking questions, writing her answers in a notebook.

"That should do it," Seth said, snapping shut his notebook. "I'll call if I have any other questions. And I'll have this typed up and bring it by to have you sign it."

He leaned forward, watching her steadily. "Derek Joiner is in the county lockup. He's saying that you misunderstood him, that he only wanted to visit the place Janice died because he missed her and knew you missed her, too." He snorted. "He's not nearly as smart as he thinks he is. Fred Denton is singing at the top of his lungs, and when he's finished, we'll have more than enough to convict Joiner of your sister's murder. And his kidnapping and attempted murder of you."

Claire searched Seth's eyes. "Did Fred Denton help kill Janice?"

"Hard to say," Seth answered. "I don't think so, but we're still talking to him." His mouth hardened. "Even if he didn't kill her, I suspect he knew that Joiner had. He's in trouble, too, Claire."

She looked away. She'd thought she would enjoy seeing Fred Denton shamed and humiliated, but the taste of satisfaction was bitter on her tongue. "You were right, you know," she said. "Monroe is different now. Or maybe *I* am. I don't need to see Fred punished for what he did in the past."

"The past has nothing to do with it," Seth answered. "He conspired to cheat the citizens of Monroe out of the tax revenue they'd get if a shopping center was built. I think Denton's days as mayor are over."

"What about Andrea?" Claire asked. "Is she all right?" The memory of the bruises on Andrea's face was still vivid in Claire's mind.

Seth smiled. "Andrea is in the domestic abuse shelter. Joiner is the one who punched her in the face yesterday, but Andrea has agreed to press charges against Vernon for his past abuse." He took her hand. "Thank you for reaching out to her," he said quietly. "My officer said you'd told Andrea about your experiences with Vernon. That took a lot of courage."

"I've made some bad decisions when it comes to men," she said. "I hope Andrea makes better ones."

"You've given her a chance," Seth answered. He looked up and smiled as Nick came into the room. "This kid of yours did all the right things yesterday. He realized you were missing and raised the alarm. You should be proud of him."

Claire looked up at Nick, squeezed his arm. "I *am* proud of him. This kid of mine is something special."

Nick rolled his eyes and Seth grinned. "I hope you don't let her talk like that in front of the other guys on the football team."

"Nah," Nick said, to Claire's surprise. "Aunt Claire is pretty cool."

Claire stood up and hugged her nephew, and Nick hugged her back. Then, clearing his throat, he left the room in a hurry. Her gaze lingered on him as he disappeared.

"Call me if you need anything," Seth said.

"Thanks for coming by," she answered. "I was going to come down to the station later."

"I wouldn't make you do that. We take care of people here in Monroe," he said quietly.

She watched him leave, then waited by the window, hoping to see Tucker's truck appear. Finally she turned away, disgusted with herself.

"He said he wasn't going anywhere," she reminded herself. "He'll be back."

She hoped. Nothing had really changed between them since she'd walked away from him. Last night he'd told her he'd stay, but she'd been injured and afraid. She couldn't hold him to a promise made under those circumstances.

It was time to get dressed and face the day. Dressing herself was awkward and uncomfortable and her arm ached by the time she was finished. She began to leave the room, then spotted Tucker's shirt lying on the chair. It was the shirt he'd used as a sling the day before.

Impulsively she pulled it on, wrapping herself in the soft flannel that was permeated with Tucker's scent. She closed her eyes as she drew in a deep, comforting breath.

Restless and dispirited, she headed back downstairs. Her job had seemed all-important to her just a couple short months ago. It had been the focus of her life.

But it wasn't going to keep her warm at night or make her laugh during the day. The existence that had once seemed perfect now felt as dull and lifeless as a stone.

But she still had responsibilities. And there were still decisions to be made about the business. She reached for the telephone.

"Thanks, Ken," she said at the end of the conversation. "Get me those estimates as soon as possible. I'll be back to check on them as soon as I can."

As she set the phone back in its cradle, she heard Nick shuffling his feet behind her. "Aunt Claire?"

"Hi, Nick," she said. "The house looks great." He'd been cleaning furiously in anticipation of Caitlyn's visit.

"Thanks," he said, clearing his throat. "I've been thinking."

"About what?" She leaned back in her chair.

"About my father. I don't care that it was all a lie."

Her heart swelled with compassion as she took his hand. "I'm sorry, Nick. Sorry that you got your hopes up, sorry that you were hurt."

He shrugged. "It doesn't matter. I wouldn't have wanted to live with him, anyway." His gaze slid away. "I want to stay with you when you move back to Chicago."

Her throat squeezed shut and her eyes burned. "You don't know how much that means to me, Nick, that you want to stay with me. I want you to stay with me, too. But we're not moving back to Chicago. We're staying in Monroe."

He scowled. "I heard you on the phone just now. You were talking about your job and going back to Chicago."

She replayed the conversation in her head, wondering what he'd heard. When she realized, she smiled and squeezed his hand. "I'm going back to Chicago so I can move the business to Monroe. This is the right place for both of us," she said. "Our friends are here. Our home is here. I don't want to leave."

"Really?" His face lit up, then the smile slowly faded. "But your condo is in Chicago. You talked about it a lot."

His mouth wobbled a little. "I know you want to go back there."

"My condo is just a place to live. Monroe is my home." The rightness of the decision settled over her. "I can work from Monroe almost as easily as from Chicago. I've been doing just fine for the past couple of months."

"Awesome!" Nick jumped up. "Can I go tell Booger? He's been really bummed about me leaving."

"Of course. Tell his mom that I'll call her later."

Nick raced out the door. Moments later he stuck his head back in. "You sure it's okay if I leave? Coach told me to take care of you."

"You've done a great job," she assured him. "There's nothing I need right now. Go on over to Booger's."

"Okay." The door slammed again and she heard his footsteps racing down the porch stairs.

Claire struggled to her feet, pain slicing through her broken arm. Her eyes went automatically to the window and the street in front of the house. There was no sign of Tucker's truck.

Maybe he wasn't coming back.

She should have listened to his explanation two nights ago. She shouldn't have condemned him because he hadn't told her all his secrets.

He'd never pressed her to reveal herself—he'd given her all the time she needed. She should have given him just as much freedom. Instead, she'd pushed him to reveal things about himself that he wasn't ready to reveal.

If she wanted to see Tucker, she would have to go to him.

And there was no way she could drive with a cast on her arm.

She kicked at one of Nick's shoes on the floor, watching as it skidded across the room. Scowling, she bent to retrieve it. "Now that was mature," she muttered to herself.

Sunlight poured through the door, and she stepped out into it. The walls of the house were closing in on her, suffocating her with memories. She needed to be outside, needed to keep herself busy.

The sun was warm on her back and the scent of the mums filled her head. Kneeling in the dirt, she concentrated on pulling out the thistles that had sprouted around the flowers. She wished all the ugliness with Tucker could be cleaned away as easily.

"I turn my back for a few hours and look what happens. That's the last time I'm leaving Nick in charge."

Tucker's voice curled around her like a warm embrace, and she swung around so quickly that she tumbled backward. He stooped close to help her rise. "I can't trust you to behave yourself, can I?"

She searched Tucker's face but couldn't read his expression. Suddenly nervous, she wiped her hands on her pants. "What are you doing here?" she asked.

"I need to talk to you."

Her heart plummeted at the serious look on his face.

CHAPTER TWENTY-THREE

TUCKER WATCHED HER steadily, as if searching for something in her eyes. Then he said, "Ted was my teammate. One day in practice…"

She put the fingers of her good hand over his mouth. "Stop," she said. "You don't have to tell me this."

He pulled her hand away from his mouth and curled his fingers around it. "You have a right to know."

"No, I don't." She untangled her hand from his. "I have no right to make demands of you."

"You don't think so?" His eyes were unreadable.

Her heart twisted painfully. "I know I don't."

"You're wrong, Claire," he said, leaning forward to tuck a lock of hair behind her ear. "You have the right to ask me anything you want."

"What gives me the right to pry into your life?" she whispered.

He studied her, one corner of his mouth curling up. "I think you know."

Her heart skipped a beat, then began to race. She couldn't speak. Her skin warmed and her throat swelled.

He bent his head and captured her mouth with his.

Beneath the tenderness she could taste the heat, the passion. And a promise she prayed she wasn't imagining.

When he lifted his head, he said, "I wanted to tell you. You have the right to know all the ugly parts of me, all the parts that I'm ashamed of. But I was afraid to tell you. I was afraid of what I'd see in your eyes. I was afraid you'd run away and never come back if you knew who I really was."

"I do know who you are," she said. "And I…" She swallowed the words. "I care about you."

"No one has ever known who I really was. No one has known the person underneath. No one has ever wanted *me,* warts and all. All they see is the celebrity, the guy with all the money. I want to make sure you know the real me."

"Tucker, I already know the real you. Nothing you can say will change the way I feel about you."

He looked away. "Maybe you should hear what I have to say before you start making rash promises."

Before she could respond, he took her hand and examined the backs of her fingers. "I've always had a problem with my temper. It got me into trouble more times than I can count. One day while I was playing for Chicago, I lost my temper with one of my teammates at practice. Ted Bromley was a good football player and a good guy. I took him down and blew out his knee. He's had three different surgeries and countless hours of physical therapy. He'll never be able to play football again. I took his life away from him."

She turned her hand to grip his. "Why don't you tell me the rest of the story? You didn't just go crazy and attack this guy."

He tilted his head. "How can you be so sure?"

"I know you," she said, her whole body quivering with intensity. "I know you wouldn't just attack someone for no reason, temper or no temper. What did this Ted do?"

"Whatever he did, he didn't deserve to lose his livelihood and the ability to play the game he loved."

"Of course not. But I'm sure you don't deserve to carry a burden of guilt, either. Tell me, Tucker. What really happened?"

He stared into the distance for a long time before he sighed. "We were both too competitive, even during practice. He was trying to catch the ball and I was trying to prevent it. It started out slow—I'd bump him, he'd push me. I'd grab his jersey, he'd give me an elbow. At the end, we were pretty much beating the crap out of each other. Then he grabbed my face mask and used it to yank me to the ground. I lost it and made an illegal tackle. That's when his knee went out."

"So he's partly to blame," she said quietly.

"I went on to play football for two more years. He spent the next six months on crutches," he retorted.

"Every football player takes chances when he steps on the field. Isn't that what you told us parents at the beginning of the season?"

He scowled. "That's different."

She smiled, happiness unfurling inside her. "We can debate that later. What is Ted doing now?"

"He's on one of those pregame television shows. He analyzes the games and the players."

"Is he enjoying it?"

"Yeah. Last time I talked to him, anyway."

"He found his post-football niche. Just like you."

"I chose to retire. He didn't."

"You retired for different reasons. Maybe you're both where you're supposed to be."

"You know, I see what you mean."

"What are you talking about?"

"You're as stubborn as a Missouri mule. I might as well be talking to one."

"Don't you forget it, Hall."

He'd come back to her and she didn't intend to let him go. "Tell me about the man who almost died."

She saw real sorrow in his eyes. "That's when I realized I had a problem. It was during a game and a guy from the other team was playing dirty. Carl Jones." He sighed. "I should have ignored it. I should have walked away. But he made an illegal tackle and I snapped. I ran him down and he hit the ground hard, broke two vertebrae in his neck. He was in the hospital for over a month."

"What happened?"

"Carl recovered. He admitted that he'd been making illegal tackles, but it didn't matter. I knew I had to get away from football. I had an anger problem and football was making it worse. I made a deal with the league—I retired and they let the whole thing drop."

"That must have been awful," she said. "Both for Carl and you." Claire took a deep breath. "You're a different man now, Tucker, and I love you," she said. "I love everything about you. And that includes your past. Your past made you the man you are today."

Slowly he turned to look at her. His gaze devoured her face, stared into her eyes. "You mean that," he said slowly, as if he couldn't believe it.

"Yes." She touched his face, leaned in to kiss him. "I love you."

He pulled her into his arms, buried his face in her hair. "I was scared to death I'd lost you," he said. "Scared to death to tell you who I really was."

He eased away from her, touched her cheek, her mouth, her neck, as if he couldn't believe she was real. "I love you, too, Claire. I never knew love could be like this." He cupped her face in his hands. "Will you marry me? Tomorrow?"

"Tomorrow?" She tried to put on a serious face. "I don't know about that, Tucker. I'm not sure I can wait that long."

He wrapped his arms around her and kissed her, a promise and a pledge. Holding her carefully, protecting her arm, he slid his hand down her back, playing with the flannel shirt. "This is my new favorite shirt," he murmured. "When I saw you wearing it, I knew I had a chance. I figured you wouldn't be wearing my shirt if you were going to tell me to go to hell."

He led her to the back porch stairs and settled her next to him. Touching her face, her hair, her mouth, he leaned forward and kissed her again. "I've started looking for a teaching job in Chicago," he said. "I've got a couple of interviews lined up already."

"Sorry," she said, grabbing his shirt and pulling him close for another kiss. "You're going to have to cancel them."

"Why would I do that?"

"I don't believe in long-distance marriages. If you move to Chicago, I'm going to be lonely here in Monroe. And I want you in my bed every night."

His eyes heated. "Did I say something about getting married tomorrow? I changed my mind. We'll get married today."

She gave him a scorching kiss. "Yes," she said, breathless. "Today. Now."

He glanced at the house, his hands tightening on her. "Where's Nick?"

Desire pulsed inside her, an all-consuming need that urged her to wrap herself around him, fuse them into one. She forced herself to ease away from him. "He's at Booger's. He'll be back any minute."

"I'm taking another rain check," he whispered, his mouth crushing hers.

Finally he stood up, moved away from her. "I need to get my mind out of your bed before I embarrass both of us. Tell me why you want to stay in Monroe. You've been counting the days until you get back to Chicago."

"I've made mistakes since I came back to Monroe," she said quietly. "One of the biggest was refusing to look at this town through an adult's eyes. I was afraid of committing to you because I was afraid of committing to Monroe."

She took a few steps toward him. "I'm not afraid anymore. I'm going to hold on to what I want. I want you, and I want Monroe. It's the best place for Nick, it's the best place for you and it's the best place for me."

He leaned back to look at her. "You have a business in Chicago. I can teach anywhere."

"I can move my business to Monroe, but I can't move my friends to Chicago," she said quietly. "I have neighbors I want to get to know better. Nick has friends in Monroe." She kissed him. "And you have a football team that needs you. Who else is going to keep their parents in line?"

Happiness swept through her as she saw the relief he tried to hide. She had no doubt he would have pulled up the roots he'd established in Monroe and moved to Chicago for her. And she had no doubt that staying in Monroe was the best thing for all of them.

"Tell me again about having me in your bed every night," he said, easing his hand beneath the flannel shirt.

"Out here? In the backyard?" She angled her body in front of his, let her hand trail down over his chest, his abdomen, below his waist. "Where do you want me to begin?"

"You're doing just fine," he said with a groan.

He swept her into his arms, devoured her mouth with his. Their hearts beat in rhythm, their whispered sounds of pleasure melted together, and he moved against her with undisguised hunger.

When she fumbled with the button on his jeans, he set her away from him. "Out here? I'm shocked, sweetheart." His mouth curled up in a hot, wicked grin. "What will the neighbors think?"

"They'll think I'm the luckiest woman in Monroe," she said, her fingers curling into the waistband of his jeans.

"I knew you were trouble the moment I saw you." He

brought her hand to his mouth, held it there. "Promise you'll still be shocking me fifty years from now?"

"Count on it, Hall."

"I'm counting on a lot of things," he murmured against her palm. "Including that I'll love you forever."

He hugged her and turned her to face the house. "Do you want to live here? For Nick's sake?"

"Oh, Tucker. You'd give up that beautiful house of yours for us?"

"I'd give up anything for you."

Tears shimmered in her eyes as she leaned into him, kissed him. "I love you." She swallowed, smiled through her tears. "And you love that house. I won't let you give it up for us. We'll make a fresh start there, away from all the ugly memories of this house from my childhood."

"My house needs a family," he said, gazing into her eyes. "And that's what I want with you. A family. A home filled with love and a bunch of kids." He brushed her lips with his. "Nick is going to be a great big brother."

"Yes," she whispered. "That's what I want. I can't believe I didn't want to come back to Monroe. Everything I want and need is here."

He studied her. "Are you sure?"

"The only thing I'm more sure of is that I want to marry you. The snotty city girl is gone for good."

He gave her a mock frown. "But I love my snotty city girl."

"You'll have to get over it. I'm not a city girl any more. I'm a hometown girl now, and I'm here to stay."

NICK APPEARED out of the woods in the back of the house, stopping when he saw his aunt wrapped in Tucker's arms. After a moment, he walked toward them.

"Did I give her enough coffee, Coach?" he asked.

"Absolutely," Tucker said. "Great job. You got her softened up just right."

He grinned at Nick and gave him a wink, and Nick relaxed. "I came back because I forgot to feed Joe this morning."

"You should have called me," she said. "I would have fed her for you."

"Nah. I want to feed her."

The screen door slammed behind him, and she heard him open the can of cat food. After a moment, Nick began calling for the cat.

"That's odd," she said, easing away from Tucker. "Joe usually comes running as soon as she hears that can open."

She headed for the house, but before she was through the door she heard Nick yelling.

"Aunt Claire! Aunt Claire! Come quick!"

She and Tucker exchanged worried looks, then Tucker surged to his feet and followed her into the house.

"Where are you, Nick?" she called.

"Up in my room."

She hurried up the stairs with Tucker close behind her, stopping at the sight of a grinning Nick. He was on his knees next to a pile of dirty laundry.

"Joe had her kittens!" he said. "Look!"

She knelt down next to Nick and saw four tiny kittens huddled next to Joe. One was an orange tabby, one was a gray tabby that looked like its mother, and the other two were black-and-white. Joe watched the humans carefully for a moment, as if assessing their intentions, then turned and began licking the closest kitten.

"Can we keep all of them?" Nick asked. "Please?"

"Five cats is a lot of cats," she began.

"I'm not sure my house is big enough for five cats," Tucker said.

Nick tossed a puzzled look over his shoulder. "What does your house have to do with it?"

"Tucker and I are getting married," Claire said. "We'll all be living in his house."

"You're marrying Coach?" Nick sat back on his heels, studying both of them.

"Would you mind if I married your aunt?" Tucker asked.

"Mind?" Nick's eyes lit up and his face glowed. "Nah. That's awesome." He gave Tucker a sideways glance. "So what am I supposed to call you?"

"Whatever you're comfortable with."

"Do you want me to call you Dad?"

Claire saw the sheen of tears in Tucker's eyes and tightened her grip on his hand. "I'd be honored, Nick. You're a great kid and I'll be proud to be your dad."

Nick's face filled with sudden anxiety. "I *am* going to live with you and Aunt Claire, aren't I?"

"Of course you are," Claire said. "We're a family."

"Then that settles it," Nick said. "We can't give away any of the kittens," he said, a sly look on his face.

"Why is that?" Claire asked.

He gave her a triumphant smile. "Because they're a family, too. Just like us."

Tucker's arm tightened around her. "A smart kid can be a real pain in the rear," he said.

Nick grinned at him. "Aunt Claire said the same thing once."

He turned back to look at the kittens just as Joe settled into position on her side and the kittens began to nurse. "Isn't that the coolest thing ever?" Nick asked, staring at the kittens.

"Almost," she said, looking at his face, love swelling inside her. She turned to Tucker, pulled him close. "The only thing better is being a family."

* * * *

Don't miss the next instalment of the
SUDDENLY A PARENT *series.*
An Accidental Family *by Darlene Graham*
is available in September 2006.

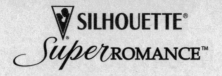

SILHOUETTE®
*Super*ROMANCE™

AN ACCIDENTAL FAMILY by Darlene Graham
Suddenly a Parent

Counsellor Rainey Chapman has three young boys in her care.
When the boys are witness to a crime, Rainey's difficult job
becomes deadly serious. Until the criminals are caught, she
must hide the boys at a secret location, known only to Seth
Whitman, a small town cop with a secret of his own

PREGNANT PROTECTOR
by Anne Marie Duquette
9 Months Later

The test was positive. She was pregnant. Lara Nelson couldn't
believe it. How had she, a normally level-headed cop, let this
happen…especially as the soon-to-be-father was the man she
was sworn to protect?

HIS CASE, HER CHILD by Linda Style
Cold Cases: LA

He's a by-the-book detective determined to find his niece's missing
child. She's a youth advocate equally determined to protect an
abandoned boy in her charge. Together, Rico Santini and Macy
Capshaw form an alliance to investigate the child's past…

FORGIVENESS by Jean Brashear
Mother & Child Reunion

Ria Channing fled home years ago after committing the one sin
her loving parents and sister could not forgive. Now she's back,
in dire straits, but the family she knew no longer exists. Sandor
Wolfe is drawn to Ria and wants to help, except his loyalty to
her mother, who took him in when he was down on his luck,
keeps him at a distance.

On sale from 18th August 2006

Available at WHSmith, Tesco, ASDA, Borders, Eason,
Sainsbury's and most bookshops

www.silhouette.co.uk

The child she loves…is his child.

And now he knows…

HER SISTER'S CHILDREN BY ROXANNE RUSTAND

When Claire Worth inherits her adorable but sad five-year-old twin nieces, their fourteen-year-old brother and a resort on Lake Superior, her life is turned upside down. Then Logan Matthews, her sister's sexy first husband turns up – will he want to break up Claire's fledgling family, when he discovers that Jason is his son?

WILD CAT AND THE MARINE BY JADE TAYLOR

One night of passion doesn't make a marriage, but it could make a child. A beautiful daughter. Cat Darnell hadn't been able to trample on her lover's dream and kept her secret. Joey was the light of her life. And now, finally, Jackson Gray was coming home…was going to meet his little girl…

On sale 4th August 2006

First comes love, then comes marriage...

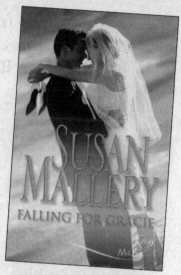

That was Gracie's plan, anyway, at the ripe old age of fourteen. She loved eighteen-year-old heart throb Riley with a legendary desperation. Even now that she's all grown up, the locals in her sleepy town won't let her forget her youthful crush.

...but it's not as easy as it looks.

And now she's face-to-face with Riley at every turn. The one-time bad boy has come back seeking respectability – but the sparks that fly between them are anything but respectable! Gracie's determined to keep her distance, but when someone sets out to ruin both their reputations, the two discover that first love sometimes is better the second time around.

On sale 1st September 2006